A Still Life

BG Knight

This is a work of fiction. Names, characters, businesses, places, events, locales, and incidents are either the products of the author's imagination or used in a fictitious manner. Any resemblance to actual persons, living or dead, or actual events is purely coincidental.

If you have enjoyed reading this book, then BG Knight would be grateful if you would provide feedback direct to bgknight2020@gmail.com

"That God is colouring Newton does show,
And the Devil is a black outline, all of us know."

To Venetian Artists – William Blake

PROLOGUE

The studio is warm; a fire burns in the small grate to one side. A pure white sheet lays rumpled across the divan and the model reclines with her back facing the artist, her head turned slightly to look at who had entered the room. Her eyes open wide in alarm and she immediately grabs the sheet to cover her nakedness.

The man who has entered moves with speed, greater speed than might have been expected for such a large frame. The artist jumps to one side, narrowly missing his easel, trying to place it between him and the whirlwind that is bearing down on him. The intent is obvious to everyone in the room, and the slight figure of the artist is clearly no match for the muscular leviathan who is now within an arms distance.

The model shrieks at the attacker, but he ignores her desperate pleas – he has heard them all before and is having no more of it. His focus is on the man who has shamed his name and reputation and has come to finish his cuckolding forthwith.

The artist ducks under the powerful, flailing arms of the larger man. He has almost made his escape towards the door but the untidy sheet lying on the floor catches his foot and trips him. He sprawls below the looming shadow and shuffles backwards until the divan blocks his progress. The model loses her sense of modesty and kneels behind the prostrate figure attempting to protect him from the onslaught. The man roughly brushes her aside and she falls backwards from the divan onto the floor and lays stunned.

Large, powerful hands close around the soft neck of the artist who squirms and tries to rasp a plea for mercy. All his efforts are to no avail. His lungs can neither inhale nor exhale. Panic sets in upon the recognition that his life is ending. His eyes bulge, and small blood vessels burst under the immense pressure. He looks directly into his murderer's eyes but there is no sign of mercy. Slowly the fight, such as it is, ebbs out of him, the hands unrelenting in their force. His heart falters, his lungs scream for air and he slips from consciousness.

I stand silently apart from the tableau before me and witness the extinguishment of a talent ahead of its time.

It was not meant to end like this. I had failed to avert the unexpected.

I, who relied upon the unforeseen and inexplicable, could not accept such an oversight.

PART 1

I
New Arrival

"You're new. Haven't seen you before"

The young priest turns and looks at the old man seated in the window, silhouetted against the pale blue of a clear spring sky. His head is bent over his sketchbook, his eyes rarely leaving the page upon which his hand is feverishly working.

"I am Father Pietro's replacement," the priest replies, extending his hand towards the old man. His gesture is ignored and so he reluctantly withdraws it.

"So I gather. We are to be your new flock, I presume." He continues to draw, looking up briefly to inspect his subject.

"Yes. Well actually, you are my first flock. I arrived yesterday."

There is a long pause until the old man grunts. It's unclear to the priest as to whether this is a sign of approval or a dismissal. He perseveres.

"Are you an artist?"

"No." Then, as an afterthought, the old man enquires, "Are you God?"

The priest is flustered at the direct question,

"No, of course not. I am merely his servant."

"Mmm." The old man continues to shade an area of his drawing. "Well I merely draw to fill in time before I depart this place."

"Is your departure imminent?"

"Not unless you have come to tell me anything different." The old man stops what he is doing and studies the young priest carefully. The priest hovers uncomfortably under the hard stare of the man. The old man looks down at the page before him. Satisfied, he turns the sketchbook round to face the priest.

"What do you think?"

The young priest takes a step forward and bends to better see the drawing.

"That is extraordinarily good." He continues to stare at his image on the page. "And you say you are not an artist. I am afraid I must contradict you, Signore, based upon this piece of work."

The old man shrugs his shoulders and snaps the book shut.

"Art is in the eye of the beholder. I merely render unto the page what I see. It is for the observer to decide if it is art or mere vanity."

The priest steps back in surprise at what he perceives as an accusation from the old man.

"Am I vain to admire a drawing of me?"

"Depends. Are you admiring the drawing or the subject?"

The priest foresees being drawn into a debate that he might not win. On his first day he does not want to antagonise his wards. His discomfort is allayed as the old man rises shakily from his chair, using the arm for support. He picks up his sketchbook and the tin of pencils.

"I am tired."

He moves slowly away from the window and for the first time the priest can see his features. The lines on his face are deep, but they are lines of mirth and joy rather than bitterness or pain. His eyes are clear blue and have a bright sparkle to them. His skin is tanned indicating some years living in a sunny climate. Frail he may be, but the priest surmises that the life that led to such frailty has been full.

The old man calls over his shoulder,

"Come and talk to me again. I may have need of you."

"I would like that, Signore." As the figure recedes into the corridor that leads from the room, the priest calls, "Can I have the drawing?"

"No!"

II
Foggia

It is the morning when the young priest returns. The old man's room is large, and the tall French windows provide a remarkable view of the lagoon with the campanile of San Marco just being visible above the mist that hangs over the languid water.

Along one wall of the room is a long, polished timber bookcase standing some four shelves high. Each shelf is filled with identical slim, black leather-bound volumes. The spine of each volume has been embossed with gold numerals that, to the priest, appear to be dates. The last shelf from the door through which the priest entered the room has space for a few more volumes – but not many.

The priest continues to survey the room. A hospital style bed stands inharmoniously against the wall behind the door, a small bedside table on each side surmounted by a shaded lamp. From the bedframe hang the controls to raise or lower various sections to assist in improving the comfort of a recumbent occupier.

A large wardrobe fills the corner of the room beyond the bed. Of the two pairs of double doors, one hides its true purpose, giving access to a private bathroom and dressing area adjacent.

The bed is out of place due to its juxtaposition with the remaining furnishings. These are predominantly antique and complement the ornate features of the room itself. The cornicing is complex as are the panel mouldings to the walls and the timber panelling to the shutters. The French doors have finely detailed fenestration, which allows the glorious outside vista to dwell within the heart of the room. Beyond the closed doors is a narrow balcony with a decorative stone balustrade.

A modest, antique desk stands to one side of the window, its tooled, leather surface clean and empty of anything apart from a brass task light and the tin of pencils that the priest had seen with the old man when he last visited. Light streams into the space as the sun breaks through the light cloud in the East.

There are no dark corners in this room.

"You're back then."

The old man enters his room, walking more freely than when the priest had last seen him. He is wearing a wide brimmed hat, and his clothes are of a style and quality that were beyond the modest stipend of the priest. In his right hand he holds a silver topped cane, in his left a sketchbook identical to those on the shelves. He was a man out of his time and looked the epitome of an Edwardian gentleman abroad.

"They said I should wait for you in your room."

"Did they." A statement, not a question, "As long as you haven't pinched anything."

The priest's jaw slackens and then resumes its position. The old man signals towards the two final pieces of furniture to adorn the room, indicating for the priest to take a seat. A small, buttoned back, brown leather chesterfield sofa stands at an angle to the end of the bed, as if to shield any visitor from the charts that hang over the ugly, exposed metal frame. A low round table before it has an intricate marquetry pattern inlaid into its highly polished surface, the differing colours of the wood veneers exquisite in their design and variety.

The old man places his cane in the corner and takes his seat behind his desk. The sketchbook is placed precisely next to the tin of pencils. He looks over the brass task light at the young priest. He waits for the priest to speak.

"This is a wonderful room. I envy you the space and view."

"Envy heaped upon Vanity." The old man looks round the room as if appreciating it for the first time. "Traits not normally associated with your calling."

The priest recalls the veiled accusation from his last conversation with the old man and wonders if all their meetings will be as confrontational.

"I did not mean it literally." He adds as if a defence, "It is just a phrase."

"So you are not envious?"

"No…well, yes. What I meant was, this is a very pleasant room with a great view."

"It is."

Silence descends between the two men once again. The priest watches a ferry head out across the placid lagoon towards San Marco and wonders why he came back to see the old man. Ripples spread out from the bow of the craft as it crosses the silken surface.

The old man also looks out of the window, remaining motionless. The priest eventually speaks to break the peace that seems to have overcome the old man.

"I don't even know your name."

The old man returns to the room from his reverie and focuses on the priest.

"Don't they tell you anything?"

The priest makes a face as if to accept that he has failed in his duties.

"My given name is James, but you can call me Giacomo."

"You're English? Your Italian is very good, but I did think I detected a hint of an accent, but I could not place it."

"Mmm." The old man returns his gaze to the view outside the window. The priest waits again for the old man to expand beyond the 'Mmm', but nothing further is forthcoming.

"How come you are living here in Italy?"

"You ask a lot of questions." The old man never takes his eyes from the lagoon, the ferry sliding into the mist and out of sight.

"Sorry. Would you like me to go?"

"No. You're here now."

The old man slowly turns to the priest and then rises from his seat behind the desk. He reclaims his cane from the corner and walks over to the bookcase. He runs his manicured finger along the shelves and then selects a book. Removing it from its allotted space, he opens it as if to check that the tooled date on the spine is accurate.

"I was here a long time ago."

He returns to his seat, having handed the closed book to the priest as he passes. The cane is carefully replaced in the corner and he lowers himself into his chair. The timber joints creak slightly as they take up the burden.

The priest turns the book over in his hands and looks at the spine. '1944'. He is uncertain if he should open it and look inside without the express consent of the old man.

The man looks out across the lagoon again and nods his head.

"You can open it."

The priest takes his cue and reveals the flyleaf. In capital letters is written; 'FOGGIA'.

He flips past this page and slowly starts to work through the volume. There are drawings on each page, sometimes more than one to a page. The right-hand leaf is the right way up, while the left page is upside down. The priest keeps rotating the book to take in the contents.

Portraits of young men, flying officers in the main, some in uniform and some in shirtsleeves with glasses of ale and almost all with cigarettes to hand or mouth. These faces were intermingled with building facades and interiors, aircraft both complete and lying damaged like beached whales with broken spines and missing fins. This was an anthology of a time unimaginable to the young priest. Each image was beautifully rendered, and all looked like they had been produced in the last few days, so sharp were the pencil marks.

"What happened in Foggia?" asks the Priest.

"It's the sodding marshalling yards again, chaps," the Flight Sergeant announced as he took a deep drag on his cigarette and exhaled a plume of blue smoke.

We had operated twenty-six of the last thirty nights due to the fine May weather. The majority had been over the marshalling yards and the enemy were getting wise to our nightly visits.

"Usual departure routine. Meet you all here at 15:00 hours for transport." He turned to leave and with a stream of smoke trailing is his wake he said, "See you later."

My heart sank and I felt sick. We all knew that our chances of survival were diminishing with each sortie that we completed. The odds were stacked against all of us, but some more than others.

"Come on, Penny. Let's get some grub before the rest have eaten it all."

Dick Kilroy had christened me 'Penny' when he discovered my surname was Farthing and the rest of my crew had adopted it. I had been assigned to Bomber Command when I inadvertently displayed a talent for shooting. I had hoped to be taken on as a navigator but due to my prowess I was placed in the ranks of the 'tail-end Charlies'. This select, and short-lived, band comprised of the rear gunners in heavy bombers, and specifically in my case, a Wellington.

The crew normally consisted of six but due to shortages we were down to five. Three of them sat up front with the pilot operating the wireless, navigating and bomb aiming or manning the front gun turret. I was the chump at the back and had replaced a jovial Irishman whose blood still decorated the deeper crevices of my turret.

Dick had no need of further sustenance, already being almost too big to climb through the access hatch at the base of the fuselage. We had buddied up shortly after I joined them. Along with a healthy appetite, Dick displayed a black sense of humour. Death, or worse, potential maiming was all a joke to him. It was his way of hiding the fear. We all had our own methods. Mine was to draw.

Over the weeks that we had worked as a crew we had become a closely bonded team. A crew formed a mutual trust in each other. The prospect of failure never surfaced or was discussed. The lost Irishman rarely mentioned save if he was an integral player in an amusing anecdote.

These flights were bloody cold. You plugged yourself into the inadequate heating system, but the isolation was numbing. It was not all action as in the books, the hours dragged by and the noise reverberated through your brain. As you scoured the sky your eyes played tricks on you and you saw what was not there.

I clambered across the wing spars that separated me from my fellow crewmen, ducking low as the fuselage tapered towards the tail. I hung my parachute on the hook on the side of the fuselage - outside my enclosed gun turret. Raising my hands to grasp the top of the frame, I swung my legs into the turret and landed my bottom on the hard seat. I closed the two small, metal, sliding doors behind me and I was in my cocoon that had proved to be a coffin for so many.

Having checked my guns and that the hydraulics worked the turret, I watched as we taxied towards take off. The earth rushed past me and we lumbered into the air, the airfield diminished beneath me - hopefully to be seen again in the morning.

It was my role to defend the bomber from attack from the rear, and it was always from the rear. I had downed two fighters who had had the temerity to try, but plenty of others had escaped my attentions. But most of the time it was stultifying boredom. If there was no action you just sat and froze, hoping that the adrenalin would keep you awake. Sleep was not something that was tolerated.

"You all right back there, Penny?"

The skipper checked in at regular intervals to make sure I was awake rather than any genuine concern for my well-being. He relied on me to deliver their deadly cargo – they all did.

"Fine, Skip."

"Not playing with anything you shouldn't be, are you, Penny?"

I recognised Dick's distorted voice and the chuckling from other crewmembers.

"No need. The girls back here are very accommodating."

"Hope you have risen to the occasion!" More chuckling and then the radio clicks and silence follows. I return to my lonely vigil until the enemy announces their presence from the ground. Beams of light cut through the black and illuminate the night sky. I put the dark lenses down over my goggles. I can see to my left one of our aircraft has been caught in a searchlight. Without warning it is surrounded by puffs of smoke that look innocent, almost pretty, but each has deadly intent. The exploding contents hungrily sought out fabric, airframe, engines, fuel tanks, or flesh. It was indiscriminate as to which as long as it destroyed its prey.

I watched mesmerised as the aircraft bucked and weaved as the pilot attempted to take evasive action, each change in direction made in hope rather than knowledge. Writhing under the multiple attacks, like an insect overwhelmed by a swarm of ants, the machine eventually succumbed to the barrage. An engine burst into flames and almost simultaneously the wing disintegrated and spun away from the remainder of the aircraft. The Wellington lazily turned onto its side due to the imbalance created by the loss of the wing. I willed the sight of parachutes opening but nothing appeared. I tried to look into the rear turret as it spun away from me but there was too much smoke and debris.

Automatically, I swung my turret from side to side to make sure I still had full mobility.

"Christ, Penny. What the hell are you doing? Is there a problem?"

My Skipper swore again as I centred my turret, each sweeping motion making the aircraft turn as the drag hit the side of the turret.

"Sorry, Skip. Just checking around. Everything clear here."

"Well keep still will you, there's a good chap. I have enough to contend with up here without you flailing around."

I swept the sky with my eyes, craning my head around the turret.

It came from nowhere.

The sudden burst of light and the deafening crash. I slid forward in my seat as the plane climbed steeply. Pushing myself back, our upward flight slowed as we fought gravity and neared stalling point. Beneath me, pinpricks of light flickered where fires raged from the incendiaries and bombs of the first wave. We reached our zenith and the nose tipped down and we simultaneously rolled to the right as we commenced a steep descent.

Apart from a howl of air past my turret, the aircraft was eerily quiet. The engines had either packed up or had been feathered to avoid any spread of fire. I was tight up against the sliding doors that provided my escape into the fuselage. I tried to turn around to open them, but they seemed jammed by the impact of my body against them. I uncoupled myself from the heating tubes and wireless and stood as best I could to face the recalcitrant doors. Panic began to enfold me in her embrace.

And then I heard it. A quiet voice that said to me,

"*It's not your time.*"

It gave me comfort and it gave me strength. I knew at that moment that I was to be saved, but how?

Fighting with them, I kicked the bottom of one of the doors and they suddenly released. I avoided tumbling headlong into the body of the aircraft but could see the appalling damage inflicted. The centre of the fuselage above the bombs was on fire and I could not see through the flames so was unaware as to whether anyone else was still alive. The smoke blew down to my position and filled the gun turret and then rushed out of the slots where the gun barrels protruded through the canopy.

"Skipper? Skip?" I shouted into my mouthpiece but to no avail as I remembered that I had unplugged myself to get up from my seat.

The aircraft seemed to be levelling out albeit at a crazy angle. Escape through the fuselage was impossible unless I wanted to run the gauntlet of the flames. I had seen the results of that and immediately rejected it.

Grabbing my parachute that had miraculously remained on its hook, I struggled to put it on as the aircraft bucked and yawed. I sat back down and did not bother to close the two doors as I tried to turn my turret. Nothing happened and it was clear that the hydraulics were shot to hell. I had to resort to the handle that substituted for mechanisation and madly wound it until I felt the turret slowly rotate. The sweat collected, cold and clammy, against my chest. I continued to turn as far as it would go so that the open doors gave onto thin air. This was the only alternative. I took a deep breath and tipped myself backwards out of the opening.

The only recollection I have of my descent was looking for my aircraft as it slowly turned in the air. No parachutes appeared until there was a searing flash and the whole thing exploded into a fireball.

The young priest listens intently.

"Did anyone survive?" he asks softly.

"None"

The priest crosses himself and mumbles a blessing.

"And you?"

"I was fortunate, but I did land heavily which broke my ankle and shattered my wrist."

The old man holds up his hand and the priest can see the misshapen bone structure and scarring around his wrist.

"I hobbled around for forty minutes with no idea where I was. Eventually a group from the resistance found me and sheltered me until they could get me back to my unit."

"So, you are a war hero?" The priest realises too late that this is a naïve question.

"I am not a hero. They are the heroes."

"And the voice?"

The old man looks at the priest, the tears not escaping his rheumy eyes but reflecting the light like a beacon.

"You tell me, you're the priest."

Silently, the priest closes the book and crosses his hands on the cover as if it is a bible.

III
Luncheon

The young priest liked to get out after Mass and his favourite escape was to the small island of Burano. He loved to walk through the narrow streets with their brightly coloured fishermen's cottages. He would then wander back across the footbridge to Mazzorbo with its quiet orchards and hidden gardens. One such garden is the oasis of tranquillity that surrounds the Romanesque church of Santa Caterina. A quiet hour reading with his back to the stone wall, sheltered against the chilly wind with the warm spring sun on his face is an indulgence only exceeded by the prospect of a modest lunch at the small trattoria that sat by the ferry stop.

He walks with a measured pace across the bridge and enters the garden through the narrow wooden gate that leads off the path along the water's edge. He seeks his usual position but is disappointed to notice that someone has already taken the bench. As the young priest approaches, he immediately recognises the person who has usurped his sanctuary, head bowed and deep in concentration over his sketchbook.

"How did you get here?" The priest asks incredulously.

The old man looks up and squints into the sun as the priest stands between it and him.

"It's my priest, I assume. I cannot see you if you stand there."

The priest moves to one side and the old man lowers his head back to continue with his sketch. The subject is the delicate façade of the Santa Caterina, drawn in intricate detail. The priest marvels at the drawing.

"I have drawn this church many times over the years, but it never disappoints." The old man's pencil moves across the paper with rapid but expert precision.

"It is beautiful."

"The church or the drawing."

"Both."

"Good answer."

For the first time the old man gives a flicker of a smile towards the priest and signals for him to sit beside him.

"What brings you to Mazzorbo?" The pencil continues to work on the paper.

"Peace, a bit of a walk and lunch." He watches as another detail within the drawing is completed.

"Me too. Shall we go?"

The old man snaps the book shut and packs his pencils into the old tin. He wraps a red ribbon around both the sketchbook and tin to hold them together. A soft leather shoulder bag is lying by his feet and the book and tin are placed carefully inside and the flap closed.

"Did you come alone?" The priest enquires.

"Of course. Did you?"

"Yes."

"Well then, we will have to put up with each other's company, won't we?"

The young priest surrenders to the will of the old man and follows in his footsteps out of the garden. The brass ferule of man's silver topped cane clicks rhythmically against the paved surface. His cloak is of a light material that hangs from his shoulders as naturally as the cagoules worn by the tourists. They pass him by, casting admiring glances towards the elegant old man with his stick, dressed in his hat, cloak and dapper suit. Leather shoes adorn his feet, polished to a shine that competes with the sun.

The proprietor of the restaurant immediately comes to greet the old man and shows the two of them to a table outside, overlooking the canal, beneath a fresh leafed tree. He takes the old man's cloak and hat and holds his chair away from the table as the old man lowers himself into position. The bag and cane the old man places at his feet.

"Buon giorno, Geogio." The Patron smiles; flattered that the sophisticated Englishman remembers his name.

"Buon giorno, Signor Farthing."

The priest was not so much ignored as overlooked.

"Due prosecchi, per favore."

Geogio starts to leave to fulfil the order but pauses as the old man calls after him,

"Frizzante, Geogio. Frizzante."

The proprietor nods an acknowledgement and hurries away.

"Must be semi sparkling. Anything else is too gassy and makes me fart."

The priest giggles like a schoolboy at the surprising admission from this English gentleman with such impeccable manners.

"I have never seen you here before, and I come most weeks."

"Perhaps you have never looked for me." The old man takes his crisp white linen napkin and shakes it open. He places it on his lap and smooths the material to his satisfaction.

As if a perfect explanation, the priest accepts this as an obvious omission on his part.

The proprietor brings the two glasses to the table, places them precisely on the white tablecloth and retires. The priest waits for the old man to take up his glass and lift it to his lips. He does so and hesitates; the glass is held just below his nose. With a sharp, and noisy, intake of breath he inhales the bouquet that emanates from the wine and sighs with satisfaction, his eyes closed in anticipation.

Conversation is sparse, but this does not worry the old man who sits and enjoys his aperitif, quietly watching the world go by. The priest also looks about him and makes no comment as the old man efficiently orders their lunch, discussing with Geogio the merits of various dishes as he proceeds. The younger man is not sure if he is the guest of the older man or not. The expansive attack being made on the menu is far greater than his normal modest needs. He worries that his share of the bill will not be easily covered by his meagre stipend. However, he has to admire the appetite of the man before him whose frame would imply much lesser requirements to sustain it.

"What did you do after the war?"

"Do?"

"Well, what I mean is, what work did you do? Or did you remain in the RAF?"

The old man's mouth tightens, and his face becomes harder. The priest settles back with his glass as it is clear that the old man is preparing to elaborate.

"I worked in the City, London that is, for forty years until I was put out to pasture."

"Put out to pasture?"

"It's a phrase in English, rather lost in translation. I was retired."

"Not your choice, then?"

"Not my choice."

The conversation ceases for a while and the men drink their aperitif.

The dishes come and go. The old man eats slowly but with an exactitude that becomes a fascination to the priest. Each dish is divided into sections and each mouthful constructed on the fork or spoon to provide a precise mixture of tastes and textures. There is no hesitation in the consumption; the profound sense of enjoyment obtained from each element of the dish is evident. He eats delicately, laying his implements down on the plate at regular intervals to take a sip of the chosen wine or the water – still, not sparkling, of course.

"Do you have family in England?"

"Is your conversation limited entirely to asking questions?" The old man suddenly sounds irritated.

"I am sorry. I do not mean to pry. I am just curious. You are not like the other residents."

"You mean I am alive and not dribbling in a chair from which I cannot escape?"

"That is slightly harsh. Not everyone is infirmed."

"Not everyone."

The old man takes another quaff from his glass and leans forward to replenish it. Before he can reach the bottle, Geogio materialises at his side to take over the task. Pouring the last of the bottle into his glass, Geogio asks,

"Is everything satisfactory, Signor Farthing?"

"Perfect, Geogio. Perfect."

The priest nods his appreciative agreement at the proprietor, who does not notice. Geogio retires with the empty bottle into the background once again but remains ever vigilant as to the needs of his customer.

"I was repatriated to England from Foggia to try to sort out the mess your medics had made of my wrist. They thought that I was going to have to have the hand amputated until I explained, pleaded in fact, that it be saved."

He sips the wine and continues.

"Stress and mental well-being were not common parlance in those days. If life was tough you just got on with it. Nowadays, any slight tribulation is met with cries of woe and a need for specialist counsellors." The priest sips his water as he listens.

"Fortunately, I had a pal who had perfected the art of teetering between sanity and insanity. He was a master at it and as such avoided most of the horrors of war. I copied his technique to convince the surgeons that for the sake of my sanity, and livelihood, they had to attempt to save my wrist. I suppose they felt that if they failed, they could always revert to the original plan. However, having been set the challenge, they made a pretty good fist of it."

The priest looked quizzical.

"I do not mean a fist, they repaired – as best they could – my wrist and saved the hand. God, you priests take everything so literally." The old man twists in his chair, raising his right hand to Geogio as if to demonstrate that it was in good working order. "Il conto, Geogio, per favore."

"You said your livelihood. So, you were a commercial artist?"

"No. But I had to make them realise how important drawing was to me."

"So you never pursued a career in art, or made a living from it."

"I said not, didn't I?" His voice rises in exasperation.

The priest reverts to a tense silence and waits.
The old man pays the bill.
The priest relaxes.

IV
Cornwall

The old man is sitting on his balcony in the early afternoon sunshine drawing. The young priest has not appeared for a couple of days. He wonders why but does not enquire. A half-drunk Aperol spritz is on the table by his side, the ice long melted, but droplets of condensation run down the outside of the glass. Out of the corner of his eye he notices movement at the door to his room.

"Where have you been, Priest?"

The shadow freezes and then alters its course to move in his direction.

"I did not realise you were in here." The priest walks across the room and out of the far set of French doors. He places his hands on the balustrade to fully take in the view. He breathes in the fresh air and slowly exhales as if to relax his knotted shoulders.

"You look tired." The old man takes a sip from his glass.

"Sorry, I am."

"Don't apologise. It is part of your calling to take on the sorrow of others."

The priest blinks, tenses and looks across at the old man in surprise.

"I know that look," the old man says.

"What look?" The priest asks, leaning on the door frame onto the balcony.

"The look that says you cannot explain to a family why their only child has died. The look that says you cannot offer the devoted widow the love and comfort of a lost husband." He continues with his drawing, without missing a stroke of his pencil.

The priest stands and looks out towards San Marco, slowly shaking his head from side to side.

"You are no stranger to tragedy?"

"I am no stranger to loss." He closes the volume on his lap and places it on the side table by his glass. "Take a seat and I will fix you a drink."

Involuntarily, the priest looks at his watch.

2:30pm.

He should abstain but the old man is already on his feet and crossing the threshold into his apartment. He returns a few minutes later with another Aperol spritz and hands it to the priest. In his other hand are a couple of volumes of his drawings. Checking the spine of each, he chooses one and places it in the lap of the priest.

"I was fortunate. I had the benefit of an idyllic marriage to the most beautiful woman in the world."

The priest takes a sip of his drink, puts the glass on the table by his chair and takes up the volume.

‘1950’.

The old man watches him and waves his hand for the priest to open the book.

The first thing he sees is the striking portrait of a stunning woman. Young, vivacious and full of life, the fresh laughing face almost leaves the page and the priest lets out a whistle of appreciation.

“I did say she was beautiful.”

“She most certainly is. This is your wife?”

The old man nods thoughtfully, as if reminiscing over joyful, carefree days. The priest turns the pages, each obsessed with the girl in every pose imaginable and all demonstrating her obvious zest for life. The backgrounds varied. In the early drawings there is little to see, but as he progresses through the book the backgrounds started to take on a more defined character. This did not infer any less interest in the main focal point of each sketch but seemed to be placing the timeline in context. Below each drawing, the date, and sometimes the place, were recorded and, as ever, in the right-hand corner the elegant initials ‘JF’ appeared.

“We married in ’50. May 17th.”

The priest looks sharply up from the page he is scrutinizing.

"But that is today."

"Is it?" The old man takes another small sip of his drink. "Happy anniversary to me…to us." He takes a further sip, leans back in his chair, closes his eyes and seems to go to sleep. His glass is balanced in his lap. The priest continues to silently turn the pages so as not to wake the old man.

As he passes through time within the book the drawings chronicle a romance, a wedding and a honeymoon in a town called Salcombe, which he assumes is in England. Enclosed within the pages is a cutting from a local newspaper reporting the marriage of Mr James Farthing to Miss Livia…. The surname is missing, the page having been torn badly across the end of the announcement. At the back of the book is an old black and white photograph of the happy couple standing outside the door of a church. The young, old man is wearing a baggy suit and his bride in a modest skirt and jacket, holding a small bouquet of flowers. They both look so happy and pleased with themselves.

The priest returns the photograph to where he had found it and closes the book. He looks across at the old man who has not moved but whose eyes are open and watching the priest.

“I thought you were asleep.”

“No.” He still does not move. “Just thinking.”

“Did you have any children?”

“Yes. A boy. Stephen.” The old man straightens in his chair. “He would be over sixty now if…” His voice trails off. The priest does not probe any further as he suspects he knows what was to follow.

The old man takes the second volume and with a slight reluctance holds it towards the younger man. The priest rises and swaps it for the volume he has already looked through.

The priest opens the book at random and is immediately shocked at the intensity and darkness of the drawings. Any finesse is absent, the images disturbing.

We had always taken the cottage in Cornwall for a month and this year we thought it would be fun to have the whole family down for a week. Stephen and Melissa had been delighted as it gave them the chance of a break, with the grandparents doing some of the looking after of our two energetic granddaughters.

The boat had been tidied up and Livia and I had spent a wonderful first week sailing around the various bays and swimming in the cool, clear water. The ingredients for picnics were bought from the local village shop, prepared and stowed for each voyage. Having spent the money overhauling and refitting the yacht, I began to appreciate why Livia had been so keen to buy it. I was not a natural sailor, but Livia had done it as a child, and so obtained her master's qualifications and even managed to garner a degree of enthusiasm from me.

The weather that week was superb. Clear blue skies from when we woke until the time we wearily retired to the comfort of our cottage. The sea was, thankfully, calm and the breeze manageable, even for a landlubber such as me. Life was good and Livia and I relaxed and laughed together more than we had for some time. The memories of the unpleasant ending of my career seemed far away.

My son and Melissa arrived late on the second Saturday and the two girls were excited and eager to explore the cottage and its small garden. We all had a catch up over some drinks and Livia had cooked a special supper, which we ate with relish. It proved to be a most convivial family gathering.

I was awoken early the next morning by excited whispering from the girls' room and decided to take them out to let everyone else in the house have a lie-in. We dressed quickly and crept out to walk to the village and buy some croissants and a newspaper. With the girls on either side, they held my hands as we walked up the road towards the shop. The climb was quite steep and they both decided that their grandfather needed pulling along to quicken his pace. All the while they chattered of school, friends and what they were going to do now that they were with us on holiday.

"When can we go in the boat, Gramps?"

"When your grandmother says we can. She is in charge, not me."

I looked out across the cliffs at the darkening sky and doubted that we would make it today. Clearly the weather was breaking, such was the unpredictability of summer in England. It was the luck of the draw, but I was sure that it would improve soon.

The day was spent at a local beach, the sun making only sporadic appearances, but the girls were unconcerned. They ran in and out of the water and we built sandcastles only for the incoming tide to wash them away. Stephen and Melissa took them for a run along the beach, splashing water as their feet caught the shallow ripples. Squeals echoed round the small cove as they attempted to catch Stephen and throw him into the sea. Livia took my arm and we wandered behind, watching our happy little family disappear into the distance. She turned and held my face in her cool hands.

"Thank you."

"For what"

"For everything."

She rose on her tiptoes and softly kissed me on the lips. We walked on in contented silence.

That evening Livia listened intently to the weather forecast having been pestered by the girls all afternoon, and evening, to go out in the boat. Satisfied with what she had heard, she announced that we would all be going for a sail tomorrow and had to get up early.

After the children had gone to bed, happily exhausted after a surfeit of exercise and fresh sea air, we sat down, opened another bottle of wine and played some ridiculous card game that Melissa had been introduced to by a friend. How the girls slept through the roars of laughter and shrieks of protest is a mystery but sleep they did.

The predictions of the weather forecasters proved to be accurate and the ritual of collecting croissants for breakfast was performed once again. Livia packed the picnic basket with food for the day and Stephen ensured that all the things that small girls might require for the trip were packed. Melissa was late to breakfast and looked slightly flushed.

The girls were impatient to get off and we sent them into the garden to play while we finished our breakfast.

I was about to get up from the table when Melissa said,

"Don't go yet, James. I have an announcement to make."

I relaxed back into my seat and looked across at Livia. She was obviously as much in the dark as I was. Melissa hesitated and Stephen reached across the table and took her hand.

"I am afraid that you are going to be grandparents for a third time!"

I whooped with relief, fearing that there was something worse about to befall us. Everyone got up and hugs and kisses were exchanged, and I grabbed a bottle of Prosecco from the fridge to add to the picnic.

"I won't be having any of that, James. Too many bubbles," Melissa said, seemingly forgetting the excessive amount of alcohol we had all consumed the night before.

"Oh, don't worry. This is semi sparkling. Frizzante, I think is the accurate term."

Melissa shook her head, "Nonetheless. But don't let me stop you."

"Oh, you won't," Livia assured the assembled company and put her arm around my waist and gave it a gentle squeeze.

The old man stops his narrative and takes a deep breath as if to collect his thoughts or banish the pain of memory.

"Don't continue if you don't want to."

The older man pulls himself up in his chair and sits more erect.

"No, I am fine. It was a long time ago. I should be over it now." He looks across to check that the priest's glass is not in need of being refreshed, but the priest has hardly touched it since the old man began his tale.

"They told me not to blame myself, but that didn't stop me."

"What happened?" The priest gently probes for a conclusion.

The day's sailing with the family was one of the best days we had had that season. Everyone was in a very jovial mood boosted by the news that Melissa had imparted earlier that day. The girls loved being crewmembers on the boat, without actually making any practical contribution to the sailing of it. Livia commanded the craft with skill and made the trip fun for everyone, even the landlubber. We found an isolated bay and swam and picnicked, played beach cricket and built sandcastles. The adults, save for Melissa, drank Prosecco with lunch and slept in the warm spring sunshine.

When we eventually returned to the mooring, we were all in high spirits. Stephen and I took most of the kit from the boat up to the car. He then returned for the few remaining items. As I stood by the car, I watched the five of them walked towards me. I was as contented as I have ever been in my life.

It was then that the Voice spoke to me again.

"*It's a wonderful evening for a walk. Take the path home.*"

Compliantly, I announced that I would go back along the cliff top path to the cottage. I needed a walk and wanted to have a little space and time to myself. The car had been cramped coming down to the quay with six of us squeezed in, and my absence would give everyone a bit more space. The girls protested and begged to come with me (Did I really hear "*I do not think so*"?), but it was getting late and Stephen and Melissa wanted to get them home and ready for bed.

"I will be back in time to read you a story before bed. You choose a book and be in bed ready for my return."

Reluctantly they agreed and I checked that everything was stowed safely and saw them all into the car. Livia stopped at the driver's door and turned to face me with a smile on her face.

"Enjoy your walk," she gave me a hug, "Don't be too long."

We gave each other a brief kiss, as comfortable married couples do, not out of habit but rather familiar affection.

I watched as the car pulled out of the car park and started its ascent towards the cliff top road. I commenced my climb along the rough path that ran parallel to the road before striking a different course to follow the rugged coastline. The walk normally took me twenty minutes and the late afternoon heat was just starting to dissipate as the sun sank towards the horizon. I remember checking my watch to time myself, as I like to step out and maintain a good pace on my walks.

The road is more like a single-track lane, and it cuts inland for a short time, passing between high hedges before it returns to the coast and skirts round the Devil's Cauldron, a large sinkhole created over the millennia by the pounding sea. The drive is high and quite scary for the unwary. The cliffs drop steeply to one side and there is a high bank on the other with infrequent passing places.

The coastal path passes on the other side of the Cauldron at a slightly lower level, cut into the side of the sloping bank. You can just see the road from the path, which passes over an arch that allows the sea to rush in and crash against the rocks around the base of the Cauldron.

My family should have passed this point long before I reached it but as I rounded the summit and started down the slope to the Cauldron, I knew that something was wrong. Up on the road was a small gaggle of people looking over the edge. I followed their gaze. Down at the bottom of the Cauldron, the sea was swirling and sucking at the wreckage of an upturned vehicle. All around was the debris and effects of my family's day out. Another wave ran towards the stranded vehicle and swamped it, throwing up a contemptuous curtain of spray to remove from my vantage point the scene that was set before me.

And then he says, "*I am sorry.*"

The old man sinks back into his chair and looks exhausted. Meanwhile, the young priest is simultaneously saddened and perplexed by the tale recounted by the old man. He is hesitant to ask any questions and allows some time to pass before he speaks.

"I am sorry." The priest immediately realises what he has said as the old man shoots him a look of disbelief. He immediately seeks to rectify his mistake,

"Was it an accident?"

"Of course it was an accident," the old man snaps.

"What I meant was, how did it happen?"

"Unexplained." The old man takes a sip of his Aperol but seems to have lost the taste for it.

"I need some water."

"Of course." The priest jumps up and goes into the apartment and reappears a minute later with the water. He neither gets, nor expects, any thanks. The old man takes the water and has a long draught. The lines around his eyes relax slightly.

"Never found Livia's body." He drinks again. "The girls and their parents were eventually found, dragged out of The Cauldron by the currents and deposited around the coast."

"Do you have a theory as to what happened?"

The old man shakes his head and looks down at his feet.

“You heard a Voice again? Was it the same Voice you heard when your aircraft was shot down?”

The old man nods and returns his gaze to the face of the young priest. There is another pause.

“Have you heard your Voice since?” The old man’s eyes do not loosen their grip on those of the priest.

“Oh yes.” The young priest feels a chilled draft waft across the back of his neck.

“And he’s not pleased.”

V
An Old Acquaintance

I turned into Redcross Way and, as I was slightly early, I wandered over to the metal gates of the Cross Bones cemetery. As usual, they were festooned with messages and ribbons. This was a deconsecrated graveyard for prostitutes and paupers that was one of the secrets of London that many tourists would miss. The women who had lain here were known as "Winchester Geese" because they were licenced in the 12th to 17th century by the Bishop of Winchester who, no doubt, benefitted from their earnings and, I suspect, their favours. Those who had been interred there were the last vestiges of an era when morals and scruples counted for little, pleasures were taken where they could be found, and your Church shared its table with Satan.

The young priest bridles at the allegations but thinks better of entering into a theological debate with the old man. It is late in the evening, a few days after the priest's last visit. In the intervening period, the priest has been troubled with the revelation by the old man that he hears a Voice in his head. Possession had been briefly considered but hastily dismissed. However, he remains perplexed as to whether the old man was seeking his help or not. As to whether he should consult a higher authority, this had also been briefly considered and similarly dismissed as premature.

It is an unprepossessing shrine, lying as it does amidst rough waste ground and having a forlorn look with buddleia growing all around and the rubbish from the street collecting in the corners of the surrounding walls. The ribbons and messages were damp and limp, reminding visitors of both the newly departed and those who had lain for many centuries in this foul earth. Each message was tinged with poignancy and mystery. The wording on the cards always seemed well crafted, which appeared to be in contradiction with the education and opportunity that had passed by most of the occupants. One recent addition caught my eye, written on stiff card and tied with a red ribbon similar to that used on my sketchbooks.

"Mia cara Livia".

Who was this Livia? Not my Livia but obviously another. My musings were interrupted by a booming and unmistakeable voice,

"Looking for your mother, James?"

The person standing on the opposite pavement outside the entrance to the Boot and Flogger was a picture of excess. Roger Sharpe was a big man by anyone's standards. He stood a good six foot six in his socks and weighed just less than two hundred and eighty pounds. His signature three-piece suits had to be made for him and were well tailored to flatter his bulk. The distinctive broad, pink pinstripe was well known throughout the City of London, as was Roger. Even though he was coming up eighty, he was still held in high regard by the City grandees.

I had known Roger Sharpe since school. He had set up a wealth management business some years ago that had prospered. He had a shrewd nose for rich clients and good investments. My inclusion on his client list was out of comradeship rather than profit.

I crossed the road to greet my old friend who enveloped me in a bear hug and clapped me firmly on the back. The two of us had the appearance of a male fashion shoot for Saga. My suits were more traditional in cut and my habit of wearing a hat causes ribaldry from my old friend, as did my adoption of the leather shoulder bag that he pronounced to be my private mid-life crisis.

"Come on, let's get some booze inside us." We went up the steps and into the bar that ran down one side of the long room. It was warm and welcoming, and Roger gave a friendly greeting to the small wiry haired waitress who was standing by the bar.

"Hello, Annie. Happy Christmas to you all." He waved his hand inclusively to all the staff behind the bar waiting for the lunchtime trade. They all smiled and returned his good wishes while he took off his coat to hand it to Annie. She had been a waitress at this establishment for years and regularly served us with a mixture of cockney humour and motherly chiding. She was well beyond official retirement but had the stamina of a woman half her age, serving multiple tables with extreme speed and efficiency.

We were ushered to our usual table in the corner by the column radiator that hissed and clunked when in full bore. We ordered two pints of "wallop" that were served in pewter pots. To this day I do not know who brewed it or where it came from, but it tasted good and was another of our lunching traditions. The order was swiftly given, potted shrimps from Morecambe Bay, roast beef - rare, with all the trimmings - and bread and butter pudding with custard, not cream. To round the meal off, we had the ever-present truckle of Stilton. David ordered two bottles of house claret to be opened to breath and Annie took the unnecessary menus from us so we could relax with our pots.

We covered the preliminaries - work, weather, but never family - over our pints and then, as an afterthought, Roger asked Annie for a couple of glasses of Chablis to accompany the potted shrimps.

"Have you decided what you are going to do?" Roger asked through a mouthful of toast, loaded with the buttery brown crustaceans. "Are you still thinking of spending time in Italy?"

"I think so. I would like to go back to Sorrento to see if I can find the hotel that we stayed in." I took a sip of my Chablis. "I might even go and take a look at Foggia. I have never liked to return but it might be the right time. Am I going to be able to afford to take off for a while? Or am I better to book my place over the road?" I nodded in the general direction of the cemetery and he laughed, but not loudly which I took to be a less than encouraging sign.

Roger concentrated a little too earnestly on his plate and then looked up at me.

"I am not going to lie to you, James. In normal circumstances you would be able to have a reasonably good, not lavish, income in retirement." He briefly paused and then added, as if an afterthought, "However, you might have to cut back on the clothing allowance, I am afraid."

"Never!"

I enjoyed dressing elegantly, albeit that perhaps the style was out of fashion now. If I were to define my look it would have to be more akin to Edwardian than late Elizabethan. When I was at college I was referred to as a 'young fogey', but age had allowed me to mature into the clothes that I wore. Anyway, I enjoyed drawing an appreciative eye from discerning passers-by. But this all sounds very self-indulgent, and so it is. This was one luxury that I would retain, along with my drawing.

Roger took a mouthful of potted shrimp piled up on a piece of toast, followed by a sizeable draught of Chablis.

"But I don't need to tell you that circumstances are not normal, do I?" He raised his eyebrows to emphasise his question, which he then proceeded to answer. "The current financial crisis will go down in the annuls of financial history. It is playing merry hell with the markets. A lot of portfolios have been massacred. Thankfully, I have kept yours reasonably risk averse. Even so, the losses are around twenty percent."

"That is still quite a hit, albeit I am sure that there will be a recovery. I have just got to live long enough to see it." I sipped at my wine half-heartedly.

It was then that Roger served up his bombshell.

"However, Stephen's company is going to be a casualty."

He swallowed the last vestiges of meat and took a gulp of the rich claret as he watched for my reaction. Upon the death of my son, Stephen, I had inherited a majority holding in his very successful (up until his demise) IT business, which did something that I could not comprehend.

Roger was Stephen's godfather and had invested in the company, but I was not privy as to the extent, or if he had any influence in its rise and subsequent apparent fall. Roger looked apologetic. I shrugged my shoulders to dismiss the rest of this topic of conversation. He topped up my glass before asking Annie to bring over the second bottle to accompany the cheese.

Lunch eventually finished just before five by which time I was feeling slightly lightheaded. As we prepared to depart the Boot and Flogger, we said our goodbyes, wishing each other a merry Christmas. I went to the Gents washroom as Roger bestowed fulsome seasonal greetings on everyone in the restaurant.

When I walked out of the restaurant the cold air hit me like a hammer. Darkness had fallen over the city; streetlights cast eerie shadows over the Cross Bones and the mottled collection of coloured ribbons fluttered disconsolately against the metal railings of the gates.

On an impulse, I decided to go to the Monkeychops Club to see who might be in, as I was not keen to return just yet to an empty house. I had passed the gates into the Cross Bones when I stopped and retraced my steps. I hunted through all the messages, but to no avail.

"Mia cara Livia" had gone."

The priest interrupts.

"What on earth is The Monkeychops Club? Sounds very disreputable." The priest smiles so as not to have his question misconstrued as an accusation of impropriety.

"Ah, yes. Of course, gentlemen's clubs don't really exist in Italy; it's a quintessentially British thing. However, there is nothing disreputable about either the club or its members. It is to be found in a rather fine Georgian building just off St James' Square in London."

As if this is all that one needs to know about the institution, the old man continues,

"I often went there of an evening when I was in London. It is peaceful and provides company when I need it."

“Ah, I understand. Female company?”

The old man snorts in amusement.

“Sadly not, those days are long past. No, the Monkeychops is strictly men only…..and before you ask, no I am not ‘that way inclined’ either.”

The priest chuckles while simultaneously stifling a yawn. The old man looks at his watch.

“Good lord, look at the time. I have monopolised you for far too long.” He rises from the leather Chesterfield and the priest takes his cue that it is time to leave.

“Now I will not hear what happened at the Monkeychops.”

“Nothing happened, Priest. Now, you better get back or they will lock you in for the night.”

VI
New Acquaintances

The young priest enjoys his trips to the Pescheria in Campo della Pescaria. It is his task to buy provisions each week and while he could get them on The Lido, the opportunity to travel across the water and immerse himself in the hubbub of the market, spending a morning away, is a welcome diversion.

He alights from the Vaporetto at San Silvestro, just before Ponte di Rialto, and meanders through the back streets of San Polo to avoid the over commercialised Riva del Vin. It is late for him, but the tourists are still few and far between in these narrow alleyways. Ahead, he notices an impeccably dressed figure, a tall elegant man moving with a spring in his step that belies his considerable age. The cane he uses is an adornment rather than a crutch. He has a certain swagger as he greets passers-by with a lift of his hat and pauses to exchange a word or joke. These are not tourists but residents of Venice, he is no visitor but an accepted member of the dwindling community that permanently resides here.

The young priest holds back, reticent to make himself known, preferring to observe this enigmatic character. He quickens his pace to maintain a consistent distance between them, but the old man now moves with increasing rapidity. The priest realises that he is being diverted from his mission as he follows the old man across the Ponte Storto, the numbers of people increasing as this forms part of the tourist route around the city. Some twenty metres in front of the old man a couple are standing admiring the display in a shop window. The woman is elderly in the eyes of the priest, but young to the old man. Her open bag is hanging from her shoulder. Suddenly a young man runs towards them and snatches the bag, spinning the woman round and causing her to fall to the ground with a cry. Her partner shouts after the youth who is now accelerating towards the old man. From a side street a policeman appears, takes in the scene and shouts for the man to stop. The old man slows his pace as the youth bears down on him but makes no effort to avoid or impede his path.

The thief checks his speed before sidestepping the old man. As he is about to pass, he inexplicably stumbles and falls headlong forward, releasing his grip on the bag and landing heavily on his face, his arms unable to cushion his unexpected fall. Now, blood oozing from his nose, he lies, groaning, on the ground between the priest and the old man, who has turned around and is fast approaching the stunned priest.

Is it only the young priest who has noticed that the old man had deftly placed the end of his stick between the feet of the escaping felon?

The policeman puffs up to make his arrest, but the old man has already taken the priest's arm and leads him from the scene.

"Come, let's be away."

"But he is hurt."

"Shame." The old man intensifies his surprisingly strong grip on the priest's arm. "We have earned a well-deserved coffee."

They casually leave as if mere onlookers with nothing to impart to the authorities as to the events of the last thirty seconds. The old man propels the priest down a narrow side street and into an open square with a church, capped off well, trees and a small café to one side. He slows his pace and slackens the grip that he has taken of the priest's arm. The priest looks around and cannot remember ever having visited this particular Campo.

The tables and chairs outside the café are all vacant and the old man takes one under a tree with a clear view down to the street from which they had entered the square. The old man orders two cappuccinos and two croissants and balances his cane against his leg and the table.

"Why are you following me, priest?"

The younger man flounders to answer the unexpected, and unwelcome, question.

"I wasn't," is the best he can do.

"Lying is unbecoming of the priesthood, but a habit they seem unable to avoid. It is demeaning of a young man such as you. So, I repeat, why are you following me?"

"It was a coincidence. I was on my way to the market and I saw you ahead of me. Rather than catch up with you, I... er."

"Followed me," the old man finishes the sentence for the priest. "I do not welcome such an invasion of my privacy. Please do not do it again." He reaches down and takes out his sketchbook and tin of pencils and starts to work on a new drawing of the square. The coffees arrive and the priest sullenly drinks while the old man is immersed in his task. After a while he places the open book on the table and takes one of the croissants.

"That one is for you. You look a bit peaky." He tears off a piece and dunks it into his coffee before hungrily devouring it.

The priest takes his and looks at the old man quizzically. The frailty of this nonagenarian seems diminished from when the priest first met him. Judging from the speed of his gait and the flexibility of his movements, he is clearly remarkably fit and well preserved.

"I did see you trip him, didn't I?"

"Did you? I really can't remember. That's the problem with old age, the short-term memory goes." He looks over the rim of his coffee cup at the younger man, his eyes sparkling and, although the priest cannot see the smile on the old man's lips, the creases around his eyes tell him that he is being toyed with.

"You were a witness. The authorities might have wanted to take a statement."

The old man considers the priest's apparent admonishment before replying,

"We were both witnesses. Why, then, have you not remained and done your civic duty?"

"You marched me away."

"I did not notice much resistance." He points to the croissant on the priest's plate, "Are you going to eat that?" Without waiting for an answer from the younger man he takes it and breaks bread.

"I am not keen on authority. I have never found them terribly effective." The Old Man wipes the froth from the inside of his cup with a torn piece of croissant and slips it into his mouth.

"That is a bit of a generalisation, isn't it?"

"Have you any experience that contradicts my assertion?" The old man dabs his mouth with a large, brightly coloured silk handkerchief.

"Do you have experience that supports yours?" The priest counters.

I left The Monkeychops shortly after nine-thirty having had a convivial evening with a couple of members in the bar and joined them at the club table for supper. It was a clear evening and so I decided to walk down to Waterloo and catch the train home.

The station concourse was quiet, it being the twilight zone between commuters returning to their families and the Christmas partygoers stumbling onto the last few trains of the evening.

I settled myself as usual in a corner seat. I took out from my shoulder bag my sketchbook and selected two pencils from my tin. The small flap-down table allowed me to place them there in anticipation of a suitable subject being found.

The outer doors pinged to announce that they were about to close. They began to slide shut when there was a commotion as one last straggler fought to hold them open and enter our carriage. He cursed loudly as he shoved through, the doors finally snapping shut. Initially, I paid no attention to the late arrival as he passed by, making his presence known by infusing the air with alcohol fumes mixed with the smell of stale sweat.

The train smoothly pulled away from the platform as the late arrival searched for a seat. I could see my fellow travellers willing him not to sit next to them. Eventually he slumped down onto a seat at the far end of the compartment. Ignoring the assembled company, he extracted his mobile telephone from a pocket.

I studied the proportions of his face and made my initial light marks on a clean page of my book. Instantly I became absorbed. My subject was holding a loud and angry exchange on his phone. I drew swiftly as he continued, profanities punctuating his conversation with unnecessary regularity. Nobody seemed to have the temerity to ask him to tone it down. It was not surprising as he was a swarthy, thickset man with three days of stubble on his face and a livid scar down his right cheek. The overhead lighting cast a harsh shadow across the flesh where it had healed unevenly. One eyelid drooped slightly over dark, uncompromising eyes.

He was as engrossed in his conversation as I was in my sketching of him. When he had finished, he defiantly glanced around the carriage, daring anyone to confront him. I looked away as his eyes swept past my location before returning his attention to his telephone and commenced feverishly texting. I felt free to continue and the drawing was proceeding well. I started to shade areas in differing tones to bring out the stark contrasts and shadows that provided the three-dimensional qualities to the picture. The carriage lighting was unforgiving, and his craggy features looked more menacing on the page than I had intended but I did not feel comfortable staring too intently to try to correct the image. The angle of his nose was causing me some difficulty, either because it had been broken and was strangely misshapen or because I was mildly intimidated at the thought of being noticed.

Stations came and went as people gradually emptied from the carriage. I continued to try to capture a true likeness of my subject and had been concentrating hard. Slowly I became aware of a presence in the passage by my seat and unconsciously I looked over to the subject of my drawing. His seat was empty, and it immediately dawned on me who was standing beside me. I looked around and the only other passenger was a man at the end of the carriage. I had seen him when I boarded and was going to draw him but with his head apparently bowed in tiredness, his hat had obscured his features. Instead, I had foolishly chosen the man who now aggressively loomed over me.

"What the fuck is that?" he shouted, pointing to my sketchbook. Before I could answer there was a stream of swearing and then a sudden sickening thud, which rocked my head back with a sharp crack against the window behind me. I sat stunned, unsure what had happened before the pain shrieked through my ears. No amount of remonstration appeased the man and a rough hand grabbed my jacket and dragged me from my seat.

The man at the end of the carriage stood and watched events unfold. My attacker did not seem to notice him, or care, and the silent man made no effort to come to my aid.

My belongings fell to the floor and the small table on the seat back snapped as I sought to defend myself from the battering punches. Another blow caught me in the stomach forcing all the air from my lungs and, with a gasp; I collapsed to the dirty wet floor of the carriage.

A boot swung past my head and thudded into my ribs. The sound of breaking bones could be clearly heard. I tried to shout for help, but it was too late.

Simultaneously, a blinding kick landed in my face. I heard a sound in my ringing ears like a distant, ripe watermelon exploding.

My body decided to capitulate and shut down all systems.

Two more coffees arrive at the table, together with two glasses and a bottle of still water. The old man pours and drinks to refresh his mouth. The priest notices the couple that had been the subject of the attempted mugging enter the square and walk over to the café. They take a seat close-by unaware of the presence of their saviour.

"What happened to him?" The priest asks.

"Is it your Christian upbringing that makes you favour the miscreant over the victim?"

"OK. What happened to you?"

"Thank you." He takes up his coffee cup and drinks slowly. "I spent that Christmas in hospital being put back together again. I think they did rather a good job, considering."

"Certainly, I would never have known. How old were you?"

"Eighty-one. It would have killed many my age, but I was damned if I was going to submit."

"Was your attacker caught?"

"Not immediately, save on paper. The police came to see me." He watches as the couple that had just arrived struggle to order their drinks. They are becoming flustered and the young waitress impatient as she has customers filling the surrounding tables and is busy. The old man stands and, taking his cane, walks across to assist them before returning. He takes up the tale from where he had left it.

The taller one wore a police uniform and the other, from his scruffy attire, was obviously a plain clothed detective. The uniformed officer was a fresh-faced young constable and the detective a man in his mid-thirties, his beady eyes alert but his demeanour wearily business like. He wore a shabby, poorly fitting suit, an off-white shirt (that might once have been white) and a gaudy tie loosely knotted. I wondered whether he had looked in a mirror before he left for work.

"Mr Farthing?" I nodded a submissive greeting and he continued, "I wonder if you would feel up to answering a few questions?"

Again, I nodded. I tried to pull myself into a more seated position but, after a sharp intake of breath at the acute pain in my ribs, I decided that I was better off remaining in a semi prone position. I leant back against the pillows that the nurses had so expertly positioned behind me.

"I hope I can help, although it is all a bit fuzzy at the moment." I tried to sound as positive as possible. Now that I was about to be asked to relive the assault, I started to doubt my own ability to give an accurate account of the events that had led me to a hospital bed.

The detective prompted me through the events of the evening, seeking any useful details from my account from the point when I had left the Monkeychops Club to when I passed out under the welter of blows that were being administered by my assailant. After some twenty minutes of intense questioning I felt that I had been a useless witness.

"Now what can you remember about your assailant?"

I realised at this point that I could redeem myself from the inadequacies of my previous answers.

"Can you look in the cupboard and get me my shoulder bag?" I waved in the general direction of the locker and the young constable bent down and looked inside.

"There is no bag here, Sir." He looked up from his crouched position and I asked what was in the locker.

"Only an old tin, a couple of pencils and a notebook." He pulled out my sketchbook that had survived my attacker's attentions.

"Is there no bag there? It's leather with a monogram of JF in the bottom right of the flap."

The young constable wearily glanced again into the locker to reconfirm with a shake of his head that it had not been hiding in one of the four corners.

The detective asked the constable if this was all that had been found at the scene.

He reported that neither my bag nor my mobile telephone had yet been located. The news initially depressed me, and then it angered me.

"Shit! That bag meant a lot to me."

I paused, recalling the soft, amused smile on my Livia's excited face as she lovingly handed me my first 'man-bag'.

I held out my hand to take the sketchbook from the constable. The ribbons were missing, as were the loose pieces of extraneous paper that had inhabited some of the pages.

My feelings towards my assailant were becoming increasingly malevolent.

I turned the book over between my fingers, before opening it and flicking to the final page of drawings. While not complete, the image was sufficient to bring his face back into sharp focus in my mind's eye. I stared at it for a while and more gaps in my memory started to return. His face was unmistakeable, and I held the page up for the detective to take a look.

"I think this might give you a reasonable likeness."

The constable moved to stand at the detective's shoulder to get a better look and recognition instantly flashed across his eyes.

"This is very good, Mr Farthing. Are you an artist by profession?"

"No, merely a hobby. You could say that I am an enthusiastic amateur."

"Would you excuse us for a moment?" The two law officers stared at the relevant page until the detective casually asked if he could borrow my sketchbook.

"Thank you, sir. We will check it for any prints and possible DNA that might help our enquiries. I will also take a copy of your sketch and then I will bring it back to you, I promise." Gently he took the book from me and I dropped my arm onto the bed in tired resignation.

I lay back into the soft pillows, a feeling of weariness overwhelming me.

I must have dozed off.

A couple of days later, my recovery proceeding well, the detective returned to my room.

He pulled up a chair alongside my bed and sat down heavily.

He unzipped the top of his bag to remove my sketchbook, which he had considerately placed in a plastic see-through envelope.

"Thanks for this. It was extremely helpful." I took the sketchbook from his hand and checked that the pages were all in place.

"We believe we know the person in your drawing. We have been to see him, but you will not be surprised to hear that he denies being on your, or any other, train. What's more, he has an alibi for the time of the attack."

"What does that mean?" I asked.

"It means that without any witnesses coming forward we can do little more." He looked at his feet, whether in embarrassment I could not tell, but I felt enraged.

"He is lying, and I suspect you know he is lying." I painfully pulled myself up in the bed to give a degree of authority to my accusation. The policeman looked at me apologetically and shook his head.

"What about CCTV? The station or train must have caught him?"

"I am afraid not. The systems were out of action and we have been unable to place him at the scene."

"Out of action? What does that mean, broken?"

"Strangely, no. We checked back and they were working in your carriage for part of the time but then suffered some form of interference. The authorities are looking into it but in the meantime, we have no evidence that the man we suspected was on the train."

"Well who is he?"

"Obviously, sir, I cannot give you his name." The policeman was becoming wary.

"Where does he live?" I surprised even myself with the anger in my voice. What was I going to do if I confronted a six foot two, two-hundred-and-fifty-pound thug?

"That would not be a good move, sir. He is known to us and is not someone to cross."

"What exactly does that mean?"

"He is a known troublemaker. Actually, he is a vicious thug – but you did not get that from me. I would love to have the evidence to put him away but...."

I looked at him in astonishment and he averted his eyes from my incredulous gaze.

"What are you going to do?"

He looked at me with eyes filled with tired resignation. He had heard similar calls for justice but felt impotent to act on his intuition. Paperwork and bureaucracy had stifled any freedom of action that he might have had in days past.

"So that is it? You do nothing more - and I have to be satisfied with that?"

The policeman's scuffed shoes were examined with care once again and he just shook his head in resignation.

"We need an independent witness. Without this we have only your word against his, and those of his mates who swear they were with him all evening."

Suddenly, I remembered,

"Wait a minute! There was someone in the carriage. A man. He stood and watched the attack." My view from the floor of the carriage flooded back. "I couldn't understand why he didn't come to my aid. He just stood there and stared."

"Are you sure? You didn't mention this earlier."

“I had forgotten, but now I recall it very distinctly. He was tall, in a dark coat, and wore a wide brimmed hat. I thought at the time that it was strange to wear a hat and coat throughout the journey.”

“Well, we will try to find this mystery man, but I don’t hold out much hope if he hasn’t come forward.”

The young priest is fidgeting and the church clock in the square chimes the hour. He needs to go to the market but feels he has to clarify a couple of points before he leaves.

“Did they find the witness?”

“No, of course not.” The old man looks at his gold pocket-watch and then up to the church clock as if to verify its accuracy.

“You better get off or you will miss the market.”

The priest rises from his seat,

“From what you have told me in the past, you hear the Voice in times of stress. Did you hear it this time?”

The old man’s brow furrows. His hand moves to the head of the cane and he rolls his palm over the carved silver top in a small circular motion.

"No, not his voice."

"Then what?"

The old man looks up pensively at the younger man standing in front of him. Naïve innocence personified. Not for the first time, he wonders if he has involved the priest prematurely.

"I think we have talked enough. You are going to be in trouble if you do not catch the market before the best of the fish have all gone." He waves his hand dismissively at the priest who begrudgingly turns and walks away, leaving his question unanswered.

VII
Priestly enquiries

The priest scrolls through the Google search late in the evening. He has put in "James Farthing" and found a myriad of irrelevant references and is beginning to give up on his search. He has scanned fifteen pages so far and is tired. He decides to look at one more page and then bed. It is then that he sees the headline.

"THUG CAUGHT BY ARTIST
Police take no action"

Full story on page 4

There is a photograph of James Farthing, the face little different from the James, or rather Giacomo Farthing that the priest knows. He notices that increasing age seems not to have taken any toll upon the old man. The article was short and bemoaned the fact that attacks on public transport were on the rise and that the police seemed powerless or apathetic. A drawing of the attacker showed an unpleasant looking character and there was a brief reference to an unknown witness who had not come forward. The newspaper stated that from their exclusive investigations the drawing was sufficiently detailed to enable them to identify a known villain, but for legal reasons they were unable to divulge the name of the suspect. Instead, they published a grainy photograph taken with a long lens of a man standing by a large pick-up truck.

It was impossible, even upon magnifying the photo on the screen, to see if it was the same person as in the drawing.

A spokesperson for the police confirmed that they would follow up the lead the newspaper had provided but that without an independent witness they were unable to take the investigation any further.

As a result, the whole case revolved around the missing witness. Obviously, the newspaper had not managed to identify or find him either.

The priest sits back in his hard chair and rubs his tired eyes. It was not surprising that Giacomo had lost confidence in the legal authorities. There is something nagging in the priest's mind that he cannot quite grasp. Something about the old man's dismissal of him from his company earlier that morning.

An inset box to one side of the article caught the priest's eye. He had thought it was an advertisement but realised it was a critical assessment of the sketch by a renowned art critic. He waxed lyrical at the deft hand that had produced such a vivid, albeit unfinished, portrait. The critic used its incomplete state to explain the social deprivation the subject has obviously been subjected to and whose circumstances were the result of incomplete and inadequate education and social responsibility in times of austerity. The critic compared Giacomo with other artists, many of which the priest had never heard of, save for one, the Venetian artist Favretto.

The priest is unsurprised by the enthusiasm for the drawing having seen a number of similarly sensitive and, at times, disturbing drawings in the sketchbooks that chronicled the life of the old man. It was strange to read about someone you know being feted by a famous art critic.

The priest prints the article to take to the old man when he next goes to see him.

VIII
A Commission

“That article was not helpful. The police thought it was an attack against them at my instigation.” The old man tosses the page of print across the table to the priest. Paint smudges soil the article and the old man takes up his palette again and returns to the canvass standing on its easel.

“I didn’t know that you painted as well. Can I see?”

“No, not yet. When it is finished and I am satisfied with it, then, perhaps.” The brush in his hand scrubs at the canvas and he is immersed in his work once more.

“Is that the only reason you have come to see me? Merely to show me a scrappy little article in a local rag.”

“Not entirely.” The priest is slightly crestfallen that the old man is not more pleased with his research and the interest he has shown in his story.

“When we last met you left me without an answer as to whether the Voice had spoken to you during the attack.”

The brush on the canvas ceases its motion momentarily and then continues as before.

"I recall that I specifically stated that I did not hear my Voice."

"You stated that you did not hear a Voice, but then left me with the clear impression that there was something else."

"Something else." He moves closer to the canvas as if examining a detail in the picture; his face is hidden from the priest seated on the leather Chesterfield sofa. He steps back suddenly and cleans the brush on an old cloth.

"I vowed that I would never find myself in that situation again. What that experience had taught me is that the law really is an ass and that you have to stand up for yourself. My old skipper back in Foggia was a tough Aussie and he instilled in his crew (and his young rear gunner) that if we had to bail out and were captured – there would be no one there to save us. He made sure we knew how to handle ourselves."

He chuckles to himself and nods towards the article lying on the table,

"Didn't help me that night." The old man shakes his head at the memory of the inadequacy of his self-defence. "As a man of advancing years, it was suggested that I acquire some specialist assistance."

He disappears into his bathroom and the priest hears water running as he washes his hands.

"Did the newspaper article produce any response as to the identity of the mysterious witness?"

"What?" The old man shouts from the next room. The priest raises his voice and repeats his question. There is a pop of a cork, the old man reappears with two glasses of Prosecco and hands one to the priest.

"No need."

The young priest cocks his head to one side and waits for an elaboration on the last response that seems to be a non sequitur, but none is forthcoming. The old man sits casually on the arm of the sofa and raises his glass.

"Cheers."

"Salute," the priest replies.

"Ah, quite so. When in Venice."

"So?" The priest continues to be persistent. "The witness?"

The old man sucks his teeth and then takes a sip of his wine.

"Why did you leave Sicily to live in Venice, priest?"

The priest splutters into his wine, "How did you know that I came from Sicily?"

"You seem to have researched into my past life. Is it so strange that I should know some of yours?"

"I only know what I found out on the Internet. You have a past; while I have no internet profile."

"Who needs the internet?" The old man sips his wine. "I have a more effective source, a source that watches and sees more than you might imagine."

The priest looks around the room and finds no evidence of a computer, tablet or mobile phone.

"Then how?"

"*Is this wise?*" the Voice idly asks.

The priest hears nothing.

Roger Sharpe's voice booms down the telephone as if he has not quite grasped the fact that technology is capable of transmitting his voice without him shouting.

"Saw the write up in the papers. It was quite a coup to get that critic to review your drawing quite so fulsomely. How are you feeling?"

"I am much on the mend, thank you."

"I wonder if we could get together. I am on the wagon for January after the usual Christmas excesses, but a coffee and a chat would be welcome."

I was planning a trip to London later in the week and so we arranged to meet up at around 11:00am.

As a reaction to my assault, I had spent the early part of the morning of our proposed meeting on an abortive trip to a speciality shop that sold all manner of walking sticks and umbrellas. I hunted for at least half an hour, searching for what I wanted, but all to no avail. Eventually, I asked an assistant and it was then that I discovered that the item I sought could not be generally purchased in retail shops. However, he suggested that I should try buying online or through a specialist antique shop. I was given the name of one in Soho, to where I had taken a taxi, and as a consequence, now sported a rather stout but refined stick with a carved silver top and polished hardwood shaft. The brass finial tapped resoundingly on the pavement as I walked to the coffee shop where I had suggested Roger and I met.

"Buon Giorno, Senor Farthing. We have not seen you for a while."

I waved a greeting at Marco and his wife, "Buon Giorno, Marco. Come stai?"

I had taken advantage of the opportunity during my recuperation to improve and add to the basic Italian that I had started to learn in Foggia. I practiced whenever I came to the coffee shop and

Marco had made a point of politely correcting my pronunciation each time I went in for a sandwich or a coffee. I enjoyed the brief exchanges and it was definitely improving both my accent and vocabulary.

Before I could order, Roger blustered in and gave me a sharp slap on the back, ignoring completely the fact that I was still bruised on most parts of my body. I winced and groaned simultaneously.

He asked what I would like and suggested that I take a seat at the table in the back of the small premises and he would bring it over. There were only two other customers, one reading the Metro and the other engrossed in her mobile telephone. Neither paid anything more than cursory attention to me, being far more impressed by Roger who noisily ordered two cappuccinos in his own almost perfect Italian. Marco and his wife were equally impressed and chatted away to him as they prepared our drinks. Roger said something sotto voce and then laughed generously and strode over to our table. He sat without taking off his perfectly tailored coat, merely undoing the buttons to reveal that the tailoring was not merely confined to his coat.

"Lovely couple" he said before looking at me for a moment to assess the degree of my recovery from the beating.

"You certainly look a damn sight better than when I saw you in that hospital. What's with the stick? Looks very dapper. Almost makes a gentleman of you!"

Marco arrived with our coffees and the two men exchanged banter again, this time Marco leaving with a chuckle and a shake of his head.

"I've just bought it. Glad you like it; it gives a bit of support when needed."

He studied the cane and then the contents of his cup as if considering what to say next. I detected that perhaps he lost a bit of his confidence or was contemplating whether to pursue the conversation further.

"We were very impressed by your drawing. I knew you were good, but didn't realise that you were that good"

I bowed my head in acknowledgement of the compliment. He continued,

"It conveyed more than just a likeness, it seemed to draw out his soul.... If someone like that has a soul? I assume the police never got him?"

I shook my head, "You sound like an art critic."

Roger laughed.

"The reason to get in touch is that we wondered whether you would undertake a commission for us?"

Without answering, I raised my eyebrows for him to continue.

"We wondered if you would be so kind as to do a portrait of our Chairman for us. It is to be presented as a gift at the end of his period in office. He appreciates the arts, paints a bit himself and he saw the article in the paper. He happened to comment on it to one of my colleagues with the utmost enthusiasm, and that set us thinking that this would be a unique gift for him."

I exhaled my suspended breath and laughed. He sat up straight and his face hardened as he tried to judge whether my reaction conveyed a rejection of his request.

"Surely you could get a proper portrait artist to do this?"

Again, he paused and stared into our, by now, empty coffee cups. He decided that two more were required. Marco appeared at his shoulder as if by magic, pre-empting his requirements and whisked away the empty cups. He returned almost immediately with two more fresh cups of steaming cappuccino. This was a level of service that I had never received in the fifteen years that I had been frequenting the establishment.

"Why me?"

Roger spoke apologetically,

"Please don't take offence, but we wanted something unusual, not the standard formal portrait but something truly unique. The circumstances of your newly found artistic fame make you a natural choice."

He raised his cup but did not take a sip as the liquid was obviously too hot. He held it in suspension, hovering just above the saucer.

"I have to tell you," I said, "that I have never done or anticipated doing a portrait by way of a commission."

The barely audible Voice took me by surprise and whispered,

"Why not?"

Roger saw the look of consternation on my face on hearing the Voice, a voice to which he was not privy. Mistakenly, he took my reaction as wavering on rejection. He lowered the hovering cup onto the saucer with a sharp clink of china. He was not used to indecision and had no time for false modesty.

Equally, I had become unaccustomed to hearing the quiet hoarse voice in my head and wondered if Roger had heard anything. Obviously not, as he continued to argue his case,

"Look, from what we have seen, you clearly have the ability and the fact that you are an amateur without formal training or any other drawings in the public domain makes the gift even more appealing to us." He waited to see if I was going to raise any other objections and when I said nothing, Roger pushed home his advantage,

"We are not expecting you to do it for free," and then added as a hasty afterthought, "but obviously as an unknown artist you cannot expect a great deal."

"Do it! Have I ever let you down?" Now the Voice was insistent.

"I am flattered and intrigued as to whether I could do it. No responsibility if it is a disaster?" Why I said this, I was not quite sure but this time the Voice was shrill and admonishing.

"Now that was both insulting to me, and foolish of you!"

I jumped once again at the interruption and spilt the coffee into my saucer. I sought to cover my surprise at the continued interjection of the Voice with a number of swift questions.

"Who's the subject? When and where can I see him? I'm afraid I am not too good at working from photographs."

Roger was not sure about my behaviour, his face showing concern as to whether my recovery was as advanced as I had suggested.

"We would prefer that the subject did not know that you were commissioned by us until the presentation is made." He felt inside his coat and produced a white A5 envelope, which he hesitated in handing to me. "We would like to do the presentation at our board meeting at the end of January. That's the week after next. How long do you need to produce your drawing?"

"In total, I'd estimate that it would take me around a day or two, the majority of that time being the final details to get the tonal quality right to bring the portrait to life."

Roger leant forward over his cup and spoke conspiratorially. "I do appreciate that this is very short notice, but the subject is attending a reception this evening to promote some of his charitable work. A number of supporters and press will be present and so you will be able to attend without raising any suspicion."

"I cannot allow you to refuse." My voice retained its note of insistence. There was a

compulsion that I seemed to be incapable of resisting.

"I could probably turn the drawing round over the weekend and deliver it to you by Monday evening. I have little else to do." I spoke without realising what I had said. The conversation and acquiescence to Roger's request seemed beyond my control.

"Where, and at what time?"

"Splendid!" Roger suddenly leant back with apparent relief while his chair fought to maintain the balance of his bulk on its rickety legs. He extended his arm across the table and handed the envelope into my care. "You will find an invitation and all the details in the envelope. I have provided a couple of photos as well, which might help but, from what you have said, I think that they may be superfluous for your purposes."

He rose and buttoned up his coat against the chilled air outside and offered his hand. I rose, shook it and in a slight daze heard him say,

"Until this evening, then."

He turned smartly and marched out of the café with a spring in his step and a cheery wave to Marco and his wife. When he had gone, Marco looked over and called across to me,

"Do you want the bill or another coffee?"

I swore quietly, "Bugger me, he didn't even pay." Not so quietly, apparently, that Marco did not hear, and he laughed.

I ordered another coffee and resumed my seat as I realised that we had not agreed a fee for the drawing. In some irritation I turned over the envelope to open it and took out the stiff card invitation. The venue was, surprisingly, The Library of The Monkeychops Club, which at least meant that I was going to be in familiar surroundings. I looked at the photographs in more detail and vaguely recognised the face but was unable to put a name to it.

I returned the items to the envelope and put it on the table while I drank my coffee. I used my mobile telephone to refer to Google to find out that Sir Brian Haleborn was a captain of industry and a generous philanthropist who supported through his Haleborn Trust works of conservation throughout the world. He had made his fortune in the biotech industry resulting in the sale of his business to a multi-national pharmaceutical company for an overly large fortune. With this money he had set up the Haleborn Trust and now spent all his time promoting its many good works. He was gifted, popular and well connected.

"Your Voice is a guide? It speaks to you regularly?" The priest is aghast and gets up from the sofa to move away from the old man. He wants to distance himself from – he doesn't know what. The old man remains seated; his demeanour is implacable to the priest's trepidation.

"You seem nervous, Priest." The glass is raised to the old man's lips and he drinks.

"Have you talked to anyone else about this voice?"

"No. Why? Do you think I am mad?"

The lack of an answer confirms that the priest is at least considering the sanity of the old man.

"Does your God speak to you?" The old man enquires of the priest.

"Not as a voice that I recognise. God is my leader and advisor by the way I live."

"So, is it your God that speaks to me?"

"God's love is everyone's love."

"Poppycock! Now you are spouting an indoctrination." The old man rises impatiently; he seems irritated by the conversation.

"I am going to refill my glass." He stumps out of the room. "You can let yourself out."

IX
An Encounter

As I walked North, the evening air was crisp and so clear and sharp that the view from Waterloo Bridge looking left towards the Houses of Parliament or right to the City of London was a myriad of bright, twinkling lights from ever-taller buildings, each increasingly dwarfing the dome of St Paul's Cathedral. Red lights on the tips of booms delineated where spindly cranes were constructing the new skyline.

I arrived slightly early at the Monkeychops Club and went into the bar. There was no one there that I knew and so I retired with a drink to a quiet corner. I had had to resort to carrying my sketchbook and tin of pencils in an old, bulky briefcase since the loss of my shoulder bag. It was an inconvenience, as it did not leave me with a free hand sincc thc earlier addition to my attire of the stout, silver topped cane. I admired my new acquisition, which was both tactile and practical. The Victorians certainly knew how to do things properly.

I heard Roger arrive long before I saw him. He greeted everyone in his vicinity and asked one of the stewards (the members had stewards, not waiters) if I had arrived. He was shown into the bar and I rose to welcome my old friend to my Club, although from his manner you would have been forgiven for thinking that I was the guest and he the member.

He was clearly in a hurry as he refused my offer of a drink.

"I wonder if I could ask you to come with me so that I can pop you on a table at the back of the room, but in full sight of your subject?"

I dutifully accompanied him as he chatted away. There were a number of strangers circulating around the corridor to the library, but fellow members seemed to be singularly absent.

We entered a wide room with magnificent moulded plasterwork to the ceiling and cornices, the surfaces heavily gilded wherever you cared to look. Round tables with green baize cloths surrounded with delicate, gilded chairs were placed before a raised dais that was in front of the high bay window that looked out over the street. The heavy damask curtains had been drawn closed. The walls were lined with shelves full of books as befits a library with a collection that had been started in 1825. Incongruous with its genteel surroundings was a large television screen at the rear of the platform and, placed on one side of the screen, was a large, gilt framed chair upholstered in red velvet. Not quite a throne, but pretty close to it. On the other side were a few of the gilded chairs arranged in a short line.

Roger deftly weaved a course between the tables until we arrived in the far corner. This table was smaller than the rest and was also positioned on a platform so as to be slightly higher, giving a commanding view across the whole room and the assembled company. Three chairs were strategically positioned around it.

“I suggest you sit in the centre. I will sit to your right and Sir Brian’s chauffeur will be on your other side”, he pointed to each chair as he explained the seating. I moved around the table to where he wanted me and sat down, placing my briefcase at my feet and my cane in the corner behind me. It was a remarkable view and even though I was seated at an elevated position, I doubted that I would be noticed as all attention would be on the raised platform that dominated the front of the room.

“I will go and gather together the other guests and get everyone settled. Have you got all you need?” It was a rhetorical question because he had gone before I could reply. My mouth felt dry and a sudden nervousness rose up through my body. I realised that I had agreed, perhaps inadvisably, but in compliance with the prompting of my inner Voice to do something that might prove to be outside my capabilities. A great deal was being expected of me and neither flight nor failure was a realistic option. Up until this point, I had viewed the task as a bit of an adventure, a unique experience, but as the time approached for the arrival of my subject the challenge loomed large, no longer just a bit of fun.

People were filing into the room. Roger had unaccustomedly melded into the background and was nowhere to be seen. I fussed with my case and tried to look as inconspicuously confident as possible.

The surrounding conversation was increasing in volume in nervous expectation. Any laughter that did erupt sounded superficial. I desperately wanted to take out my sketch pad in order to have something to do with my idle hands that flapped from tabletop, to pockets, to briefcase catch and then back to the tabletop again.

As if from nowhere, like a magician appearing from behind a puff of smoke, Roger materialised onto the stage and raised his arms, flapping his hands up and down, to silently call the room to order. The noisy chatter subsided until he held the floor and their rapt attention. He spoke with quiet authority and, despite the size of the room; he was perfectly audible to every corner. He explained what was to happen and the timing of the evening's event. I listened but did not hear, altering my position slightly to ensure that I still had a clear view of the gilded 'throne'. The distance for an accurate sketch was slightly too great for comfort but I felt that I should be able to add any detail from the two photographs. The purpose of this evening was to try to find and to capture the essence of Sir Brian's true character in an attempt to make my drawing unique. I quaked at the thought of not being able to fulfil the task. Such thoughts had to be instantly banished. I needed to concentrate and prepare myself for what was probably going to be the most tortuous couple of hours of my life. I had to remind myself that this was an opportunity that most amateur artists would have given their right arm for and here was I fretting that my inadequacies would be displayed for all to see.

The Chauffeur took his seat next to me without acknowledging my presence. He sat on the edge of his chair to maintain, if required, a clear path into the body of the room. He was a surprisingly squat and powerfully built individual and I wondered if chauffeuring was his only role. Having carefully scanned the room and satisfied himself that all was in order, he did eventually nod a brief greeting in my direction. He then resumed his perpetual scanning of the excited guests as well as the doors to and from the room.

To my right, beyond the chair that Roger would take, was a pair of tall, double doors that gave access into a room that on normal days would have been the breakfast room for those members who were staying overnight. The uniformed stewards were quietly coming and going, sliding through a single, barely opened leaf.

There were around thirty tables all occupied by existing benefactors and potential supporters of the charity that was the subject of the reception. Roger was circulating, speaking to various members of the audience, reassuring, answering excited questions and generally settling down the crowd as we all awaited the appearance of Sir Brian Haleborn. Guests seated nearest the dais were those that I presumed were the primary targets for largesse, while a member of the press and a photographer occupied a single table on the other side of the room to where I was seated. I decided that I could safely remove my sketchbook from my case and, trying to look like a diligent member of the press corps, do a couple of quick warm-up sketches to limber up my fingers in preparation. My presence remained unnoticed and inconsequential as I started to discretely draw quick vignettes of random members of the crowd. These were quick single line sketches, immediacy being a discipline that might come in handy later. I even took a few notes on the room, even though I knew it well; it was usually lit in a subdued manner and the harsh lights shining onto the dais altered the dynamics of the space.

After a couple of pages of relaxing line sketches, the imminent arrival of our host was announced. The event proved to be perfect for my purposes because there were a number of short presentations by various representatives of the charities supported by the Haleborn Trust (do not ask which charity as I was concentrating too hard to recall). My principal subject sat patiently and listened intently to other speakers before giving his keynote address. I studiously drew.

To my delight, my nervousness that had almost overwhelmed me earlier had subsided and I started to enjoy my task. With every passing moment my pencil moved more surely. It was as if I was being guided by an external force, my observational senses heightened, my manual dexterity accelerated. Eventually, I decided that I had sufficient material to enable me to work at home on a final portrait drawing of Sir Brian. However, I continued for a further five minutes completing some more detailed elements of his clothing and his hands. I was surprised at the speed of my work as I filled page after page of my sketchbook.

I relaxed, content with the numerous pages of sketches that I had swiftly gathered. There was a limit to how much I needed without losing spontaneity. Almost like an athlete might gently wind down after an intense period of exercise, I continued to draw other guests over the final fifteen minutes of the formal proceedings.

At a table directly in front of Sir Brian was seated a woman in her mid-forties with large, sparkling auburn eyes sheltered by flowing, raven black hair, high cheek bones, pale skin and a wide mouth with full, rouged lips. Her mouth was slightly open; a slight smile hovering that created dimples on the outer edges of her lips. She was almost overwhelming in her beauty that shone out amongst the wan, bland faces of those who surrounded her in the crowded room. I had been so absorbed in what I had been doing that I had not seen her until that moment. The slim neck held her head proudly high, verging on the haughty, but her eyes were soft and approachable.

I could not resist and set to work, finding my fingers effortlessly steered in their task. I concluded that the excitement of the evening and the adrenalin surging through my body was intensifying my visual senses, my eyes coordinated effortlessly with my pencil as graphite of varying intensities was transferred with surprising fluidity onto the paper. The face of the woman jumped out from the page and I was slightly in awe of my own creation. I sat back and stared in wonder at the sketch and then looked up to my subject as if to check that she was as striking as I had created her.

She was looking directly at me with an imperceptible hint of amusement in her eyes and on her lips. Did I imagine the slight dip of her head as if in salutation? Was she inviting me to share a secret – her secret?

The formalities had come to an end and the doors to my right swung effortlessly open announcing the start of an informal drinks' reception. Everyone stood as Sir Brian made his way towards the open doors. His chauffeur had left our table and appeared by his side, eyes continually roaming over the faces that watched the great man make his way from the room. He exchanged pleasantries with some of the people as I resumed my seat to watch him pass in front of me and into the adjoining room. I unexpectedly observed a couple of mannerisms and details that had not articulated themselves to me earlier. Immediately I returned to my book to sketch them down while the throng burst into noisy chatter as they followed in their host's wake.

People were milling around, each moth nonchalantly striving to make its way towards the host's candle. I moved from my table to better watch the flow but knew that I was really trying to see if the raven-haired woman was still in the room. She was not visible, and I was disappointed not to have gained a last look at her. I turned to recover my briefcase and put my sketchbook back, when I sensed a presence, an infinite rise in body heat, indefinable but detectable to my subconscious. Perhaps there had been a gentle brush against my table. I do not know.

Lifting my eyes, I saw that she was standing to my right, leaning gently on, but not supported by, the open door. She appeared hesitant, watching the flow of people but holding back from joining their number. There was a slight puckering of her lips as if she was blowing a secret kiss to a departing lover. The glint in her eyes had evaporated to be replaced with a doleful air that was at odds with the rest of her demeanour. She rotated her head slowly to look in my direction and tilted her head slightly to one side. I returned her silent stare; she opened her mouth as if to speak but then appeared to have second thoughts.

I could do little but gaze at her natural and almost overwhelming beauty – it was even more captivating close to than it had been from across the room. Her skin was flawless and like alabaster across her high cheekbones, her long hair a lustrous black that hung in curls and ringlets partially obscuring one eye. She seemed to be inviting me to initiate the conversation.

"Good evening," was the best I could do, even when accompanied by what I hoped was my most endearing smile. It was as if I was not really standing in front of her. Even though she now faced me, her sight was not focused on me but somewhere just behind me. After what appeared to be a calculated pause, her soft voice was so distinctive, overlaid with a clear Italian accent. The words were spoken with clarity and precision,

"And mutual fear brings peace,
Till the selfish loves increase:
Then Cruelty knits a snare,
And spreads his bait with care".

"That is beautiful. What is it?" I tentatively asked, unclear if she was really speaking to me or not. Regardless, I was bewitched at hearing my wife's voice apparently issue from another.

"William Blake's 'The Human Abstract'."

My heart rate rose, my body seemed to be overheating. I grabbed the back of a chair to steady myself, all the while not permitting my eyes to leave the face that now was undulating slightly, as if a reflection in rippling water. Before I could respond a group of excited stragglers flooded up to the door, enveloping her and sweeping her away. The human wave spread across the carpet, gradually slowing until they coagulated into smaller groups, eager to mingle and socialise. Greedily they grabbed from the trays of circulating canapés and drank heartily from glasses that were forever full.

I desperately hunted around the groups for a sight of her, but she was nowhere to be seen, a mirage that had tempted my thirst but not slaked it.

I desperately wanted to follow to search for her but my instructions from Roger were clear in that he wanted me to wait behind in this first room. I continued to crane my neck in search of any sign of her amidst the throng, but she had disappeared.

Roger strode out of the doors and gave me a slightly curious look. He asked with undisguised concern if I was feeling well as I was looking a bit pale. I assured him I was fine and, while not wholly convinced, he nervously asked whether all had gone well. I nodded my head and somewhat distractedly affirmed that it had.

"Can I see what you have done?"

I showed him the outline sketches that I had completed over more pages than I had realised. He carefully turned over each one and studied the work with consummate care until, eventually and to our mutual relief, he expressed his delight with what he saw.

"I assume that this stuff will provide you with the where-with-all for you to complete a formal portrait?" His question had a slight inflection, signifying that he hoped my working sketches were not going to be the finished article.

"No, no," I assured him, "these are the working drawings." I took another quick glance over his shoulder into the room beyond, but still she was nowhere to be seen.

As an afterthought, he casually asked if I had done anything else. It was clear to me that he had spotted me warming up with some general sketches as we awaited the arrival of Sir Brian. Ever the diplomat, I had done him early on during his briefing and found the page to show the result. It was a swift, single lined caricature rather than a portrait, but he seemed to be taken with it and asked if he could take it. Fortunately, because of my particular method of only using the right-hand page and then turning the book over to repeat this until I got back to the front page it could be detached without taking any other drawings with it. I cautiously tore it from the book and handed it to him. I continued to flick through the practice pages for him and he chuckled where he recognised faces.

We reviewed the principals' pages a second time and as I came to the end, I turned over the page to reveal the woman who had so captivated me. He placed a large hand on the page to stay me turning it and a slight frown fleetingly gathered over his eyebrows before he returned his attention to me.

"My word she is a beauty. Who is she?"

"I was rather hoping that you could tell me," I replied in the sure knowledge that he would have known everyone who had been invited.

"I have no idea, I am afraid," and took another brief look at her face. He lifted his hand to release the page into my care and, taking one last glance at the woman, he returned to the business in hand.

"Well, that all looks splendid and I look forward to seeing the finished article."

"Good," I replied and packed my materials away in my case. "I shall get on with it then."

I waited to be dismissed but Roger was obviously trying to recollect something that he had overlooked. It suddenly came to him,

"We've not spoken about a fee for this. Any ideas?"

I thought for a moment,

"Really, Roger, I hadn't intended to charge anything, apart from my travel expenses, perhaps?"

"*Nothing!*" The Voice snapped its disgust.

I involuntarily turned to look behind me and then realised from where the voice had emanated.

Roger stared at me with renewed concern.

"Are you sure you are alright?"

"What about a hundred quid?" I blurted out to distract him.

"Are you mad? He would have paid at least double that!!"

"That sounds splendid," delight spreading across Roger's face at such an unexpected bargain. He took another brief, admiring look at his own image on the torn page and absent-mindedly thanked me for my assistance, and turned to return to the reception.

"When and where do you want me to deliver the drawing to you? I could have it ready on Monday after I have had the weekend to work on it." I picked up my briefcase, put the valuable sketchbook carefully inside and secured both of the catches.

"That would be great and fits in well with my timetable. Shall we say 4.00pm here, at the Club?" He delicately slid my caricature of him into the inside pocket of his double-breasted jacket.

"If you ask the doorman for me," I said, reasserting my credentials as the true member of my Club, "I shall let him know to expect you."

"Until Monday, then."

He turned smartly, in true military fashion, to return to his duties and was soon engulfed in the free for all in the adjoining room.

I hovered on the periphery of the multitude following his departure. I was not sure if, as the hired hand, I should be so presumptuous as to claim a couple of glasses of champagne but decided that it was not inappropriate. I put my briefcase behind my chair for later collection and gathered my cane from the corner.

Taking a glass from a tray expertly balanced on one hand by a steward, I meandered alone into the shallows of the sea of faces. Nobody noticed me or spoke to me. I briefly saw Sir Brian expertly working the room. He approached a carefully stationed group of people, discrete staff members quietly briefing him as to the composition of the group and who in particular should be flattered or picked out for special attention. I watched in awe at the expert handling of both guests and our host to achieve a blending of wealth and patronage.

My hesitancy to leave was in the hope that I would have one last chance of seeing the subject of my last sketch.

Why?

Really, I had no idea. I had to confess that I was intrigued and even a little captivated by her. I was buzzing with the success of the evening and wanted to have the opportunity to share the experience with someone. Subconsciously, I knew that I wanted the opportunity to study her afresh, to imprint her image onto my mind and then to lay her onto my paper and enfold her within my book. My hopes were not to be fulfilled, she was nowhere to be seen and so I reluctantly picked up my bag and retraced my steps back to the cloakroom where I collected my coat and hat.

It was late and I felt invigorated and excited. The adrenalin was still coursing through my veins as I walked across London to catch my train home. The unexpected events of the day had been almost surreal – and I had rather enjoyed it. My only regret was not seeing the woman again.

"*Patience, my friend. Patience.*"

I slept fitfully that night.

X
Venetian Delights

The view beyond the tall, open balcony windows of the ballroom was of a clear blue sea with soft white clouds speeding across a pale cerulean sky. We appeared to be floating, the building swaying rhythmically upon a slight swell. Brightly dressed dancers, their faces masked, and harlequin knaves were unavoidably jostling me, moving around me, obscuring from my view the object of my quest. She glided gracefully ahead, beyond my reach, in a black taffeta gown, the skin of her exposed back, shoulders and arms white and misty. She circulated effortlessly amongst the other revellers but spoke to none, repeatedly looking back over her shoulder towards me, and raising her eyebrows as if she was inviting me to follow. Her eyes glistened to the point of tears, but her mouth was set in determination. Her expression was a veneer of mystery and intrigue. I was sure that she wanted to speak to me. The gulf between us increased, I could not keep up with her progress around the gilded room. I tried to hasten my pace, but my feet would not move me through a shifting floor of deepening sand that was becoming increasingly heavy. Dark, swirling water soaked up into it; a rising tide by which only I was engulfed. Slowly, I could feel my balance become unsteady as I inescapably subsided into the wet sticky floor, the water thick, cold and clawing against my calves. All the dancers and knaves around me were inexplicably lifted onto a higher, safer plane. She hesitated and held out a distant hand towards me, as if to try to save me from the swirling morass, but it was too late. My eyes slipped beneath the surface, the vision of perfection became diffused as the cold, saltwater rushed into my lungs. I caught my breath sharply and…

"Wake up! Wake up!" The priest is shaking the old man who has fallen asleep on the sofa. The old man's eyes open suddenly, and he looks about him as if his surroundings are unknown to him. He focuses on the face of the young priest and shakes his head to clear his brain of the dream.

"You were having a nightmare." The priest releases his hold of the old man's muscular shoulder. He continues to be surprised by the fact that the old man is not emaciated like other people of his age. In fact, he looks increasingly well fed and trim, a picture of fitness and health.

The easel remains in the corner of the room, but a pure white sheet shrouds the canvas. The air is cold, and the radiators gently click as they expand to warm the space.

The old man gets up with a flowing movement from the Chesterfield sofa. He walks across to the bookcase and slides out a new volume from his collection. He returns to the priest and passes the book to him.

"Excuse me for a minute."

The priest is left alone, and he sits behind the desk in the opposite corner to the easel, next to the window. The light is fading and the water in the lagoon reflects the last of the sun's rays as it sets behind San Marco. He places the book on the table and starts to look through the pages that the old man had described before he dropped off to sleep.

He flips page after page, this book being more worn than earlier ones. A page is loose and proud of the others. The priest turns to it and sees the woman staring up at him, as if seeking his cooperation in an unknown errand, begging him to pay her some attention. He looks into her glistening eyes, the indistinct reflection of someone or something hidden within their depths.

Unlike previous volumes, where the pictures of faces, buildings or landscapes were isolated on their allotted pages, this was a complete rendition. It was a departure from all the old man's other efforts. Every part of the page was covered in graphite of varying shades and intensity. The detailing of the architectural features in the background were exquisitely drawn. Tall open windows provided a vista of the water beyond, lit as if by moonlight. The windows had arched frames, ornate carved architraves and deep, rich drapes materialised, as did shadowy figures, half-hidden in dark alcoves around the edges of the room. The impact was startling, and the priest found his hand shaking slightly at what he saw on the page. The woman's portrait seemed to stand in relief against the backdrop, proud of the surface of the page upon which it had been drawn.

She looked out at him. She knew him and he knew her.

The priest cannot remove his eyes from the face and wonders what had happened to lift the quality of the old man's drawing to a wholly new and higher plain. This drawing was like no other and exceeded even the old man's hitherto high standards.

"It is a reality," the old man says as he re-enters the room, "that the more you practice a thing, whether it be playing a musical instrument, or drawing, or painting, the better will be the final result."

"What I am looking at here is quite exceptional. It is far beyond anything else that you have shown me. Is it the woman that inspired you to new heights in this particular drawing?"

The old man picks up his cane and walks with grace (or was it a swagger?) over to his desk, places the cane in the corner and takes his seat behind the leather inlaid table. He stretches his legs out beneath the surface and leans back in the chair, his hands interlocked at the back of his head, his barrel chest pushed out as if to emphasise his age defying strength. The young priest continues to be mesmerised by the picture.

"As you can see, I have dozens of sketchbooks on these shelves containing thousands of drawings, some with very acceptable likenesses, but never have I been so overwhelmed or awestruck as I was that evening with my rendition of this magnificent woman. I felt at that moment that I had arrived at the zenith of my creativity. When I completed that drawing I sat, like you, and marvelled at what I had managed to produce. I had captured the very embodiment of the woman I sought to portray – sophistication and beauty with a hint of mystery."

The priest is reluctant to turn the page, not wishing to leave the image that has seduced his senses. Could he detect in her clear, sparkling eyes a trace of pain or apprehension? It was impossible to decide which prevailed, or to know if such emotions were an imposition or an observation by the artist. Had his self-proclaimed infatuation been guilty of romanticising the image?

"She has an enigmatic look. I feel that I know her but then again she is remote, aloof almost." The priest feels that he is struggling for the right words and seeks to clarify his interpretation of the drawing. "She seems to want to impart something to the observer but you, as the artist, have been unable to ascertain what this might be, whether she is happy or desolate. From the background it would appear that she is in a grand room, where is that?"

"I have no idea; it comes from somewhere deep in my imagination."

"There is a familiarity to it that I cannot quite put my finger on. Is it in Venice?" The priest studies the bottom of the drawing. It is dated January 2009, but there is no identification of the location. The neat 'JF' cipher sits in the lower right-hand corner.

"As I say, it is a figment of my imagination. I drew it almost automatically, it sat so naturally with the main subject of the drawing."

"Is it somewhere you had visited in Venice before you drew it?"

"No. I had not been to Venice in January. I only came here in February of that year."
"And it is not an addition that you added later?"

"No."

"Did you ever see her again?"

I finished the portrait of Sir Brian over the weekend as promised. My concern that Roger would find my offering unacceptable dissipated. Confidence was accruing with every added detail as I had proceeded with both Sir Brian's portrait and that of the elusive woman. Alternating between the two, I found that one enhanced the other, the two diametrically opposed subjects having a symbiotic relationship the one with the other.

Satisfied that I had exceeded my usual high standards, I travelled to my meeting with Roger to hand over the portrait with a spring in my step. Even though the day was damp, dreary and depressing, my spirits were high as I knew that I had done a good job. It was a mixture of artistic pride and a consequential release of tension.

I climbed the worn Portland stone steps leading to the glistening, black, panelled front door. The modest, highly polished brass, plaque with its black inset letters, informed anyone interested that this was the home of The Monkeychops Club. The heavy door opened smoothly on its well-oiled hinges and I entered the small vestibule with the usual huge vase of tall blooms strategically placed on a polished side table. To the right was a small desk behind which sat a uniformed porter – strangely the porter was not referred to as a 'steward' – why had never been explained to me and I had never questioned why there was the differentiation.

The perfume of the flowers enveloped me in an aroma that combined with wood smoke, wine and a whiff of decadence. The calming atmosphere as one entered the building provided a welcome that was in contrast to the noise and pollution that infused the rest of London. It was more akin to a visit to the country house of a close friend for a pleasant weekend.

"Good afternoon, Mr Farthing," the Porter said, "It is good to see you again."

I gave a perfunctory nod in acknowledgement, informed him that I was expecting a guest and asked that he be directed to the Firepit.

"Is he a member, Sir?"

"No."

"Then I shall arrange for him to be accompanied."

I left my coat and hat in the cloakroom and took my briefcase and cane with me through to a large room at the rear of the club. This was a rarity in London, and a sanctuary for many members on a cold winter's evening.

High, double doors opened into a large circular room with a wide bay window down one side. The main feature, however, was a huge firepit in the centre of the room, with a monumental, brass cowl over it that collected the smoke and directed it upwards, through the centre of the building and out into the night air. I had not seen anything like it before and it was unique within the centre of London. How it had escaped the attentions of the authorities was a mystery only known to the Secretary of the club who seemed to have obtained an exemption from all regulations.

The embers of the fire emitted a thin spiral of smoke that magically rose in a straight, vertical vortex without any spilling into the room. The hearth was a perfect circle around which a number of chairs and tables had been positioned for the coming evening.

Although I had taken refuge in this room many times, still I marvelled at the scale of the fireplace, and the engineering ingenuity that allowed the cowl to hang as if suspended on invisible wires. It defied gravity and had been the subject of a number of articles over the years in architectural and other similar magazines.

Across the hall from the entrance to the Firepit was a further set of more modestly proportioned double doors into a room used for smaller gatherings, sometimes of members and sometimes hired out for functions acceptable to the Secretary. One of these doors opposite opened and another member of staff came out holding a tray of empty glasses. A sound of animated conversation and the crescendo of polite laughter slipped out alongside him. I could see fifteen or twenty people standing in a group, most with glasses in their hands.

“Who’s in the Clarence Room?” Some name or other identified most rooms in the building.

“It’s an outside group, sir.”

I took the hint, most members being slightly disdainful of the use of any of their rooms for ‘outside groups’. However, their annual subscriptions were kept to a modest level due to the income the Secretary obtained from these lettings.

I stood with my back to the Firepit and observed my surroundings while watching the door opposite to see if it would reveal any more than the steward had imparted. The room in which I stood was remarkably empty of members. Usually, even on a Monday, there would be at least a couple of people sleeping off a long, alcoholic lunch. But today there was no one. The fire crackled softly, and the Steward returned to take up his duties in the room opposite, his tray empty. He looked over to where I stood and entered the Firepit.

"Can I get you anything, sir?"

I was momentarily tempted to ask for a glass of champagne but decided that I should await Roger's arrival and settled for nothing.

"As you wish, sir. We are a bit quiet today but if you should need anything, just ring."

He motioned towards the bells that were positioned around the four quadrants of the room. Members did not like to have to move too far from their table to summon service as competition for prime tables around the fire was fierce and success highly prized. An absence for any time was likely to result in a loss of position to another member, however gentlemanly their apparent character.

The steward quietly slipped through the doors into the cacophony, the merry sounds from across the corridor being muted as he closed them behind him.

I was left alone in the Firepit once again and stood in silence, a million miles away from the roar of traffic just outside. All along one wall hung a mass of framed portraits of men, each with a small brass plaque at the base of the frame. The legend comprised of a name and two dates that recorded when that person had been the President of the Club. It was a fascinating collection, the subjects of earlier portraits having large whiskers and frock coats. The later ones eschewed the whiskers for thin pencil moustaches and slicked back hair. As I moved along the wall the signatures of the artists caught my eye. Pietro Annigoni, de la Mare, Hockney, Lucien Freud, Ronnie Wood, Kray, to name but a few. I was always slightly intimidated by this array of talent, but not today. I felt that I could add to this assortment of venerable portraits and hold my head up as being just as competent, and perhaps more so than some of the more eclectic or avant guard offerings.

I was admiring the simplicity of one of the drawings when I heard the hum of conversation escape from the room opposite and turned expecting to see the steward. It was to my considerable surprise, and delight, to see the woman from the previous Friday evening reception slip silently into the corridor, looking around as if unsure where she should go. I presumed that she was unaware of my presence as she took a deep breath and rubbed the back of her neck with a slender elegant hand, perfectly manicured, the nails a bright red. A ring comprising of a huge diamond and encircled by rubies set in white gold sat on her wedding finger, the stones trapping and reflecting the light from the bay window overlooking the garden.

I stood transfixed by her statuesque frame; her beauty undiminished from the other evening. She stood at around five foot ten, a slim but curvaceous figure. Her silky black hair cascaded down her back and engulfed in waves of soft curls the hand that was still massaging the back of her neck. Her complexion was of porcelain, the high cheekbones, the large bright almond eyes set below dark, arched eyebrows. Her nose was slender, slightly pinched at the end. Her full lips showed a hint of lipstick but otherwise her face appeared devoid of unnecessary cosmetics. Diamond drop earrings hung delicately from her small ear lobes.

I involuntarily took a sharp intakc of breath. Rather than any sign of surprise, she slowly raised her eyes to study me and smiled in the manner that had so captivated me the previous Friday. She briefly glanced down the corridor in which she was standing and then advanced into the Firepit, closing the doors behind her to provide an intimate privacy. The reality of her presence here before me was even more dazzling than the image I had imprisoned in my mind and on the page of my sketchbook.

"I'm sorry," she apologised in a soft tone that did not sound apologetic.

"I needed a break from the great and the good." She indicated with a minute flick of her head towards the room across the corridor. Still maintaining eye contact, she gracefully lowered herself onto one of the comfortably upholstered chairs by the firepit and crossed her legs. She was wearing a simple, but perfectly tailored dress, which settled modestly around her as the soft cushions yielded to her weight. She retained the distinct hint of an Italian accent, while her clothing exuded the sophistication that comes so naturally to that race.

I tried to regain my composure and stumbled over my words as I attempted to assure her that her presence was most welcome. My phraseology sounded stilted and slightly pompous and she radiated a childishly, innocent grin to devastating effect.

"Are you here on work or pleasurable affairs of state?" A slim, artistic hand languorously caressed her leg as if to smooth an unseen wrinkle in her sheer stocking. I gawped like a stupid teenager and found myself lost for any sensible, let alone witty reply.

"Oh, for God's sake!"

I was unnerved. Had I said that out aloud? She stayed perfectly still, so I assumed that the Voice remained in my head. She waited patiently, eyes unblinking, for my answer.

I faltered and my brain scrabbled to find the words that are so simple.

"I am meeting a friend," I stuttered. "I have a…" I corrected myself, "something to give him."

"That's pathetic. Hardly an impressive introduction."

I rubbed my perspiring hand across my chin and wondered what to say next. I was overtaken.

"I'm an artist and have been completing a commission. I'm here to present the finished article to my friend."

This time she definitely heard me and looked intrigued. I was intrigued for a different reason; I did not recall having spoken.

"How very exciting – an artist." She re-crossed her legs and sat forward slightly on the chair as if to study me better, now an item of interest. I was uncomfortably aware of her attention and uncertain what to say or do next.

"My name is James Farthing." I extended my hand and she lifted hers for me to collect. It was cool and soft to the touch and a sensation of a mild electric shock between us was fleeting as she gently withdrew it from my hold. There was no reciprocating introduction and so she remained nameless for the moment.

"May I enquire what you are doing here?" The question sounded impertinent, particularly with the emphasis on the 'you'. It was none of my business, but I really did want to know. She waved a dismissive hand in the air and was evasive in her reply, stating that she was merely killing time. She reverted to the role of inquisitor,

"Are you famous. Should I have heard of you?"

I floundered again, too diffident to either admit or deny the suggestion.

"Well, you may have seen some of my work recently," I listened to myself and wondered where this was leading. The statement was true but not in the manner she obviously took my overly confident response to mean.

"James Farthing." She closed her eyes as if trying to remember my name. Her lashes were thick and as she opened her lids, they revealed in slow motion her sparkling, amused eyes. She knew how to use her eyes to devastating effect. She watched with self-absorbed delight at the effect she was having upon my deportment.

"That is a charming name and I am sure that it sounds a chime, but I cannot recall why."

The slip in her English revealed a linguistic naivety that was charming and accentuated her Italian roots. I did not feel in control of the conversation to the extent of being excluded. I managed a wan smile that I knew to be pitiful against her spontaneous bursts of sunlight. She watched me with undisguised amusement for a moment longer, her head held slightly to one side.

"Now I look at you, you do look slightly familiar. Do you think we might have met before?"

"Not formally met, but I was at the reception last Friday and we did briefly speak."

"Really? Were you there to draw or donate?"

"To draw." I could not help myself. She slowly extracted from me the information she required.

"Ah, now I think I know what you have been doing. Can I see?"

"Sadly not. I would love to, but I think on this occasion it would be inappropriate, not to say unpopular."

"Pity, I have some interest in art and artists. Some might see me as a patron so I would like to form my own judgement." She pouted, playfully playing the petulant child. "If, as you say, it would not be popular with your client then I will have to be patient. But don't keep me waiting too long, I might lose interest."

She rose from her seat and unexpectedly announced, "I am Contessa de Wolfherz. I hope that one day we will meet again, and you will feel more able to show me some of your work."

I felt my spine tingle and I was sure that I blushed. She showed no sign of witnessing my lack of social etiquette and her certainty of us meeting again thrilled me.

"I would like that. Do you live in London?" I was not sure how you addressed a Countess and I felt that my question was verging on the impertinent, if not flirtatious. I was trying, unsuccessfully, to insist that this inquisition must stop before I got out of my depth.

"Relax, I am in control."

The Contessa hesitated, whether to consider the appropriateness of my question or to allow my discomfort to grow I do not know. Slowly her smile dissipated, and she ruefully ran her hand gently across the surface of the table in front of her.

"No. I am here on an errand with my husband. We are staying with some of his friends." I noted the unenthusiastic reference to her husband's friends as she continued, "I am not much taken by London, I am afraid. And you? Where do you live? Do you have a family?"

My confidence seemed to have evaporated. Had my Voice departed from the room? I was left alone to make polite conversation with this exquisite but inquisitive stranger.

But she was no stranger.

I knew her well and by having drawn her in such detail I had created a self-styled familiarity that drew us together in search of a mutual purpose that I could not yet define. I momentarily regained my composure and attempted to perpetuate the conversation.

"Me? I live alone, some thirty miles west of London," I was uncertain if I should elaborate further and my voice trailed off leaving the sentence hanging in a static atmosphere full of uncertain expectation. Her face softened and she let her eyes reveal a sadness that was unexpected.

"I know what it is to lose those you love." I was not sure that I had heard her correctly, or what had prompted her to say such a thing. "There have been so many, but few such as that which you have lost."

I became confused but before I could get any clarification my Voice had returned.

"Do I detect a slight hint of Veneto in your accent, Contessa?"

The Contessa was shaken from her brief, uncharacteristically doleful mood and smiled broadly at the observation.

"Why, yes. How clever of you. Do you know Venice?"

"I expect to be travelling to Venice in the near future. I have not been before and I could not resist."

The Countess clapped her hands with excitement and her eyes lit up. I stood with what I hoped was not too astonished a look on my face at her sudden burst of energetic enthusiasm.

"Oh, it's my most favourite city. I have had such happy times there," she faltered, looked briefly towards the door from whence she had come, but then regained her fervour. "I spent many happy summers there, swimming at the serene Rima's floating baths." She chatted, divulging a reverie of memories to which she was not sure I should be privy. Suddenly she refocused upon my presence, "I wish we had time to speak some more, but really I ought to be getting back." The Contessa again looked expectantly at the door but continued speaking, "For an artist such as you it is the most sublime city."

As she rose from her chair and walked slowly towards the door she spoke swiftly of restaurants and galleries that I should visit, the names of which were impossible for me to catch. Seeing my confusion, the Contessa asked for a pen and a piece of paper. I only had my sketchbook and pencils in my briefcase and scrabbled inside to hand both to her.

She wrote swiftly and smoothly on the fresh new page I had presented to her,

"Galleria D'Abrinzi has fond memories for me. It is exceptional, if modest. You must go there; I believe that you will find it of fascination and antiquity. You might have to forego a swim at Rima's, as the baths are only open from June to September. On another visit perhaps?"

In her excitement to impart her information to me her English became more fragmented and less fluid. She hesitated in handing the book back to me and slipped a finger between the page she had written on and the one before. Immediately I detected that she was going to turn back and see the drawing that I had done of her the previous Friday evening. I panicked and roughly grabbed the sketchbook from her hand. She looked hurt and I tried to apologise for any offence that I might have caused. She pouted peevishly and gave me an admonishing flash with her bejewelled eyes.

She had written the name of the gallery in a clear strong flowing script and I reverted to the conversation before I had so rudely dispossessed her of the book.

"*I'll be certain to visit the...,*" I looked down at the page again, "*Galleria D'Abrinzi.*"

"You must. You really must." She was so insistent upon the point that she was on the verge of agitation. I assured her with my most ingratiating smile that I would make every effort.

She calmed and politely, almost quaintly, repeated that she must take her leave of me. She extended her hand one final time and I held it again. The contact was brief but exhilarating. I thought that something indefinable passed between us - a link, a knowing.

"I feel sure that we shall meet again," she slipped her cool hand from mine.

As silently as she had arrived, she departed from the Firepit closing the door with a barely audible click, leaving me in breathless, confused isolation. The exchange had been surreal, and I was unsure if it had really happened. Her appearance, the conversation all seemed as if in a dream. I stood before the Firepit and her absence was heavy in the room, like some musk perfume that stimulated the senses, hung in the air, but showed no physical presence. All I could remember was her name, Contessa de Wolfherz. The only evidence of our conversation was the hastily written address of the gallery in my sketchbook.

I stared at the writing, unseeing of the words, before my contemplations were interrupted by the arrival of Roger a few minutes later, who stormed into the room and he was clearly in a hurry.

"James, I am really sorry that I am so late and that I have kept you waiting." Such an apology from Roger was rare and he must have been flustered. "The office is like a mad-house at the moment. The markets are all over the place."

He shook my hand swiftly and waved me towards a seat. I lowered myself into the Contessa's chair, the indent still warm from where she had been seated. I pulled my briefcase onto my knees to take out the portrait. He looked around the room with obvious appreciation.

"Do your members have any idea of what you have on these walls?" Roger asked as he examined some of the signatures on the portraits that stared down at us.

“I have to admit that we all get a bit blasé about them and do not notice them much, until a guest or visitor like you comes along.” I had taken my drawing out of its protective sleeve and he waited expectantly as I unwrapped the stiff sheet of handmade paper. I passed it across to him for his approval.

He whistled quietly and looked up at me from the drawing, “This is magnificent, James. Oh, yes. Sir Brian is going to love this. I really am most grateful to you.” I gave him the wrappings and he carefully placed it back in the envelope by his side while he retrieved two fifty-pound notes from his jacket pocket.

“I think this is what we agreed, was it not?”

I took the crisp clean notes and heard my inner Voice scornfully say,

“You’ve been blinded by the aura of fame.”

“What did your Voice mean?” The priest had been sitting for a long time and wants to leave but cannot interrupt the old man while he is reminiscing.

“I didn’t know at that point but was to find out.”

“Were you truly unaware of what you were saying, what words were passing from your lips. Had the Voice really taken control, or did you just not recognise your own self-confident mood at that point when speaking with the Contessa?"

The old man sat looking at his desktop without really focusing.

"I am not certain if I am ever really in control."

XI
Retribution

The old man is dressed in a light-coloured suit, with a silk handkerchief fluttering from his top pocket. On his feet are polished, brown loafers and on his head a white straw hat with a bright purple band. The ever-present cane is held loosely in his hand, swinging gently to and fro as he stands on the quay on La Giudecca. A funeral barge is passing before him and he removes his hat and lowers his head as it moves across the water. He adopts a relaxed stance with his legs slightly apart and the stick no longer swinging but grounded in front of him as a mark of respect.

He replaces his hat when the funeral cortege has moved away across the choppy water.

"Are you following me again, Priest?"

The priest is standing just behind the old man, having seen him as he returns from an errand he was running for his Bishop.

"There is something particularly moving about a Venetian funeral cortege. It is timeless and unique." The priest is in a reflective mood, aware that the occupant of the barge was one of his flock.

"Death is death. Once the last rattle has been expelled all that is left is an empty container, a husk." The old man turns to face the priest.

"What of the soul?"

"I am not as convinced as you are that there is a soul."

"Everyone has a soul."

"Not everyone. Some leave memories, some have legacies, and some just die."

"And those that 'just die'?", the young priest stands next to the old man, both are staring out over the water, neither looking at the other.

"As I say, they just die."

"Whom do you refer to? Who are these people who just die, and who decides that they just die?"

The priest senses another theological discussion that he is not in the mood for and wishes he could change the subject.

"You and I can decide that they just die." The priest turns his head and looks at the old man's profile. The creases in his face are lighter, the skin infinitesimally tighter across his cheeks. The old man does not return his stare,

"It just takes motivation."

Shopping had never been a pastime that I had enjoyed and as I wandered around my local town centre I knew why. People pushed and shove to get their purchases in a quantity that seemed to defy logic. Parents dragged reluctant children from store to store, purchasing a myriad of goods that were beyond both their needs and means.

When I wandered around the various stores, people noted that I used a cane and assumed that I was impaired in some unseen manner. Most were sympathetic and gave me space, or even on some occasions an undeserved privilege such as a place in a long queue. My stick had become part of my everyday life and a constant companion on any trip made beyond the confines of my home. Since the attack, it provided me with the degree of reassurance that I wanted. It was elegantly sturdy with its brass ferule and silver top and, in the intervening period since the assault, I had become adept in its use and now travelled with confidence.

With each step that I took, the stick resounded solidly on the concrete floor of the multi-storey car park. I had come to buy my weekly provisions from the supermarket that was located beneath the building. Weaving my way through the rows of vehicles, I tried to navigate a direct line to the scratched and battered door giving access onto the stairwell. When I pushed the door open the stairs smelt of urine and the lighting was overly bright.

I started to descend the stairs and I could hear someone climbing up towards the landing. Before I reached the bottom of my flight of steps, the climber had started to turn onto the landing beneath my feet. He looked up and stared me straight in the eye. I froze. He stopped in his tracks and a malevolent smile broke out over his scarred face.

"Well fuck me! If it ain't me old mate, Picasso!" A cackle of ugly laughter reverberated round the empty stairwell.

Adrenalin surged into my stomach, but I stood my ground a couple of steps above him. I looked around to see if anyone was in the near vicinity to witness what was inevitably about to happen. He swaggered up the final step onto the landing, my leather bag nonchalantly hanging from his shoulder. He saw me looking at it and could not fail to perceive the anger in my eyes.

"Oh, you noticed. Do you like me new bag?" He took it from his shoulder and held the strap in his hand so that it swung gently forwards and back towards me.

"You should get one, it would go well with the rest of your fancy gear."

I listened, unmoved by his taunts. I tightened my grip on my cane and, spotting the white of my knuckles, he paused in his advance.

"Now you're not going to do anything silly are you, old man?" His other hand went to the back pocket of his filthy jeans and there was a click as the blade of his knife snapped open.

I did not hesitate and swung my stick towards him. In the confines of the stairwell the force was not as strong as I would have liked. As it approached the side of his head, he dropped the bag and caught the shaft, the wood slapping hard against his palm making him wince.

"You silly, old fucker!" he yells and starts to pull the stick towards him. I twist the handle against his grip and swiftly withdraw the long rapier blade from its innocuous looking wooden sheath. His mouth drops open and his eyes widen as he focuses on the pristine, razor sharp edge that has been carefully honed and now glinted in the harsh lighting.

"What the f…."

"Shut up and drop the knife." I snapped.

His bravado partially returns, but the smile is unsure.

"What you going to do old man?"

"You are going to return my bag to me."

"Fuck off!"

I take a step down so that the tip of the blade is now pointing directly at his Adams apple a mere fraction from the skin. I notice it give a convulsive jump and the colour drains from the thug's face.

"You wouldn't dare. You ain't got the bottle."

As if to demonstrate that I would, and did, I flick the blade infinitesimally, a wave of motion snakes fast along its length so that the point cleanly slices his skin. A thin trickle of blood escapes and starts to run down towards his collarbone.

He grabs his neck, and then looks at the blood on his hand. His face displays undisguised hate, but his eyes show fear.

"The knife?"

He looks at his other hand as if he had forgotten what was in it. Slowly he releases his hold on the blade and it drops with a clatter onto the floor.

"The stick please?"

As if not believing what was happening to him, he hands me the remains of my stick.

"You're a fucking idiot. Do you think I'm gonna let you walk out of here? No way. I'm going to ram that fucking sword right up your arse."

"*Unlikely, frankly. I have control now, don't you think? But rest assured, you won't be capable of following me.*"

He looks at me with incomprehension,

"What's with the scary voice?"

"*What scary voice is that*?"

"I'll still get you. I know where you live. I'll fucking cut you up in bits and feed you to my dogs."

"*In that case, we have little alternative*." The voice in my head is quite insistent.

The point of the long blade remains motionless at his neck. I can see the blood pumping through the veins to either side as he enters fight or flight mode.

"*My bag, please*?"

The thug lowers his body to a crouch and the rapier follows him down. He feels for the strap, his eyes black and murderously never leaving mine. He rises and holds out the bag.

"Just toss it lightly in my direction, but don't think to move or you will be skewered." He swings the bag to and fro a couple of times and then let's go. It falls in easy reach onto one of the steps just above my feet.

"*Now, what do you want to do*?"

"Do?"

"*Walk away or not*?" I know he is not going to walk away.

"Oh fuck. Whatever."

He turns and bends to pick up his knife.

"*Uh-uh. You can leave that here*."

He stops mid-way and looks up at me again. He is weighing up his chances, still not believing that I have it in me.

Suddenly he lunges for the knife simultaneously making a charge up the stairs. He is far too slow. I slash the blade downwards with a flick of my wrist. There is a strange whistle of air as it slices smoothly across his throat, splitting his voice box and opening the pulsing veins. He stops instantly and watches as blood spurts from his neck. He silently mouths in my direction, no longer in anger but unbridled terror.

I do not need to linger, as I know the outcome. I kick his knife towards him as he sinks to his knees and tries to stem the torrent of blood that flows from his body.

I return the blade to its scabbard, pick up my bag and turn back up the stairs.

The whole encounter has taken no more than ninety seconds.

It is not until I am driving down the spiral exit road from the car park that I hear a scream.

"You killed him?" The priest is horrified.

"Ssshh! No need to announce it to everyone."

The two men are walking along the waterfront as the old man recounts the latest episode in his tale, idly watching the activity on the wide canal between Giudecca and the Fondamente delle Zattere.

"Did he die?"

"I hope so."

"But that is murder?"

"Self-defence, dear boy. Self-defence."

"Did the police come to see you?"

"No. Bearing in mind that he moved in some very unsavoury circles, it was assumed to be a gangland killing of some sort. The police never even came to tell me whether the poor chap had died."

"Poor chap?! But you killed him!"

"I like to think it as a dispatch. I dispatched him."

"What difference does it make what word you use?"

"A great deal. You dispatch a rabid dog, and there was no one more rabid than that young man. He needed to be removed from society."

"But that is not your role. That is the role of the legal system. That is what makes us a civilised society."

The old man stops walking and turns to face the priest.

"You are so naïve. Life has a lot to teach you."

"Why are you telling me this?" The priest is becoming distraught and feels that the situation is beyond his experience. He is slightly frightened of the old man and looks down at the stick in his hand.

"Is that the murder weapon?"

"Will you stop using that word? Yes, it is. Forever with me for just such eventualities."

The priest shakes his head in disbelief,

"I need to sit down."

The old man looks around and sees a bench to which he gently steers the overwhelmed younger man. They both sit and while the priest seems exhausted, the old man is erect, alert.

In the silence the priest struggles with the implications of what he is hearing, unclear as to precisely what he should do. The priest eventually regains some of his composure.

"Have you told anyone else about this?"

"No. I never felt that there was a need." The old man replies, and then adds, "Not until recently."

"Why now? Why me?"

"I am an old man and will die. You are a priest and as a priest you have strong ethics when it comes to confession."

"You are treating this as a confessional?"

"Yes, I suppose I am."

“Then come to the church. Come to the confession box. See me there.”

“Why? It is more convivial to do it out and about. I don’t like the strictures of religious rites.”

The two men revert to their respective silences, one man at peace, the other in turmoil.

“Are you on the run from the British authorities?” The priest tries to speak in a soft tone, conciliatory and almost comforting. The old man wonders if the priest is trying to extricate himself from the entanglement that he finds himself in, to erase the information that he now holds.

“I did say that the police took no interest in me. Didn’t even inform me as to whether the boy had died.”

The priest seems to relax slightly.

“What are you going to do now that I have made my confession to you?” The old man emphasises the ‘you’ in his question, seemingly more curious than concerned.

The priest has been churning this question around in his mind before the old man asks it. While in no way does he wish to condone, or to show any sign of approval of the old man’s actions, he does have a slight degree of sympathy. It seems from the account given that the other man was intending to harm the old man. But how was he to know whether the story was true? The young priest places his hand over his mouth and rubs at the soft stubble on his chin.

"I need to think this through." The priest gets up and looks down at the spritely old man who shows no symptom of distress or remorse. He is merely regaling events as he remembers them.

As the priest turns to leave the old man catches his wrist in a tight grip.

"*Don't take too long. I need to speak to you further.*"

The old man's voice is hoarse and sounds familiar but ethereal. The priest's heart jumps a beat and he hurries away to pray.

Intermezzo

"Thank you for sparing the time to join me in this charming little gallery.

I feel that you might like me to explain myself as I think it might be of assistance to you. My role in this saga is dictated by necessity. By some I am revered, perhaps even by you, while for others I am something to be feared. But this is ill founded and a mere product of ignorance. You will all make the same journey, only for some there is little perception of the path being travelled until, perhaps, the final steps. At that time, I shall be on hand to provide assurance and lead you – onwards towards the final mandated conundrum.

However, this old man's journey is of a different nature to most. He has been chosen, much as you have chosen to witness the events that will unfold. As such, I must request that you expand the narrow preconceptions and logic of your everyday existence, dispel the numbing grip on your capacity to peruse the world from different perspectives, with different eyes. You must draw upon what you see, not what you discern.

But I digress, the necessity to which I referred earlier is to undo what has been done, to ensure that the correct paths are redefined for those who were misdirected and cast adrift.

Now come, I see my lecturing puzzles you, which is not my intent. We have only a short time together, so let me try to cast some light on my dilemma.

Walk with me a while as we cast an eye upon the works that hang here.

Ah. Observe. Here she is! Such beauty, such poise; how could any man resist her undoubted charms, or any artist not be inspired to capture her very essence on each canvas that we now see before us? But mark my words; do not be deceived, she is not without a fulsome awareness of her attributes and the methods by which she can turn them to her best advantage.

Who is she, I hear you ask?

Why the young Livia, of course.

Allow me to elucidate a little further, if I may?

'Temptation or Seduction', she knows the price of both having been born to a poor, but hardworking family in the hills. That early life of poverty was counterbalanced with paternal love and pride. However, her obvious ambition overwhelms both of these. Her father recognises the stifling effect rural life will have upon his beloved daughter. Unaccustomed to seeking assistance from his Liege,

he finally conjures up enough humility to approach his employer and explain that he wishes to find a better life for his young daughter.

The master knows of the girl and of her beauty. Generously, he offers to take the child to work in his palazzo in the city and provide her with the chance of education and betterment. The father expresses his gratitude to the man that he had served for all of his life, comforted in the thought that no harm could come to his innocent offspring in such a fine gentleman's safe keeping. Such blind naivety is the curse of many fathers. Trust is sometimes misplaced in the desperation to give what one hopes is the best for one's child.

Don't misunderstand me; the master was an honourable man and good to his word. The young woman was employed in the service of his wife. She appreciated having the pretty, attentive and amusing maid as company during her husband's long absences from the city on affairs of state. She teaches her to read and write, how to dress her mistress and appreciate the fine clothes that they buy together. The maid watches and learns and begins to dream of attaining a vastly more superior status than her current position. The secrets of her mistress are privy to her, not least the attentions of a young man who adoringly implores the love and consummation of his wildest reveries. The mistress plays her admirer, meeting him secretly behind masked face and false chastity. She knows that he will eventually satisfy his voracious appetites but demonstrates to the maid that the chase is sometimes more satisfying than the kill. At a time of her choosing she will succumb to his charms - and willingly so – but at this time the anticipation remains delicious to her taste and she has no strong desire to prematurely bring that sensation to a climax.

Hence, one of Livia's roles becomes that of clandestine go-between, running messages to and from the two parties. In so doing, she discovers the many and varied streets of the city and becomes conversant with the numerous communities that inhabited the different districts, or sestieri. She brokers many friendships outside the palazzo with those who work in, and demand leisure from the city. The latter is readily available to those who seek it and there are plenty who will aid the search for those less confident in navigating such darker conduits of delight.

I know what you are thinking; I always know what you are thinking. How can such an innocent immersed in this apparent depravity not become sullied? Rest assured, our young maid maintained her virtue. Simultaneously, she learnt the ways of those who worked the city, as well as those of her capricious mistress. However, as she develops her appreciation of the finer things in life her peers in the palazzo begin to become jealous of her rise. One such was the controller of the finances and staff within the palazzo for the family.

If you look at the picture now before us, we shall concentrate our attention on the depiction of his accommodation. He has furnished it with a few fine pieces that were surplus to the needs of both the family's country and city palazzos. It is not an ostentatious room. The walls are painted with a light lime wash and a polished mahogany corner cupboard stands to one side of his leather-inlaid desk and high-backed chair. The desk seems to be covered with invoices and ledgers with which he attempts to maintain a tight control on the budgets that are within his responsibility. Behind the desk hangs an unexceptional portrait within a gilded frame. His hat and long black coat are draped neatly from a coat stand, while his delicate ebony handled umbrella stands open at the base, water running from its ribbed surface onto the stone floor, forming pools of reflected light from the high window opposite his desk. As is his habit, he wears a dark suit with leather shoes and a starched white shirt. He considers himself fortunate to have such a position, privately acknowledging to himself that he is not the most accomplished bookkeeper or administrator. But by dint of hard work, he holds down the position, possibly only due to the fact that the master is away so often that he does not have time to pay close enough attention to the tasks required of the man.

The young Livia rarely had occasion to attend this part of the palazzo and so, when summoned, enters with some trepidation. The man has long admired the slim figure that regularly accompanied his mistress but has supressed the desire to make any advances. He is a man of figures, you understand. He does not have the smooth ways in matters of love and desire, as do his counterparts in the world of poetry, art, literature or architecture. His manner is used to being deferential rather than forward, a product of an upbringing in servitude. However, the young maid is beginning to assume airs and graces that he considers to be inappropriate for her station in the house. That, together with the constant presence of this beautiful but innocently vulnerable young woman, results in an unrequited passion building within his breast. He desires her more than any woman before, including both his wife and mistress.

Ah, yes. I understand your confusion. How can a man such as this have not only a wife but also a mistress? Forget your preconceptions about modern day sensibilities. We are in a city of unadulterated vice, in an era when the moral norms are ignored, if not eradicated. Young, old, rich, poor – they all follow a path of self-indulgence and excess – even our ineffective accountant. The only difference is the degree and overt brazenness of such excesses. The richer you are, the more with which you can afford to get away - or have covered up.

Forgive me, are you comfortable at this pace? I am not going too fast for you, I hope? No? Then, if I may, I will continue?

I suspect you can guess what is coming. So, before we move on, let me assure you that this young lady does not succumb to the man's ever-insistent advances. She is incensed at his presumption that his elevated position within the household gives him a lien upon her virtue. That will be relinquished at a time of her choosing and such a valuable commodity will command a high price. Much more than this man can afford.

Her mistress has taught her well. An immediate rebuttal would be detrimental to her situation, the balance of trust and authority with her master and mistress still being against her. But young Livia is not beyond redressing imbalances. She establishes a hold over her besotted paramour in anticipation rather than satisfaction. This she manages for some months while she insidiously infects the mind of her mistress, and hence her master, as to the man's voracity and whether he is conflicted between his own financial vulnerability and the fortunes of the household. She causes sums of money to 'disappear' or items of expenditure to go unreported. The errors compound themselves and increasingly the ledgers do not balance. The man is confused and distracted due to his single-minded pursuit of Livia. He becomes sloppy in the diligence with which he would normally attend to his duties. She finds it increasingly easy to befuddle the poor man and leads him into murky financial waters.

Eventually, at the appropriate time, she springs her trap. Angry at the obvious maladministration of his affairs, the Master summarily dismisses his chancellor. The poor foolish man is ruined and falls into a poverty-stricken existence. Livia, while not being wholly without conscience, does not feel any guilt at his demise.

Let us progress; there is more to see and my time is short.

I mentioned that young Livia moves freely through the city streets and, with increasing familiarity and knowledge, her acquaintances become many and varied. Wealth and privilege fascinate and beguile her. She starts to formulate her next strategy, namely, to enter a higher ranking within society. She meets and subtly interrogates the many staff members of other patrician families. She visits the major palazzos within the city under the guise of her mistress's social needs. Each is assessed and evaluated; slowly she whittles the likely candidates down until she is clear which one she is to concentrate her efforts upon.

This is a price that is worthy of her virtue.

And so, see here. 'The Entrance of a Patrician's Home in Venice'. Look who enters and who is watching. At the door to the house is a man with his back towards us. He hides from the surrounding poverty beneath a scalloped parasol that also protects him from the harsh late morning sun that fills the narrow alley leading up to his faded front door. The gaggle of women to his right appear reasonably well attired but still hold out their hands for alms. Opposite the begging women stands a stable lad, bridles in hand, and next to him a young, dark haired beauty. The other women know her, but her true intentions remain a secret from them. The patrician gentleman is totally unaware of the beautiful Livia, for that is who stands beside his door.

His fingers fumble with the keys as he seeks to get into the cool of the interior. His dark, formal day clothes are hot and clinging to his skin as the fetid air rises from the alley. Stuccowork has fallen from the walls to expose the spalling brickwork either side of the entrance. Standing guard over the door is the grizzled face of some unknown deity, carved into the keystone, hanging ponderously, barely balanced, defying gravity's pull.

But this is the house of a wealthy patrician and the exterior belies the opulence that lies behind the door. The air is cool in the interior, marble flooring and shaded courtyards echo to the soft sound of crystal-clear water running along channels. The style and features are those more usually found in the architecture of the East. The incorporation of such elements of design exemplifies the depth of education and breadth of travel that the owner has experienced during his privileged life.

Livia knows his face, but we do not. From our vantage point we can see that he is of muscular stature, but clearly not young. Livia has quickly concluded that older men have had time to cultivate their personality - and enhance their wealth. This patrician, which she has marked out as her quarry, is a Count. He has not married young, as others might have done, but has completed his army service with distinction and honour. He relishes the discovery of the natural beauty of the world and has experienced more than most of the citizens that live in his sullied city. He has achieved position and respect in society, becoming a politician who is ruthless in his hate for corruption and dishonesty in all its forms. This is a rare commodity in those days, and perhaps also now.

However, a narrow-minded society wonders why he has not chosen to wed and consequently rumours abounded that he is not drawn to women as other men might be. This slur is an irritation to him, but nothing more. Livia views this slander as a virtue as, if true, he would not be too demanding upon her young body. He was neither hideous to the eye nor overtly violent – also a rarity at this time. He has led a blameless, quiet existence that suits her purpose and would, if ensnared to her satisfaction, enable her to lead a carefree existence to entertain herself as she saw fit.

Having chosen her target, she needs to put in place a plan to turn his head in her direction. As a mere lady's maid, she could easily accept the role of a mistress, to be used and abused while her youth and beauty remained pleasing to the needs of her benefactor. But if the rumours were true, then this was not a route open to her either. Besides, the role of mistress did not suit her needs and ambition – her focus was on becoming his Contessa.

Come. Let us move on, see here – 'Waiting for the Bride and Groom'.

She succeeds, having wooed her prey with an efficiency and fervour that overwhelmed the Count. She is married at twenty-two (the Count is forty years her senior) and they honeymoon at his palazzo in Venice. Subsequently they share their time between his palazzo in the Tuscan hills and that in Venice. Livia is mistress to both but prefers the temptations of the city to the solitude of her childhood in the hills.

This painting shows a simple wedding, not the grand service of blessing that might be expected of a Count. Perhaps, as a man of consideration and understanding, appreciative of the fact that he was marrying a young woman of known low social standing, he felt the pomp of a large society wedding would be overwhelming for both him and his bride.

His bride discovers that the rumours as to his lack of interest in female company are wholly untrue, although he proves not to be a demanding husband; his attentions being somewhat flaccid and lacking in any true passion. Contessa Livia does not resent the loss of her virginity to this man as she has achieved a station in society that fulfils her dreams. The other ladies in Venice sneer at her position and are prickly towards her due to her youth, beauty and lack of birth right. The Count pays no attention to this snobbery as he adores his Contessa and, while not encouraging profligacy, allows her to spend relatively freely and move around the city with ease. In return, she remains almost faithful while maintaining in all that she does as discrete a demeanour as her husband.

This does not preclude affairs, but these are fleeting and on her own terms. Some just fizzle out while others, where her favours are abused, result in harsh retribution for her erstwhile lover. One such instance culminating in the suicide of an unfortunate army officer who miscalculates how ruthless she can be.

Her life was pleasing enough but over time she feels that it lacks something indefinable, beyond the mere fleshly pleasures or the amassing of material objects. She tolerates the company of her maid, but never falls into the trap of becoming over familiar, thereby exposing herself to the weaknesses of her former mistress. She appreciates that the Count is the master of the house and aware that the maid is not her confidante, but his.

Are you tired? Let us sit here a while and contemplate 'Encounter on a Bridge' – a rather unassuming picture which seems to have been painted in haste. It discretely camouflages the identity of the people involved. However, I know that this is one of many encounters that change the Contessa's life and provide her with something that had been missing for so long. As I stated a moment ago, the Contessa has been careful to lead a relatively blameless life, blameless that is within the context of Venice at the time of our story. She is approaching her mid-thirties and laments the fact that the firm musculature of her lithe body is starting to soften. The shallow laughter lines that frequently visit her face are beginning to be visible as permanent features. Her ageing husband remains remarkably resilient to the ravages that afflicted old age, but he has become increasingly possessive of his young wife. He does not overtly restrict her movements but often questions her upon her return to the palazzo from her many excursions. Sometimes he partakes in long, probing conversations with her maid and this merely serves to prove to Contessa Livia how wise she has been to keep her maid at arm's length as to many of her more personal activities.

But let us return to the bridge. Here we see a couple deep in conversation while a second fellow stands to one side, leaning idly on the balustrade. Is he listening to their discourse or is he merely there by coincidence? The white-gloved hand of the lady is held tightly in the other man's grip and his head is angled slightly to one side as if he is questioning the woman. He holds a walking cane in a slightly threatening manner. It is unclear if this is an accusatory encounter between husband and wife or one between lovers. Perhaps if you look at the image further you might conclude that the truth is, in fact, an illicit meeting peremptorily interrupted between the loiterer and the lady. Did the couple swiftly separate upon the unexpected arrival of the husband, hoping that their encounter was unseen?

The artist leaves us in a quandary, save that the lady's face does not seem to have the countenance of one who is staring at the subject of illicit affection. It is submissive, even apologetic, perhaps to a deceived husband. Is the man who is innocently leaning on the balustrade the artist, unsure whether to flee or remain and provide protection to his paramour?

I can elucidate and remove any uncertainty. Contessa Livia met the artist at a small private Venetian gallery where, as a patron, she was exhibiting some of his work. For the first time in her life she was able to converse with a man without any apparent hidden agendas or intents. He was not statuesque or handsome but simply open and passionate about his art. She had not met such a person before and became fascinated by his world. Her beauty absorbed him, as it did with all men, but rather than conquer her body, he sought to capture her countenance through the medium of paint upon a canvas. The Contessa was well aware that to be seen in any painting that had not been commissioned by her husband would immediately suspend the trust the Count had in her and cause an unwelcome scandal. However, the unique temptation to sit for the artist was too great. She arranged secret assignations at his studio on the top floor of the gallery owned by his friend. The artist was exasperated on each occasion that she sat because she insisted that her true beauty and identity be clouded from view, despite his promises to never allow anyone to see any of his portraits of her.

Hence the 'Eighteenth Century Venetian Lady' - over there - has her head turned away from the artist, her hair a flaxen colour covered with a diaphanous scarf, flowers over her right ear. These were all changes that were insisted upon by the Contessa, to maintain her anonymity.

During each sitting the two would talk freely and openly and the Contessa found the experience one of enormous release and enjoyment. To say that it exceeded the lustful cravings of her younger years was not true, but the sensuality of the voyeurism and method by which the artist expropriated each one of her delicate features and softly lay them onto the yielding canvas had an innocent eroticism that she found exhilarating. She spoke of her early life in the hills, in service and her ultimate social elevation with absolute honesty – the artist imbued in her a confidence that fed the inspiration for his work.

For example, you see over there we have 'The Mouse'. You see? There, further along the gallery. This is the depiction of the instant when her maid saw a mouse and none of them could catch or kill it. With tears running down her cheeks, the Contessa regaled how eventually, because of the hue and cry they were making, the exasperated Count was reduced to summoning two small boys to find and remove the mouse that had sought sanctuary in her linen cupboard.

Over time and, perhaps inevitably, the sittings became more frequent and slowly and insidiously, but without intent to harm, the artist succeeded in getting his muse to undertake ever more daring poses. 'After the bath', up there to your left, was one such pose. This beautifully delicate work was undertaken with a touch of each brushstroke that denoted more than mere voyeurism. Once the threshold had been crossed then she became ever more liberated and liberal with her life modelling, but always on the same terms. The artist prospered and their friendship grew and eventually blossomed into something more than that which might exist between pure artist and model. He became a gentle, grateful and considerate lover, mixing his work with his adoration of her body. She found him intelligent and caring, not a strong, forceful character but one who respected her feelings and valued her opinions. He taught her to draw and paint, and over time they became entwined one with the other, their lives separate but indivisibly linked through their art, thereby developing a dependency upon each other.

The artist's name, you ask.

I doubt you will have heard of him. He was Signor Giacomo Favretto, a citizen of Venice and, by virtue of my good offices, to be inextricably linked to the hero of this tale.

XII
Venice

PRIEST,

YOU LEFT IN A HURRY WHEN WE LAST MET AND HAVE CHOSEN NOT TO RETURN AS I HAD REQUESTED. CLEARLY, I UNSETTLED YOU, BUT DO NOT EXPECT AN APOLOGY FROM ME. I HAVE DECIDED TO CONTINUE WITH MY PURPOSE BY WRITING TO YOU, AS YOU DO NOT COME TO SPEAK TO ME. I AM NOT GOING TO REFER TO THE EVENTS ALREADY TOLD FOR OBVIOUS REASONS. I REMAIN WITH THE INTENTION OF CONTINUING TO CONFIDE IN YOU AND SO THIS SHOULD BE READ IN THAT VEIN. WHEN YOU HAVE CONSULTED WITH WHOMSOEVER YOU NEED TO CONSULT, AND THEY HAVE PROVIDED YOU WITH THE COMFORT, SUPPORT AND GUIDANCE THAT YOU NEED, THEN YOU CAN RETURN. UNTIL THAT TIME, YOU ARE OF LITTLE PRACTICAL USE TO ME.

GF

Arriving at Marco Polo airport is like any other international transport hub with all the frustrations and idiocy of modern air travel. Any sense of adventure from both the anticipation and actuality of travelling to some exotic or mysterious location has been lost for the sake of security and commercialism. A tawdry trade in tatty consumables has replaced the exotic, and any mystery is solely the preserve of the baggage handlers who determine the ultimate destination of your luggage.

There is a six-minute walk along an anodyne, first floor corridor with long, moving walkways, piped Vivaldi and a view of a bland car park until escalators deposit you down onto a bleak concourse. As an introductory welcome to Venice, the modern, stark brick columns exude a brutality of architectural form that screams to be demolished and replaced with something more sympathetic to better complement the stepping off point to La Serenissima.

I presented to one of the two men controlling the chaotic scene before me the inevitable piece of paper that ensured my transportation into the deep embrace of Venetian hospitality. I was directed to Pier 4, which was off to the right. The waterman was dark and swarthy with two days stubble on his chin. He looked me up and down, taking in my travelling attire with an admiring look normally reserved for his fellow countrymen and, more particularly, women. He smiled in greeting and took my bags. He concluded from my walking cane that I was more disabled than was the case. Consequently, he extended his hand to aid my boarding and I thanked him as I was ushered into the saloon and encouraged to take a seat on the upholstered bench.

Riva launches arrived and departed, like industrious bees around a busy hive. Each had varnished timber decks and lit interiors, they slid through the water that bucked and splashed around the low, concrete jetties, each rising and falling to the swell. Vertical poles marked their mooring points and denoted the course to be followed out into the lagoon. The powerful engine burbled as we backed out from the pier, turned and left the melee behind us.

The distant roofline punctured by spires and softened by elegant domes wistfully hovered, just visible, above an ethereal winter mist that hung over the silken lagoon. The wan morning sun had risen a few hours ago above an indistinct horizon and weakly attempted to dispel the chill of the night air. Lights flickered on the far shore, the city enticing the weary traveller, tempting him to approach her, breath in her heady perfume and wantonly explore her. Venice is a seductress, the watermen her pimps, delivering ever willing customers to her pleasures while simultaneously sliding her hand inside their wallets to relieve them of their hard-earned currency.

It was this first view of the city that made me involuntarily breathe a little faster, plumes of condensation catching in the cold air as if from an exhaled cigarette. The tranquillity of the distant mistress was in stark contrast to the bustle of the water taxis and their voluble pilots.

The sharp curved bow sliced through the surface of the lagoon and powered me towards the far lights, cutting the distance between us by the second, the detail of the buildings being teasingly revealed through the veil of mist as we approached. I could not remain in the saloon, nor resist the opportunity of standing by the boatman in the open cockpit as we rode the wash from other boats returning to the airport for their next fare.

As soon as we were out of the confines of the airport channel the driver opened up thc engine and with a deliciously deep roar, we accelerated forward. The wind blew into my eyes producing tears that brushed down my cheeks. The fresh morning air released from within me a deep sense of freedom and relief, mixed with an expectant exhilaration. My adventure had begun and even though I was a solitary traveller, my expectations were eddying within me and the ecstasy of the moment was greater than I had ever anticipated. I was in love already and I had only just met my beloved Venice.

We passed the walls to the small island that formed the cemetery and slowed as we entered a wide basin. In turn, this led to a canal between pastel shaded buildings, our wash lapping against their foundations. I looked back towards the airport. I was leaving the 21st century and being enveloped within an earlier era, a time of elegance mixed with poverty and immorality. Here was a city that had no scruples and brazenly exposed her failings, gaily applauded her paradoxes, and dared the innocent and the naive to succumb to her allure. Her aged, cracked and crumbling visage looked down upon me, painted and gilded, as I slid into the timeless setting - a willing prey to her voracious appetites.

As we progressed along the waterway, I could see a wider canal before me with the early morning traffic moving goods back and forth. The ornately baroque, white façade of Casa Pesaro witnessed my arrival from the opposite side of the Grand Canal. We expertly edged our way past a lone gondola, black and gold with vacant red velvet cushions on the seats, gliding towards a small pontoon. The gondolier was wearing a thick coat over his traditional stripped shirt. His boater lay discarded on the seat in front of him. He returned my gaze and imperceptibly nodded a welcome to his domain. No smile, no overt expression of greeting but merely a knowing acknowledgement that I somehow belonged in this watery idyll. I broke eye contact and returned my attention to the front of the boat.

We emerged into the grandeur of the Grand Canal. The image so oft captured by Canaletto remained remarkably untouched by modern times; the buildings would have been as recognisable to him as they were new to me now. The whole scene was awe-inspiring such that I let out a whoop of sheer joy. The driver did not turn in surprise but merely smiled. Another satisfied customer had succumbed to his mistress's charismatic beauty – he had seen it all before.

I had barely had time to take in any of the detail before we had eased our way across the Grand Canal, sliding between delivery barges and vaporetto crowded with early tourists or those making their way to work. Gently we drew up to a pontoon outside a building with an ochre red façade, an incongruous timber, first floor bay window and a shallow, columned second floor balcony. On the pontoon were a number of small metal tables with chairs either side for any hardy guests who sought to take a coffee or grappa overlooking the Palazzo Fontana Rezzonico and Casa D'Oro, or House of Gold, on the opposite bank. But all this was unknown to me at the time of my arrival and was yet to be discovered.

A yellow light shone through the glazed doors that opened onto the pontoon. A smartly suited porter appeared to supervise my arrival. The Riva gently kissed the side of the timber platform, with its cross-poled balustrade. Two stripped vertical poles denoting the disembarkation point. The boatman deftly made the craft secure while the porter stepped forward, greeted me by name and offered me his hand to assist my transfer to the pontoon. I turned to retrieve my bags from the floor of the launch, but he insisted that I leave them where they lay, assuring me that he would safely deliver them to my room.

Using my cane for support, I steadied myself on the gently undulating pontoon and looked up at the façade of the building.

Beyond the glazed, double doors into the building were heavy damask curtains held aside by swatches of gold rope with tasselled ends. This had once been a comfortable, if not sumptuous home that reluctantly, or in greed for the tourist dollar, had been forced to become a boutique hotel. I found the interior strangely familiar and comforting; the richness of the rugs that deadened my footfall, the striking wall tapestries, the varied paintings that hung from every wall of the hallway, a ceiling of low, dark beams, and a selection of display cabinets and tables set against the wall supporting a wondrous collection of Murano glass. To the left was a small, rather incongruous bar and TV room that was ill lit and devoid of windows that might provide its guests with the advantages of an outlook over the canal. This room sat awkwardly within the body of the house and, for some inexplicable reason, I felt disappointed at the use to which it had been put.

At the far end of the hall, an intricately carved reception desk was sited beneath two huge, gleaming Murano glass chandeliers. Their droplets of facetted glass sent coloured rainbows flickering across the surrounding surfaces as the draught from the open door to the pontoon swept through the building.

A suited receptionist stood behind the marble topped desk waiting to greet me. Beyond the desk was the main landward entrance to the hotel and I could see a small sunlit courtyard planted with decorative foliage, the leaves shivering imperceptibly in the light morning breeze. The bright light from the open doors placed the receptionist in silhouette.

"Mr Farthing, welcome to San Cassiano. I hope that your stay with us will be enjoyable."

"I am sure that it will. Thank you." My answer was somewhat stilted as hesitantly I began to exercise my Italian. I had used the period of my recuperation prior to my departure on this trip to brush up my conversational skills learnt so long ago when I was in Foggia. I was delighted that I understood his greeting and, more importantly, that he had understood my response. I felt very gratified at this small achievement but sadly the receptionist made no acknowledgement of my accomplishment.

He held out his hand and asked for my passport and slid a form across the desk together with a silver pen for me to complete my details. As I filled in the form the porter who had first welcomed me and seen me ashore, appeared by my side with my battered and frayed bags. He patiently waited while the formalities were completed. The luggage sat at his feet, soiled and ill matched to the once palatial surroundings.

The receptionist took a key from the rank of wooden pigeon-holes that were behind the desk and, addressing the porter, gave him some instructions and the number of my room. Dispelling my initial delight at my linguistic success and, due to the speed of his speech and a dialect that was different to what I had expected, I was not able to catch either.

The porter was not a young man but was powerfully built. He had a haughtiness that Italians, no matter what their station in life, seem to have mastered. He insisted on taking my bags and led the way back to a stone staircase to the upper floors. As we climbed, he spoke in slow, precise Italian, encouraging my attempts to speak in his native tongue. Having ascertained that I had never visited Venice before, he extolled the advantages of the location of the hotel and its accessibility to all the usual tourist hot spots.

"You know that this is Carnival time here in Venice, Senore. You will find many varied exhibitions and entertainments in the squares and churches. For example, at Campo Santo Stefano there is the big open market. You must see that, Senore, it is quite a sight."

I agreed happily without knowing or caring as to the whereabouts of Campo Santo Stefano. I just wanted to absorb the atmosphere and the spirit of all that surrounded me. I was a free agent and I had no responsibilities or ties for seven whole days.

My room was located on the first floor, down a long corridor with doors off to one side. The inevitable artwork continued to adorn the other. At the end of the hall the porter slid my key into the lock and when I entered, my eager anticipation was rewarded with accommodation that transpired to be a magnificently proportioned suite.

I appreciatively surveyed my home for the next week, but more than anything, I could not contain my excitement at the fact that it was on the front of the building overlooking the expanse of the Grand Canal. My broad grin was met with a delighted smile from the porter who placed my bags onto a trestle and proceeded to give me a guided tour of all the facilities. It was the style of room that I had very rarely, if ever, had the good fortune to stay in before, and probably never would again. I expressed my effusive appreciation and somewhat clumsily gave him an overly generous tip for his trouble. This was an investment well made as it happened, and his almost overwhelming gratitude was touching. I was assured that if there should be anything I should need, anything at all, then I had only to ask and he would arrange it for me. He handed me my key and, with a modest bow, withdrew and left me alone in the tranquillity of the room.

I could not resist the obvious temptation to fling open the windows and shutters and to lean out from the frame to breath in the morning air and take in the sights and sounds of one of the most glorious locations in the world. Below my vantage point the pontoon with its metal tables and chairs was just visible. A mooring to my right had a variety of small craft tied up and they bobbed on the surface as if eager to get away and move across the choppy water. A small Rio, or canal, ran down the side of the hotel and every so often a motorised boat loaded with vegetables or indistinguishable boxes would disappear to my right at an alarming rate, guided inch perfect by its driver between towering walls.

After a short while of absorbing the mesmerising activity below me I realised that I should unpack and not waste the day. I finished the task in no time at all having always travelled light. I had not anticipated the need to bring any clothes for any specific occasion. The greatest weight was probably from a smaller bag containing my drawing materials. If I was guilty of over packing, then it was in respect of the excessive number of additional sketchbooks I had brought – some of which would inevitably return unused. These I placed on a writing desk that stood to one side of the window, the light flooding across its polished surface. I carefully arranged them for ease of access and use.

My time was now my own – an experience that was both exhilarating and perturbing at the same time. I was aware that it would be very easy to meander randomly through the alleys and squares and I needed to maintain some form of structure to my visit. While to wander aimlessly was appealing in part, I knew that I would then regret not taking in at least some of the tourist sites that my guidebook had told me were awaiting me. I lay my map out on the bed and tried to create a route for the first outing, but the tangle of streets and alleys made this more difficult than I had anticipated.

It was not until noon that I eventually dragged myself away from my map and emerged from my room. I enthusiastically entered the maze of narrow alleys that surrounded the hotel. I had my map with me but, contrary to my earlier intention to structure my visit, I decided to leave it to fate to dictate where my ramblings would lead me. On more than one occasion I found myself ducking under low-slung beams forming a roof to a damp dark cul-de-sac that deposited me at the water's edge of a silent canal. The buildings rose up on either side with dark entrances opening directly onto the rio, some with stone steps and others with nothing but the lapping water against the foundations of the building. Many of the entranceways were long unused for everyday access and the timber doors rotten at their base. In some instances, iron gates were chained closed. No matter how many times I studied my map, it was impossible to get my bearings without retracing my steps.

Streets that appeared to be dead ends only divulged their true intent once you had walked their full length, finally turning through a camouflaged ninety degrees corner that immediately opened out into an unexpected square or a wider street. Others abruptly closed and sent you back to start anew.

Invariably the squares, or Campi, had a centrepiece comprising of a capped off stone sided well that once provided the citizens of Venice with their fresh water. Others were dominated by a columned ecclesiastical façade of immense proportions that dwarfed the surrounding buildings. Each church unassumingly contained fabulous wealth in terms of the art and sculptures by the old masters that innocuously decorated their walls. High vaulted ceilings softly echoed with the sound of hushed conversations of visitors to these hallowed places.

I relished the quietness of the area in which I had found myself and was surprised that a city I had understood to team with tourists was relatively untouched by their presence once you escaped the main thoroughfares. I had no idea where I was, nor did I care. The mist had lifted, the sun was shining -

albeit weakly - and the temperature was most pleasant.

I was in Venice and I had no commitments or cares, having left any unpleasant memories back in England.

"Signore, have you decided?"

I stirred from my thoughts as the waiter asked again what I would like. I was seated in a pretty enclosed courtyard to the rear of a back-street restaurant. A dwindling crowd of late lunchtime clientele surrounded me, mainly comprising of artisans and local residents, all come to eat, drink and exchange the latest news and gossip. I asked for a small beer and, as he left, the waiter placed a menu before me, more in hope than expectation, that I would expand my minor requirement into something more substantial.

It was already mid-afternoon, and the lowering sun played upon the upper leafless branches of the small trees within the courtyard that must have provided welcome shade in the hot summer. The tables were simply set with paper table clothes and I casually looked through the menu but without any real appetite for food, even though I had walked a considerable distance. I reverted to my map and tried to work out yet again where I was. The waiter returned with my beer and I asked him as best I could to indicate the location of his premises.

He swiftly pointed to a small street that was only a short distance back from the Grand Canal. He hesitated in the anticipation of an order for food, but I apologised and stuck with my beer. He removed the menu and attended to his more profitable customers while I returned my attention to my map. I saw that it appeared to be only a relatively short walk to the Campo Santo Stefano on the other side of the Grand Canal. I was sure that I remembered that the porter from the hotel had mentioned this square in his introduction to Venice and so I decided to walk there to remind myself of what it was that he had urged me to see.

I strode with purpose to the beautiful, timber decked Ponte d'Accademia arcing high over the gentle sweep of the Grand Canal as it enters the Bacino di San Marco. Exquisite vistas were revealed in all directions. I was transfixed on the peak of that bridge, standing, holding onto the parapet and taking in all the activity on the surface of thc flickering water below. The scene was set in aspic from all those paintings that one had appreciated of early Venice, the mechanisation of the launches and barges unable to modernise the panorama that stretched before one.

A chill entered my bones as the sun slowly descended behind the ancient facades and the daylight began to retreat from the alleys and tributaries that led off the main thoroughfares. Lights appeared in windows and on the boats, and I realised that the warmth of the day was lost, and I was without either my coat or, unusually, my hat. I involuntarily shivered, tightened the grip on my cane, and hurried my way down the far side of the bridge towards Campo Santo Stefano.

The path was well trodden by visitors and locals alike, the conversation rising and falling like a lyrical tide on a sea of words, a sea that I was increasingly able to sail, following the currents that were becoming progressively more comprehensible to my ear. The ebb and flow of the voices was both calming and melodic. As I turned into the wide-open space that formed Santo Stefano, I could hear a piano being played, the sound from open windows wafting to and fro on the eddies of the cool evening air. A tenor voice rose above the accompanying piano and it mixed with the hum of transient conversation and was accompanied by the beat of the footfall of those who passed me by. I walked as if in a dream, the activity within the square silently yielding to the softly lilting music. The multi-coloured stalls with their wares on display tempted those who wished to buy a gift for a relative, friend or newfound love. I passed by, observing the whole while not seeing the specific. The scale of the market and the flood of sounds and colours urged me to take up a brush and paint – but I had no easel and had no materials – to lose the opportunity seemed to me to be a tragedy. I found myself overcome with an emotion that I had not experienced for a long time. It was an amalgam of deep love with deeper sadness. My eyes filled with tears; the music, the lights, the smells, sights and the touch of the chill air had overloaded my senses and accentuated my loss of my family – of my wife.

I am not an overly sentimental person, but I realised at that moment that this beautiful city had emotionally vanquished me – and all in such a very short period of time. I was a prisoner to her unfailing charms, her strong will and her voracious desires.

A familiar voice, unsympathetic and mocking against the distant music, dried my tears and quickened my heart,

"Venetian! All thy colouring is no more
Than bolster'd plasters on a crooked whore."

"What does that mean?" I asked, as an elegant be-whiskered gentleman with a silver topped cane – not dissimilar to my own - gave me an alarmed look and hurried on his way.

"Something Blake wrote. It seemed apt to strike a note of realism."

"You demean a place of grace and beauty, an architectural marvel, unparalleled in the modern world."

"Blame Blake, not me. But I told you it was worth coming."

"You were right," I replied, absorbing the almost physical aura that enfolded around us. Like an excited child, I extended my arms and spun around to obtain a full three-hundred-and-sixty-degree view of my surroundings. As the dusk had descended and the stalls were lit, they cast shadows across the stones beneath my feet. The people moved now in silhouettes, their clothing appeared more akin to the costumes of a bygone era, the men escorting crinoline enclosed women, gowns and cloaks whispering across the ground, heels of bejewelled shoes exposing slim ankles and petticoat hems. The very history of this square was coming alive in front of me and I was part of the celebrations of a time that would live with me forever.

Reluctantly, I dragged myself away from the square back into the narrow streets that were lined with a myriad of small shops selling calligraphy tools and more Venetian masks. Restaurants and bars were being prepared for their guests and all the while the voices echoed down the low-ceilinged alleyways and from the high overhead balconies. I walked like an automaton, no longer uncertain as to my coarse but being silently guided by some inherent knowledge of the form and layout of the passageways. It was as if I had passed this way a million times before, unerringly true in direction until, unexpectedly, I found myself standing before the entrance to my hotel. The journey had been completed, but I could recall none of the sights or events that had occurred in the intervening hour of that journey. I had left the square, walked and arrived at my destination. It was dark, I was cold, and my clothes were damp from the night air and my exertions.

Later that evening, I contentedly sat in the corner of the small bar, even though I was denied a view of the Grand Canal with the lights reflecting from the buildings on the opposite bank onto the ever-moving water. I had had a hot bath upon my return to the hotel, which both revived me and prepared me for an excellent meal at the near-by family run restaurant recommended by the porter, who I now knew as Maurizio. While the hotel provided accommodation and breakfast, it had no formal restaurant, but gave a secluded refuge from the frenetic excitement of my first day in Venice. I felt full and comfortably relaxed. I had retired to the modestly stocked bar and had indulged myself with a large, pale malt whisky, served in a gleaming cut-glass tumbler that now sat on the low table by my side together with my tin of pencils.

Maurizio was dressed in a well-tailored dark blue suit and a crisp white shirt with red tie. His handsome face was lined and tanned from the summer sun. His ready smile was slightly crooked and constantly on show as he assisted guests with their requests. I quietly sketched Maurizio as he busied himself with his duties. His face was one that had experienced life to the full, what most would probably glibly refer to as typically Italian. A degree of sophistication and suaveness was in evidence, but with the hint of wickedness from the serpentine smile and the youthful glint in his clear blue eyes. Both were reserved, in particular, for the female guests, no matter what their age, beauty or state of decrepitude. Each was treated not only with accomplished servility but also with an unashamedly flirtatiousness mixed with an air of authority. Over the years, Maurizio must have caused many a heart to flutter within the breast of those to whom he paid his gracious attentions.

The bar was reasonably busy for so late and guests looked over at my solitude. However, seeing that I was busy, they left me to my own devices. Maurizio maintained his distance but from behind the bar he was constantly checking that I had all that I needed. Whether it was my sketching or the level of the liquor in my glass, I could not be sure. Clearly, he was intrigued as to whether he was the subject of my doodling and so was fighting the urge to prematurely offer to refill my glass while simultaneously taking a sneak preview of the results of my efforts. After forty minutes he could contain himself no longer and sidled over to my table, unnecessarily brushing some non-existent detritus from the shining surface. Admittedly my glass was almost empty and so he used this as the excuse to come to my assistance.

His eyes moved furtively from glass to page, but not long enough to really appreciate what I felt was a rather fine portrayal of his Venetian features. The shading of shadow and lining was almost complete although I could probably have continued working on the picture for a further hour or so.

"Would you care for a refill, Signore?" He bent forward better to view the page and in so doing was not concentrating on taking hold of the glass. He misjudged the distance and he dislodged a pencil that rolled off the table onto the floor.

"Mi scusi, Signore." He swiftly picked up the pencil and placed it back in the battered tin.

"Grazie, Maurizio. That would be very pleasant, but perhaps not quite as generous on this occasion?"

He took the glass, but my abstemious request had obviously fallen on deaf ears, as the measure he returned with was from no optic that I had ever experienced. I did not object and the warm fuzzy feeling that was enveloping me was not unpleasant.

"Are you an artist, Signore?"

"No. I am what you would call a happy dabbler." I had no Italian for the word dabbler and so used the English. He hovered; unsure as to what a dabbler might be, contemplating as to whether to openly ask to see my current drawing. I decided to relieve him of his obvious uneasiness. We had struck up a comfortable friendship in the short time I had known him although I think he found the fact that I was unaccustomed to my lavish surroundings engaging. He had taken it upon himself to protect me from that which normally assailed the unwary traveller. I was under his wing and he wished to ensure that the experiences I encountered would leave me satisfied and desiring more.

I turned the sketchbook so that he could better see the page I was working on and his image. He smiled in appreciation.

"You are more than an amateur, Signore. That is magnificent," and added, with a smile at his feigned arrogance, "No doubt aided by an exceptional model, but magnificent all the same." He continued to admire the drawing.

"Let me work on it a little more, and then you can have it, if you would like it?" His eyes lit up and he opened his arms in delight.

"I would be honoured to have such a thing from such a talented artist". I thought that his gratitude was genuinely effusive as he shook my hand and then, as if realising his station, withdrew sheepishly to his bar in order not to further disturb my concentration.

The combination of the quiet peace of the room and the mellow whisky (now regularly replenished) aided my mood and the work progressed swiftly and accurately. As the picture emerged from the page, I became slightly reluctant to honour my promise. It seemed that the environment in which I now found myself was highly conducive to the hobby that had so dominated my life. I mentioned this to Maurizio as I handed over the page that I had carefully removed from the sketchbook.

"Ah, Signore, it is not surprising you are inspired." I waited for him to make another compliment to himself but instead he continued, "This house was the home of the famous Venetian artist Giacomo Favretto. He was a prolific painter of Venice and its people in the late 19th century but died very young. You share his name. Giacomo. James. You also love the lines of the human form and the light and shade that is unique to Venice and so prized by painters who visit."

I felt a shiver down my spine for some inexplicable reason and I wanted to know more about Signor Favretto. Unfortunately, at that moment, a receptionist entered the room and called for Maurizio to attend to a late arriving guest who was waiting in the hall. He gave me a small bow and carefully placed the drawing behind the bar as he left for the reception. As I emptied my glass, I was slightly regretting the loss of the drawing because it really was rather fine. I contemplated retrieving it from where he had so carefully stowed it but dismissed this as discourteous and ungrateful. I was flattered by his comments although over the recent weeks I was beginning to appreciate that my art was better than the negligible value I had previously placed upon it. In a contemplative and pleasantly befuddled mood, I collected my pencils and sketchbook and took myself off to bed to sleep deeply.

The old man stops writing and lays down his Montblanc fountain pen by the sheets of manuscript that are spread across his desk. He wearily looks over to the ormolu clock on the bookcase and is surprised to see that it is past midnight. The glass of Chianti that had been his companion for the evening is empty, the dregs dried to a granular veneer at the bottom of the ornately engraved bowl.

He carefully screws the top on his pen, rises stiffly from the chair and stretches his back.

“I will finish this in the morning, Priest.”

The room is empty and silent as he turns out the lights. The soiled glass remains on his desktop.

XIII
Lunchtime encounter

The sun floods into the old man's room as he returns to his desk and takes up his Montblanc pen. The dirty glass remains where he left it the previous evening, but the ruby red meniscus sits halfway up the engraving. He reads through his notes before slowly unscrewing the cap to the pen. His hand hovers over the paper as he thinks about the events that he has been recalling. After a minute or two he resumes his writing.

Next morning that deep sleep was broken by a parched taste in my mouth and a head that was dully aching from just behind each eye, no doubt as a result of the injudiciously large measures of whisky that I had consumed the previous evening. I rose and stumbled into the bathroom. Standing before the mirror, I studied the face that looked out at me. The bright lighting was harsh and unforgiving. In the intervening weeks since the assault my face had healed while my beard had thickened. I rather arrogantly thought that it made me look somewhat rakish.

After having drunk nearly a full bottle of still water that stood on the table by my bed, I trimmed the stubble from my face to re-emphasise the remaining growth.

It was too early for breakfast for many of my fellow guests who were either sleeping off the Carnival excesses of the previous evening or did not experience the same sense of urgency as I did to get out into the city and continue my explorations.

As I was the only person taking breakfast, I walked down the long narrow room that had tables on either side, opened the French door and stepped out onto the second-floor balcony. Leaning on the balustrade, I had an excellent vantage point to take in the sights and sounds of the early morning, which was dominated by vaporetto travelling up and down with early risers and workers. As each minute passed, the noise rose to a crescendo of activity as barges from the fish and vegetable markets by the Rialto Bridge moved goods onto smaller boats that could navigate the narrower canals. A delivery man guided his craft bcneath the balcony into the canal to the side of the hotel, one hand on the tiller, the other holding a mobile telephone. His face was wreathed in smoke from the cigarette that he held between ever moving lips.

Builder's rubbish bags were piled high on another craft, plastic flapping in the wind while men chatted, nonchalantly seated on the pile. The boat effortlessly slid between ever-increasing numbers of water taxis and gondolas, eventually making a right turn and disappeared from view down another side canal. The rising sun lit the rooftops and sent shafts of light to catch on the foliage of the garden to one of the houses opposite. The greenery was unusual along the canal and gave a welcome relief to the intricate medieval and rococo facades that dominated. The golden light, pale against the white stone, gothic facade of Casa d'Oro, was eerie. The recesses behind the filigree of columns and pierced arches appeared dark and mysterious, tempting the inquisitive passing traveller to seek what lies within. More commercial supply barges were plying up and down delivering goods to the hotels, shops and restaurants, and timber, sand and blocks to the building sites that were located along the minor canals within the depths of the city.

Returning from the balcony, I had a swift breakfast while reviewing my drawings of the previous day. I had done more than I thought. I flipped back through the pages of quick pencil studies of the buildings and wharfs I had visited or people I had watched on my perambulations. Details of elements of the Venetian architecture were crammed into spaces between drawings of pedestrians, or groups of friends seated at pavement cafes. A couple of unfinished portraits where the subjects had obviously departed fought for space with chairs and tables, arches, windows, towers and domes.

I had been very busy. The pages crinkled with the weight of deposited graphite that now filled both sides of most. The result was building into a wonderful travel log of my disjointed and meandering walk of yesterday. Each piece of work was scrupulously dated, together with an approximate time at which I had closed the book to move on. I kept turning back, looking and examining until I reached the point of my arrival in Venice. Briefly I checked that I had not missed anything on the previous page. It was then that I saw the precise, rounded script of the Contessa de Wolfherz and her hastily scribbled note of the Galleria D'Abrinzi that she had so enthusiastically recommended. I immediately tried to find the gallery in my guidebook, but there was no reference to it. My map, however, showed a small Fondamenta, or quay, that bore the same name and so I decided to track it down after breakfast.

Having collected together all the things I would need for the day; I went down to reception. Maurizio was talking to an elderly American lady who was seeking a route to the Rialto Bridge. Without faltering in his description of the best route, he looked across to briefly acknowledge my arrival and effortlessly, and seemingly without the American noticing, pointed a finger towards the bar. I wandered in that direction, as this was obviously his silent wish. There, on the wall between the two shelves of bottles, in a dark black and gilt carved timber frame was my portrait of a contemplative Maurizio. It looked very fine and he was delighted at my surprise at seeing it hung in such a prominent position. I nodded my approval and indicated that I would come and see him later. The silent conversation being understood and completed, I exited the hotel through the courtyard garden and re-entered the maze of streets and alleys for another day's exploration.

Within minutes I had immersed myself within a new bewildering area of the city, having yet again abandoned any attempt at an itinerary, timetable or agenda. I could amble freely or sit at yet another café in the doleful sun, well wrapped against the morning chill and sip a cappuccino or watch the world spin by as people went about their daily business. What an environment in which to live and work. As a result, the pages of my sketchbook filled with the sights that surrounded and enveloped me. Page after crammed page illustrated my day, the people who took refreshment at neighbouring tables, the pediments, pillars, capitols and architraves that craved my attention and demanded to be recorded in my journal. I even found myself writing short aide memoires about a specific sound or smell that could not be drawn or committed to sight.

I was gradually moving in the general direction, as I thought, of the street that bore the same name as the gallery. However, distractions appeared at every corner and the journey took far longer than I had anticipated. A further reference to my map showed that I had yet again veered off course and I had to adjust my route. On more than one occasion, intrigued by another low, dark alley I would find my passage blocked by a new watery Rio, deserted of both gondolas and other craft.

Eventually, after many false attempts, I ducked my head beneath a particularly low arch and, crouching as I went, emerged into the errant street for which I had been searching. It ran parallel to a mean, dark canal filled with foetid water with a slick of static oil on its surface, broken by indeterminate pieces of floating detritus. This was a narrow causeway with a dead end according to my far from perfect map. It ran in front of a lengthy terrace of tall buildings that banished any sunlight from the foul water. The temperature fell as I moved down the uneven, flagstone-paved surface. My cane clicked on the rough stones, but the sound was silently absorbed by the chasm of brickwork. There was no bird song, no sounds of the nearby streets, just a heavy, enveloping silence. The structures about me seemed even older and more dilapidated than any I had seen to date, forming a solid façade with shuttered windows and uninviting dark, wooden doors of considerable age and weight. Halfway along the terrace one of the buildings was shrouded in rusting scaffold poles, the walking-boards worn and split at each lift, the toe-boards were missing and the whole structure had a neglected air. The building was bereft apparently of any life or future. In fact, as I looked back along the causeway, the whole area was deserted and seemed to be detached from the bustle of the immediately surrounding streets. The air was heavy and the silence increasingly oppressive to the extent that I felt uncomfortable with my presence in this funereal place. Having found this dour street, I knew that I had to satisfy my curiosity and so walked hesitantly along its full length. None of the properties had the characteristics of a gallery, active or not, merely a marooned pocket of deprivation and decay. It surprised me that the city fathers would allow such a state of apparent decrepitude to exist even though this inhospitable backwater appeared to be remote and well off any tourists' beaten track. I returned to the damp tunnel that ran beneath one end of the buildings and had provided my entrance, but now was a welcome exit out of the street. Once I had escaped the clawing grip of the place, I reluctantly congratulated myself with the fact that I had seen a part of Venice that I doubted many other visitors, if any, had explored. However, I felt no great desire to tarry there to record in my journal the shabbiness of this corner of my beloved City. It was as if I had found a blemish upon the face of a loved one and I wished to banish it from my memory.

It was a mere thirty paces along the low, dank alley before I was immediately returned to the brash norm of the crowds passing along the busy thoroughfares, enjoying the warmth of the sun shining into the Carnival cheer. I involuntarily shivered with the contrast in temperature and atmosphere and sought a suitable restaurant for lunch and a reviving drink. Adjacent to yet another ornate stone bridge was a pretty trattoria with outside tables covered with pristine white paper tablecloths that fluttered in the light early spring breeze. Each was held in place by shiny cutlery and sparkling glasses, and a single red flower in a silver vase gave a splash of colour to the centre of each setting.

My wife would have loved this place. But any drift of my mind in that direction was swiftly interrupted.

"Don't allow yourself such thoughts. Look around and take time to appreciate your surroundings and the people that you see."

"It is difficult to just push her from my mind," I replied, whether aloud or not I could not be sure. Nobody seemed to be aware of our conversation.

"Maybe so, but I have you here now."

"I am not sure I understand. Is this all happening at your will?"

"All will become clear but for the moment I want you to sit and relax. Why not take that table, there by the water's edge?"

The restaurant was located alongside a canal not dissimilar to the one I had just visited but on this occasion the water was clear and benefitted from bright, warm sunshine, the paving clean and busy with pedestrians. My Voice had directed me towards a solitary table-for-two that was available amongst those occupied by customers already in animated conversation about the excitements of the morning, or their plans for the afternoon and evening. Other diners were savouring the culinary delights that the place had to offer and then I realised how hungry I was. Once seated, my shoulder bag on the opposite seat and my sketchbook and pencils readily to hand on the table, I ordered the pasta of the day together with a glass of local red wine and some water.

I looked around and explored in more detail my immediate surroundings. I briefly sketched as the gondoliers navigated between water taxis and a moored builder's barge on the opposite side of the narrow canal. The builders were nowhere to be seen and I realised that the inactivity in the derelict street was no mystery but had more to do with the fact that it was lunchtime. Unlike in England, where on a fine day workmen slumped in the street with cigarettes and a greasy burger for lunch, here the men took to the comfort of a local restaurant for some idle banter and to eat the excellent food. I watched with fascination as a broad beamed barge with the legend of 'Teatro Fenice' down its side, expertly navigated passed the inconveniently moored builders' craft. The four crew members worked as a team to ensure that the scenery it was carrying did not catch the sidewalls or the arch of the bridge. With absolute precision the craft slid cleanly by and disappeared from sight.

Further along the quay in front of me, on the last table laid for lunch, sat a young woman who I started to draw. Before getting very far my main course arrived and I closed my book, partly from the waiter's prying eyes, and more particularly because the small size of the table was unable to accommodate my sketchbook, pencils and the large bowl filled with the sumptuous looking fresh pasta. The hunger that I experienced when I arrived required me to concentrate on the culinary art that lay on the plate before me. Occasionally, I looked across at the girl and increasingly I gained the feeling that there was something familiar about her. But this was not an entirely unique sensation for someone who spent most of his spare time drawing strangers who he would not see again. Inevitably, similarities of features and detail would appear, and so I concluded in this case. I continued to inconspicuously observe the face as I eagerly consumed my food.

There are a few simple, fixed sets of proportion that I followed in determining the correct structure of any face for a drawing. The distance between the hairline and the eyebrows equals that of the distance from the eyebrows to the bottom of the nose, and from that to the chin. Similarly, generally, there exist two equilateral triangles, one across the eyes to the chin and the other, when in profile, joining the points from the bridge of the nose to the chin and thence the earlobe. An ancient maxim applies that ‘between eye and eye there is an eye”, the width of which is the same as the width of the nostrils. From above, the head is an oval, but broader at the rear than to the front. Follow these simple rules and you will achieve a passable portrait. It is then necessary to identify and adjust the particular peculiarities of your sitter that might break these rules. These might be small, almost insignificant, but to the practiced eye these characteristics provide the essence of the likeness and vibrancy of the portrait.

The challenge for me, as the artist, was to find the particular unique features that set that face apart from any previous work. I had to avoid the repetition of what might be stored subconsciously in the deepest recesses of my artistic memory, trying to trick me into replicating the known instead of capturing the unknown.

Having ordered my coffee, I took up my sketchbook again and returned to the drawing of the girl that I had briefly started. I estimated that she was in her twenties, although I was becoming increasingly poor at assessing ages nowadays. The sketch progressed well, with my taking increasingly regular, but fleeting, looks at the features upon which I was particularly interested (in this case her softly rouged, immoderate lips and the delicate philtrum beneath her nose). As I looked once again, I realised that she was also observing me. Slightly flustered, and I don't know quite why because I was becoming increasingly used to being "caught" by those that I had decided to draw, I felt myself blush and I quickly looked away – and then back again. She smiled a smile the like of which I had never experienced before - or had I? Without thinking I smiled back. Almost imperceptibly, she coquettishly bobbed her head in greeting and then returned her attention to whatever she seemed to be reading, or writing, next to her plate.

I was flattered and, against all my instincts, abandoning my usual British reserve, I called the waiter over with the intention of asking him to enquire if she would join me for a coffee. He ambled over to my table and I explained to him what I wanted. Somewhat impertinently he seemed to struggle with my Italian, as if he did not recognise my perfectly adequate efforts. I suspected that he understood my request, but the conversation was becoming protracted and beginning to draw the attention of other diners. To simplify matters, I turned to point to the table at which the young woman was seated, only to discover that it was empty. She had gone.

"We cannot have a repeat of this."

The waiter shrugged his shoulders in a gesture that implied I was deluded. I did feel somewhat foolish, an emotion which was enhanced by the waiter's indulgent smile that said that here was an old fool who had been misguided enough to think that a friendly smile from a pretty, young Italian woman was a romantic enticement. Or was I merely imposing my own judgment as to my imprudence into his body language?

I asked for the bill to save me from any further humiliation. He returns to the till to regale his friend with the stupidity of old age – they both laughed, the second waiter slyly looking over his colleagues' shoulder in my direction. The apparent blandishments of the pretty young girl were no more than a self-confident and knowing smile. She was an attractive woman and I was a man old enough to be her father, or even her grandfather, flatteringly imparting her likeness onto paper in his sketchbook. No longer comfortable in my surroundings, with the impression that each diner was now looking accusingly in my direction, I hastily settled the bill and got up from my table collecting together my guidebook, sketchbook and other accoutrements into my bag.

It had not been my intention to leave the restaurant's terrace via the table so recently vacated by the girl, however I found my passage blocked by the second smirking waiter who was serving the table behind me. Without wishing to give him the pleasure of a second helping of his enjoyment at my recklessness, I walked the other way, towards where she had been sitting. I drew alongside the table and would not have looked down but unwittingly I was prompted to do so. To my astonishment, a portrait of a young man was imprinted onto rough paper that had apparently been left to lie where I had erroneously assumed there was a book that I thought she had been reading. I stopped dead in my tracks and gawped at the image. It was spectacular, not just because of the quality of its execution, but more particularly due to the subject matter.

It was me!

At least, I thought it was me. Me, that is, as a much younger man, but instantly recognisable from the eyes and general shape of the face. The beard was there, which I did not have as a young man, but otherwise the youthful visage was so precise and accurate that I knew it could only be me.

Surreptitiously I looked around to see if anyone was looking and then, standing with my back to the waiters, who were busily clearing other tables, I looked a little more carefully and noticed that chalks had been used rather than a graphite pencil or charcoal. Brown, white and a dull red. Each line was crisp, and the shading provided an intensity of light and dark that made it appear that a fire burning brightly close by had lit my face. So as not to smudge the soft chalks, I carefully picked up the rigid paper. I took one more look before placing it between the pages of my guidebook in my bag.

I thought I had got away with my act of innocent theft until I realised that a small boy was watching my every move. He put his head inquisitively to one side and I winked as I gave him a guilty grin. Turning, I hastened my departure upon hearing his piercing voice announce across the terrace in excitement that 'the man' was ripping up the tablecloth. The small boy pointed in my direction. Luckily his mother distractedly dismissed his accusations, asking why on earth anyone would steal any part of a paper tablecloth. The waiters on overhearing the boy, hesitated and looked over to where I was making my escape. I did not wait around to find out whether they were going to pursue me and disappeared back into the labyrinth of passages leading away from the scene of my crime.

As I slowed my pace and caught my breath, two thoughts simultaneously entered my consciousness. The first was the completely out of character nature of my minor delinquency that would have so appalled me back home. I had displayed a devil may care attitude that I sought to justify to myself with the conclusion that the girl had clearly left in a hurry, forgotten the drawing and that I would seek to return it to her.

Secondly, and perhaps the slightly more obvious thought, was that I had no idea who she was, where she lived and how I would actually return the picture to her. The truth, if it were known, was that I coveted the drawing and intended to keep it. Naturally, I told myself, in the unlikely event that I did see her again, I would, of course, return it to her. But in so doing, I needed to know if she had drawn it or if it was something she owned or was the work of another.

Whichever was the case, I could not get away from the fact that the drawing had, in my mind, displayed a remarkable likeness to me. This led me back in a circle to the question of whether she had been drawing it as I ate, rather than reading as I had initially assumed.

I pondered on this as I meandered through the streets.

"Perhaps she left it for you to find? A gift or token?"

"Don't be ridiculous," I answered, but the alternative suggested by the Voice did have its attractions to me. At this stage I had no other better explanation and the thought that the pretty young woman wanted to attract my attention flattered my male ego.

The conversations of those who passed me by cut into my reflections and I realised that I had become increasingly adept at understanding the fast-flowing language, even getting to grips with the variations from the local Venetian dialect. My ears picked up the dulcet voice of a passing Italian man expressing his undying love to his wife, or was she his mistress? They walked tightly coupled, arms entwined around each other's waists. A mother gently chided her wayward child, a young man spoke apologetically to his mamma on his mobile phone and a waiter complained under his breath at the inadequately meagre tip proffered by a Dutch tourist.

Each word was as clear as if it was spoken in English, albeit unequivocally Italian.

"It is to be expected as you immerse yourself in the life of the city," my Voice assured me.

Near-by a smartly dressed middle-aged woman was outside her front door, balancing a number of packages whilst looking for her keys in her deep handbag. One of the parcels fell from the pile and instinctively I ventured forward to pick it up for her.

"Signora, can I assist you?" I collected up the parcel and held it close.

She turned and hesitated before smiling, "Thank you, Signore, you are very kind." She held my gaze and went to take the parcel from me. I made no effort to hand it over and she looked concerned,

"Signore?" She held out her hand to retake possession of her belongings from me.

"Oh, si, Signora," I apologised, "I thought that we had met before, but I am obviously mistaken."

The woman modestly lowered her eyes towards the ground and then looked up provocatively through mascaraed lashes,

"I do not think so, Signore. I am sure I would have remembered." I retained her parcel.

"Please, I shall hold this for you whilst you find your key."

She took one more dive into the depths of her bag, rummaged amongst the contents and triumphantly produced a small bunch of keys. The door was unlocked to reveal a richly decorated interior with sparkling chandelier, stone staircase and a heavily patterned oriental carpet on a stone tiled floor. Placing her bag, remaining parcels and keys on a small side-table inside the door she turned and confidently looked me in the eye,

"Courtesy is a rare thing in this city nowadays. I am grateful to you, Signore," and she patiently waited for me to pass over the parcel that I was cradling. I paused and then handed it back, giving a slight bow,

"You are most welcome. Have an enjoyable evening, Signora."

"And you, Signore."

She slowly closed the door whilst holding my attention all the while with her eyes until the latch finally clicked into the keep.

I stood back confused.

"Do I see a revived James Farthing before me?"

"What do you mean?"

"You are becoming more Venetian with every passing minute. It suits you, Giacomo."

I remained standing, bemused in front of the door and, had the woman reopened it, she would have feared for her safety from the fantasist who appeared to be planning to lay siege to her home. I turned to look about me, but I was alone again in a sea of passing strangers. I cannot describe exactly how I felt that late afternoon. Confused, exhilarated, inquisitive and mystified would all be appropriate. I suddenly had a strong desire to return to the privacy of my room and have a good look at the drawing that I had taken from the restaurant. There seemed to be more to this set of events than I was aware, and my Voice seemed to have more knowledge than I at this point. I checked my own bag for its contents, feeling a stab of excitement as I saw the piece of rough-edged paper peeking out from the pages of my guidebook. I was eager to get back to the hotel room and I confidently walked towards my abode, my head spinning with the events of the day.

Before too long I was again in the courtyard to San Cassiano and was greeted by Maurizio who ushered me over to his lair behind the bar. The picture was still in its place of prominence keeping watch over proceedings. I wanted to get away to the sanctuary of my room but clearly, he had decided that as a single traveller, inexperienced in his eyes to the finer things of life, necessitated him taking me further under his wing. I appreciated his concern and his determination to ensure my enjoyment of this adventure.

"How was your day, Signor Farthing?"

"What a day I have had, Maurizio."

The concierge stood in apparent awe and then beamed widely.

"Signor, your Italian! It is becoming faultless."

I tried to cover my transformation from student to accomplished linguist,

"Ah, hardly. But I have found that it is improving."

He was clearly impressed with the speed with which I had progressed.

"You are very good, Signore," he enthused. "I believe that I can even detect a distinct Venetian intonation."

"You are too kind." I was embarrassed and wished to move on from the analysis of my newly found gift. I wondered if each spoken sentence was entirely under my control. My alter ego seemed to be increasing in strength - and hence control of my actions.

I recounted my day to him as quickly as I politely could, omitting any mention of the embarrassing episode at lunch or the stolen picture that was lodged in my bag. I found that if I tried to speak too quickly, I was overpowered by the Voice who imbued every sentence with embellishments and opinions that were not entirely of my own or were consistent with who I was. This internal being was dispelling any appearance of the English reserve in my behaviour that had been so evident upon my arrival.

Despite having started the conversation, I was ever more impatient to get to my room. But Maurizio was equally keen to hear that his city had served me well and lived up to all my expectations. However, even though he listened with rapt attention, he seemed equally to be on edge, excited to impart to me an item of news of his own. He appeared timid at the prospect of interrupting my eloquent and flowing dialogue. Eventually he found his moment and made his own announcement in anticipation of my delight at the results of his initiative.

"As part of the Carnevale celebrations, the hotel has arranged to have a masked ball on Friday evening, and I have taken the liberty of obtaining a ticket for you." He watched to see my reaction at his well-meaning boldness and looked dismayed as my face fell. I had never enjoyed dances although my wife had; it was the only gap in our relationship. Barn dances and the like made me cringe. I remonstrated that I had no suitable attire, let alone a mask – although I realised that this was a poor excuse considering that just about every shop in Venice at this time of year sold a mind-boggling array. He held up his hand to halt my protestations and explained that he had anticipated this and had an elegant solution of which he hoped I would approve.

"My brother is the costumier at Teatro La Fenice, and he would be honoured to supply you with all that you may require. He will see you tomorrow morning and anyway, no visitor to Venice should ignore or miss La Fenice."

"But Maurizio, I am the most atrocious dancer," I exclaimed. I knew this because my wife frequently reminded me of the fact, having attended ballet school in her youth and consequently showed an expertise in any form of dance. Her frustrations at my dire attempts to emulate her normally ended in her dissolving into laughter and ribaldry at my expense. I also hated the thought of entering a room full of strangers, let alone attending a ball, on my own. As if he had anticipated my reticence,

Maurizio forestalled any further obfuscation on my part.

"That, Signore, is the joy of a masked ball. The mask provides you with anonymity. You can lose your identity – and your inhibitions. In the 18th century the Carnevale was rife with scandal and intrigue. This was, and in part still is, a wild celebration before the abstinence of lent and as such the result was a period of excess in almost every form. The word Carnevale means 'farewell to meat', but not to the sins of the flesh. Then Venetian women scandalised visitors and dignitaries alike. They were shameless and fed their wanton desires to the full behind the obscurity and safety of their disguises." Maurizio suddenly ceased his flowing description as he saw the horror on my face.

Again, the Englishman's traditional reserve made this all sound outwardly chilling, but inwardly it was alluring and gradually the latter was overcoming the former. Clearly to Maurizio I did not look convinced, although the prospect of being ravished was not wholly without its appeal.

"Of course, Signore, I am not proposing or encouraging you to behave with impropriety. The act of dressing up makes the event a game and you can adopt any persona that takes your imagination."

He spread his hands in supplication and my store of excuses was exhausted. I had tried to find a convincing argument to wriggle out of what I imagined would be an excruciating night of embarrassment, if not complete ignominy on my part. However, to my consternation I heard the enthusiastically suave reply that emanated from my lips,

"That's wonderful. I am not averse at all to a little impropriety and I shall look forward to it immensely."

My own mouth had immediately ruined any of my tenuous protestations. The pleasure that my unreserved answer gave to Maurizio was obvious. Without delay, he instructed me to report to him in reception early the next morning. I agreed and took advantage of my unexpected and unwanted defeat as an excuse to retreat back to my room.

As I ascended the stone staircase my Voice and I debated my reticence to make a complete fool of myself. Eventually, against my better judgement, I was convinced that I should embrace the experience if only for the artistic opportunities such a resplendent affair would provide.

"To be frightened occasionally is good for you. The adrenalin revitalises your body, your mind

and your soul. Trust me, I am an expert on such matters."

ENOUGH!

PRIEST, YOU ASKED IF I CONTINUED TO HEAR MY VOICE. WELL, NOW YOU KNOW THE ANSWER. AT THAT TIME I COULD NOT WORK OUT WHETHER OUR CONVERSATIONS WERE IN MY HEAD AND IF IN ITALIAN OR ENGLISH. THE LANGUAGE DID NOT SEEM TO MATTER, AS I APPEARED TO BE QUICKLY BECOMING FAMILIAR WITH BOTH. THE THOUGHT THAT I HAD STARTED TO SPEAK TO MYSELF ALOUD WAS MORE DISCONCERTING, ALTHOUGH THERE WAS NO EVIDENCE OF THIS LUNACY.

THE FACT THAT MY VOICE WAS BECOMING INCREASINGLY INDISTINGUISHABLE FROM THE REAL ME WAS MORE OF A CONCERN. I ADMIT THAT I FOUND MY ALTER EGO A CHARACTER THAT IN LIFE I MIGHT HAVE LIKED, POSSIBLY EVEN ADMIRED, BUT IT WAS

DISCONCERTING TO FEEL THAT THE FORMER, OLD ME (PERHAPS NOT THE REAL ME?) WAS INSIDIOUSLY FADING INTO THE BACKGROUND. I WAS FINDING THAT MY STRENGTH TO MAINTAIN DOMINANCE WAS INCREASINGLY INADEQUATE AND MY AMIABLE COMPANION TOO RESILIENT FOR ME TO CONSTANTLY RESIST.

SURRENDER SEEMED INEVITABLE.

SIMULTANEOUSLY, MY WILLPOWER WAS WEAKENED AND DISTRACTED BY MY DEEP-ROOTED SENSE OF LOSS TOWARDS MY WIFE AND FAMILY, A SENTIMENT THAT HE SEEMED TO WISH TO DISMISS AS IF, BY RAISING THE TOPIC, I WOULD EXPOSE COMPLICATIONS THAT WERE BETTER LEFT UNDISCOVERED. HIS METHOD OF DIVERSION WAS TO ENVELOPE ME IN AN ENVIRONMENT THAT BOTH NURTURED AND SATIATED MY CREATIVE APPETITE AND ARTISTIC SKILLS. HE HAD SUBLIMATED MY LOSS TO THE BACK OF MY MIND. IF IT SHOULD REAPPEAR, EVEN FLEETINGLY, HE CONTRIVES TO ENSURE THAT IT IS SUBMERGED ONCE MORE AS

YET ANOTHER NEW EXPERIENCE IS INTRODUCED.

WHERE ARE YOU, PRIEST? YOU CANNOT IGNORE ME. YOU CANNOT ABANDON ME. TO DO SO WOULD BE TOO DENY YOUR OWN FAITH.

GF

XIV
A Decision

The Priest reads the fourteen pages of neatly, written text. The hand is strong, the letters looping and artistic, as might be expected. He raises his head from the final sentence not knowing if the account is the product of an overly febrile imagination or that of a madman, possessed by some force or power beyond the Priest's comprehension. The old man is right. He has spoken to those of a higher theological knowledge and authority, but they have given little comfort, scant support and inadequate, if not dismissive, guidance. He is also right, in that to abandon the old man now would be a derogation of his duty and calling.

Besides, the Priest is intrigued.

But also, he acknowledges to himself that he is frightened – perhaps frightened is too strong a word. He is perplexed and unsure as to whether this old man needs his help or is toying with him, playing a game to while away the last period of his life. What constantly preys on his mind is the one sure fact, or as sure as he can be. He confidently recalls that at their last meeting he had also been spoken to by this Voice. It was a hoarser version of the old man's, making him sound like he was an inveterate chain smoker, the nicotine and tar having cloaked his vocal chords with years of sticky residues. But unlike the old man's gruff way of speaking, the Voice had a suavely cold, hard insistence. This troubles the young Priest more than anything else – and confirms in his mind that the old man is recounting facts that are as real to him as the presence of the Priest at his side.

He meditates quietly in his barren room on all that has happened and all he has heard since meeting the old man. A Psalm comes to him, a waterfall of words that cascade and tumble across his mind and then slowly settle in a gentle stream through his consciousness;

> "Deliver me, O Lord, from the evil man:
> preserve me from the violent man;
> Which imagine mischiefs in their heart;
> continually are they gathered together for war..."

The Priest inhales deeply, holds for five seconds and then slowly releases the air from his lungs. He is relaxed.

He is ready.

The die is cast, the decision made. He speaks to the old man from the solitude of his chamber,

“Rest assured, Giacomo. I shall neither ignore you, nor abandon you.”

XV
The Private Suite

The priest is attending to his morning duties in the church and is quietly walking down to the side of the main body of the building. The pungent odour of incense used during the early morning mass hangs in the air, while shafts of sunlight make the motes of dust sparkle as they cross the alter from the high stained-glass windows at the eastern end of the building. Small chapels are built into the sidewalls, each dedicated to one saint or another. They are solitary places for private worship or contemplation. Between each are tables with metal frames holding fresh or expired candles. This morning it is the priest's job to tidy up each for the coming day. He is passing by one of the small chapels and sees the figure seated peacefully, his back ramrod straight, his eyes looking ahead. The cane stands vertically between his feet, the silver top shrouded by the man's two hands, his arms outstretched with the fingers overlapping, resting contentedly on the top.

The priest moves silently to the old man's side but says nothing, not wishing to disturb him. A door somewhere at the back of the church shuts and the sound resonates around the vast void that encompasses the two men.

“I decided to come to you, Priest.” The old man speaks without altering his position or line of vision. “It is quiet here.”

“Yes.” The Priest lowers himself onto the chair by the old man and takes up a similar pose, not in a mocking manner, but because it is the natural thing to do. In the absence of a cane, the Priest places his hands softly on his knees and breathes slowly and deeply. He feels embarrassed that it has taken this simple act by the man to bridge the gap in time that it has taken the Priest to reach his decision. The fact that he was intending to go and see the old man today was not worth mentioning. He would not be believed.

“How are you?”

“Fine. And you?”

The Priest is unclear as to whether this is an enquiry as to his physical or spiritual health but opts for the former as to date the old man has displayed no overt respect for the latter.

“I am well, thank you.”

“I am not here other than to make sure you are not,” the old man hesitates, choosing his words with care, “indifferent to my requirements.”

"I am not indifferent to anyone's requirements, if I know what they are."

The old man thinks for a moment. He does not wish to wound the young man further or have to repeat with another what has been achieved so far.

"I need to finish my confession."

"I am happy to take that."

"Yes, but not here. Not in that box built like a coffin. Not speaking through an iron grill; separated by a sliding trap door and veiled by a thick curtain."

"OK." The priest speaks calmly and accepts the condition imposed by the old man. He looks at his watch and says, "I have a few things to do here so why don't we meet for a coffee in the café across the square?"

The old man knows it well, having spent a number of days sipping coffee there as he watched the Priest come and go about his duties.

"When?"

"Give me half an hour."

The old man picks up his shoulder bag and stands without faltering or stiffness.

"Half an hour, then."

He bangs his stick onto the stone floor and then swings it forward as if to create some momentum for onward movement. The Priest remains in his seat and studies the bejewelled cross that stands on the simple alter in front of him, the imperious click of the old man's stick filling the church as it recedes into the distance. Further lines of the psalm filter into the Priest's thoughts:

> "They have sharpened their tongues like a serpent; adders' poison is under their lips.
> Keep me, O Lord, from the hands of the wicked; preserve me from the violent man;
> Who have purposed to overthrow my goings."

In the intervening half hour the old man sits outside the café with his coffee and a glass of still water. He draws, as usual, until the arrival of the Priest.

"I am sorry, have I kept you waiting?"

"No. I have ordered you a cappuccino. Sit down."

The young priest gathers his cassock around him and sits on the metal chair across the table from the old man. The waitress approaches from the door of the café with a single cup on a small tray. She places it in front of the Priest who thanks her with a smile.

"Did you read my letter?" the old man asks.

"Of course."

"Have you anything to say or shall I just continue where I left off?"

"I have read it a number of times and remember the stage we had reached. When did this all take place?" The Priest takes a sip of his coffee.

"My arrival in Venice?"

"Yes." Froth from the cappuccino lines the Priests upper lip.

The old man thinks for a moment. "It would be around five years ago."

"And when did you come back here to live?"

"I never left." The old man pauses again, waiting to see if the priest is going to respond. "No other questions?"

"No other questions."

Both know this last answer to be untrue but chose to ignore it.

The priest sits back in his chair and holds the cup and saucer on his lap as the old man resumes his narration.

I reached my room and wearily opened the door. The interior was sombre, but warm and welcoming while the peak of the sunset outside waned. My window framed the lights from Palazzo Fontana Rezzonico opposite, and the view of the terracotta pink building in the fading light begged to be committed to paper. But I was exhausted, 'all drawn out', and merely wanted to slump onto my bed and sleep.

With the increasing twilight gloom in my room, I cannot be sure whether I had slept or not. If I did, it was not for long as I was stirred into alertness by the sudden recollection of the young woman at the restaurant and, more particularly, the paper that was pressed between the pages of my guidebook. I sat up and slid to the edge of my bed to eagerly retrieve it from the bag that, in my lethargy, I had dropped to the floor. I carefully removed the piece of course paper from between the pages of the guidebook and took it over to the desk where I turned on the light to have a much closer look than was possible in the restaurant. I was flabbergasted, as the image had been far more beautifully rendered than I had initially thought. The marks were not in pencil or charcoal, as I had originally imagined, but in a brown chalk. The highlights had been picked out in white and a rusty red and the drawing entranced me. I dared not touch the surface for fear of smudging the exquisite draughtsmanship with its clearly defined lines and delicate crosshatched tones.

In the bottom right-hand corner of the drawing was an ornately delicate single letter 'L'.

Stored in my suitcase were a number of clear plastic folders that I used to safely keep any of my own charcoal sketches – sketches that were woefully inadequate compared to the example that I held in my hands. The paper felt thicker than the flimsy material that I was familiar with using. I placed it carefully within the plastic envelope and stood it against the lamp on the side table by my bed, the yellow light flooding down the surface of the rough textured paper. This was not commercially bought paper, but hand made. The picture had the appearance and quality of something that could not have been hastily drafted whilst simultaneously eating lunch. I lay back down on the bed to admire the piece and to ponder over the events of the day before gently slipping back into a light, contented sleep.

I invented soft focussed vignettes on a broad canvas of the girl laughing against an ever-changing background, a vista of ornate and elegant facades interspersed with the dilapidated quayside. She moved effortlessly through the brightly lit streets and dark alleys of the city with a quiet confidence that only comes from having lived amongst them for all of her life. Someone I would probably never see again had entered my dreams. I drew her over and over again in my mind, every pose different, but always with that puckish smile that had so captured my imagination.

There was a soft knock on my door that gradually lifted me out from my sleepy daydreams. The knock repeated, slightly louder this time, and a voice beyond announced room service. I assumed that they wished to turn down my bed and stumbled over to open the door. It was with some surprise that Maurizio was standing outside with a bottle and glass on a silver tray. He looked me up and down as I obviously looked somewhat dishevelled from my catnaps.

"Signor Farthing, you ordered a bottle of wine?"

I was muddle headed and could not recall having done so. However, before I could correct his error, I replied

"Si, grazie mille, Maurizio. Please, put it on the table."

He hesitated on the threshold,

"Are you feeling well, Signor Farthing?" he asked. "You look a little pale." He passed me in the doorway but all the while he steadfastly maintained his gaze upon my face. He placed the tray on a table.

"No, I am fine," I replied, *"just over did it a bit today. All the excitement and exertion of seeing such a plethora of wonderful sights."*

He nodded in understanding and I agreed to him opening the bottle, which he deftly did and poured a small amount into the glass for me to try. It was thick, rich and tasted delicious. I nodded my approval and he filled the bottom of the goblet. However, the concern remained on his face and he stood by the table while I slumped into one of the soft, velvet upholstered chairs by the window.

"Maurizio, do you know a gallery called D'Abrinzi?" I enquired.

He thought for a moment and then replied,

"I believe that there is a Quay D'Abrinzi but I hear it is an ugly little back water. I have never had a reason to visit it. I cannot recall a gallery by that name and would not envisage anyone wanting to open one there." He watched attentively as I took another mouthful of the wonderful wine.

"Why do you ask, Senore?"

Maurizio obviously felt uncomfortable at doing nothing while I enjoyed my drink. He ambled over to the bed to smooth the counterpane and generally tidy what did not need tidying. I continued to sip my wine. I placed the glass onto the table and rubbed my eyes to dispel the sleep.

Maurizio replaced the top on to the bottle of water that sat on my bedside table and stopped when he saw the drawing in the plastic folder balanced against the lamp.

"That is a very good likeness, Signore. Did you do this?" He pointed to the drawing. I had forgotten that I had left it there and hastily got to my feet to retrieve it in order to return it to my folio.

"No. I wish I had. I acquired it this afternoon." I spoke the truth but sounded furtive in my reply.

"Did it come from this gallery D'Abrinzi? It is superb. In fact, it is very similar to a print that we have in the hotel."

He was not making any sense and I possessively removed it from the table. I looked at the drawing again. The portrait that stared up from the sheet with its roughly torn edges was still of me, albeit that on a closer inspection the dark, shaggy beard and moustache was a little more pronounced than mine and the hair slightly thicker and wilder.

Maurizio beckoned for me to follow him and we left the room.

I am not sure where we went, as the hotel seemed to be a labyrinthine maze of corridors and back stairs. Eventually we entered a rather fine salon with a highly decorated ceiling and panelled walls covered in a pure blue silk. Paintings hung all around the room and Maurizio strode purposefully to one that looked down from an alcove to one side of the fireplace. It was well lit and the similarity to the drawing now in my possession was astonishing. I stood and looked at it closely and cursed that I had not brought my version up with me.

"This is a private suite that we keep for an overseas guest, but he is rarely here. He travels a great deal."

I walked slowly around the comfortably furnished apartment, my steps soundless as they passed over the exquisite Persian carpet that all but covered the floor of the room. In the opposing alcove was a painting of a young woman with high cheekbones and wide eyes, a laughing mouth and with a distinct twinkle in her green eyes.

I knew this face.

"Who is this?" I asked.

"We do not know her name, but it is likely to be one of Favretto's many models or perhaps a mistress, or a courtesan. This house was the residence of Giacomo Favretto," Maurizio then remembered that he had already imparted this knowledge to me upon my arrival. "But I have told you this already."

“Perhaps she was all three. Favretto painted it.’ I could see that Maurizio had become confused, unsure as to whether this was a question or a statement of fact. He appeared increasingly uncomfortable by my apparent change in demeanour. I found myself striding somewhat proprietorially around the apartment, surveying the myriad of paintings and drawings, straightening some that did not hang true on the walls. I spoke with an authoritative voice while not actually appearing to be anything other than an inquisitive visitor. Eventually Maurizio became more formal, perhaps concluding that it had not been a good idea to bring me to this apartment.

“The owner hopes so, Signor. Although it is believed that Favretto did have many pupils who undertook a number of drawings and paintings that closely followed his technique and style.”

Not wishing to prolong the visit, Maurizio added,

“I think we should leave and return to your room, Signore.”

“Just one more look at this drawing of Favretto. It is truly extraordinary how alike it is to the one in my room.”

I remained motionless in front of the drawing and tried to memorise every detail so that I could run a comparison with my own. However, no matter how hard I concentrated upon the face before me, my eyes were drawn to the woman.

"Come, Signore." Maurizio gently took my elbow and guided me out of the ornate salon and locked the door with a large bunch of keys that he kept on a thin silver chain attached to his belt. I was escorted back to the door of my room and Maurizio opened it for me to enter but did not make any move to follow me in. I turned and thanked him for showing me the salon and the other drawing. He smiled and assured me that it was his pleasure and suggested that I might care to get the drawing looked at by an expert as it could be worth a lot of money.

"I will try to locate this Galleria D'Abrinzi of which you speak," he offered. "Come and see me after your dinner and I will let you know what I have discovered."

I thanked him and closed the door on his retreating back. I went immediately to my folio into which I had placed the drawing after its discovery by Maurizio. I carefully removed it and poured another glass of wine. I resumed my seat by the window, the natural light outside having given way to darkness.

The drawing was very similar, exceedingly similar – but not identical. I looked on the back of the paper to see if I could detect any other clue as to the artist, the age of the paper, or the origins of the piece. There was nothing save for the previously unnoticed, and unexplainable, marks of time – marks that could not have materialised since the drawing had come into my possession. I rubbed between my fingers the edges of what I had initially thought was handmade paper. It did not have the texture of paper. It seemed to be more like pulped linen, or deconstructed fabric that had subsequently been treated with a binding agent and formed into a sheet. Not exactly a canvas, but with the same rough finish.

Puzzled, I gently returned it to its folder and replaced it in my folio case. I was hungry and slightly lightheaded from the heavy wine that I had consumed while I had contemplated the picture. I needed to find a suitable restaurant for dinner before reporting to Maurizio to see if he had had any luck with the whereabouts of the elusive Galleria D'Abrinzi. Collecting my equipment and putting it into my bag, I placed my newly acquired drawing into the small safe, securely stowed away from prying eyes. While I could think of no reason why it should have any intrinsic value, it was a drawing of exceptional quality and, as such, I did not want anyone to take it from me.

INTERRUZIONE

So, the Priest is away, summoned to Florence. As a result, I have left Giacomo to his own devices. I will have need of him again before long.

The likeness in the carefully concealed drawing is striking, is it not, between our Giacomo and Signor Favretto? I am quite proud of my little subterfuge.

Like the work of Signor Dali, what one observes from afar is not necessarily what is seen upon closer inspection. Surrealists test the eye and torture the mind with the inexplicable so, at times, none of us can differentiate between the real and the surreal.

Why Signor Giacomo Farthing is the subject of my attention is really pure happenstance. Why does a mosquito sink its malaria infected proboscis into one particular person and not another? What is the justice of a young mother being struck down with a cancerous tumour while the childless is allowed to escape? Both have a destiny that is outside their control and beyond their comprehension.

Even I cannot always control the perfidy of nature. All is down to natural chance – almost. It is a litany of wrongs - the wrong person being in the wrong place at the wrong time. And so it is with Signor Farthing, although I have to confess that, in his choice, I did indulge in a perverse desire for some sort of tenuous linkage to the task that has befallen him. He is undoubtedly a talented artist with, now, no dependants. He has the time and the opportunity, admittedly unwittingly, to serve me in my task.

I know that he grieves for his loss of family, but I cannot allow such thoughts to linger within him. What has passed is in the past, a necessity. Giacomo's future lies both with me, and the small task that he is now able to perform for me.

We are, therefore, inextricably linked and, ultimately, his future will rectify an omission from my past. Suffice it to say that I have need of his services and in so doing; we shall reach an accord and grant an unfulfilled wish that he may have until death. This is not some cheap trade for his soul or some squalid deception, but an equitable barter between one knowing party and one innocent party. I know that I have provided a strange route by which Giacomo has been drawn to Venice. That is in part my weakness for the dramatic; it is what adds interest to the job, makes it worthwhile.

It is equally true that I am as fully aware, as he is in ignorance, of what I am seeking to achieve through him. I do not consider this to be taking advantage of his innocence, but more a generosity of spirit on my part in liberating him from the frustration of not fulfilling his true destiny.

He continues his immersion in the people, buildings and culture that the fair city of Venice has to offer to all those who seek true fulfilment. My absence is irrelevant to the enjoyment of his day, but needless to say, he has been in creative ecstasy. As a consequence, the endowments that I have lavished upon him, his accomplishments have soared to a higher plane than ever experienced before. Normally such virtuosity can only be attained through inspired tutelage and years of diligent practice. My friend has neither available to him and so he must rely upon my own talents to accelerate his progress.

Naturally, he puts this extraordinary self-improvement down to the inspirational and mental stimulation that is all around him. Who is to disabuse him of this conclusion?

XVI
La Fenice

"I've been in Florence. It is such a beautiful city. Have you been?" The priest is back in the old man's room sitting on the battered, leather Chesterfield once again. It has become a comfortable retreat from his daily duties, even when the old man is somewhat grumpy.

"Went a few years ago. Didn't like it, too many tourists."

"And so you settled for Venice?" The priest's voice sounds unintentionally mocking, but the old man takes it as criticism.

"I accept that Venice appears more infested with tourists than rats, but the rats prevail in plenty of quiet corners that the tourist maps and guides overlook. You just have to find them."

"Talking of tourist hot spots, which you say you choose to avoid, when last we spoke you told me that you had asked Maurizio to find your Gallery D'Abrinzi. There was something about La Fenice as well."

"Ah, so you have been listening?" The old man looks pleased.

“Naturally. I have been giving your story a great deal of thought over the last couple of days. In fact, it has been with me constantly. Go on. Tell me what happened.” The priest expects the old man to take up his story but is surprised when he is asked,

“How long have you been away?”

“Only a day.”

The old man raises his eyebrows in what appears to be disbelief at the priest’s answer.

“It seems longer.” The old man is remotely pensive, “Yesterday was a strange day. Yet again I wandered aimlessly around Venice as if I was in a trance. It was almost an out of body experience. I felt a newfound freedom, a sense of release. It is difficult for me to explain.” The old man seems more unsure of himself, vaguer than when the priest had previously seen him. His face is tired and pale, his eyes a little more sunken. He wipes some spittle from the corners of his mouth with a large handkerchief and then continues, the present becoming melded with the past.

“When I rested, I drew with even greater fluidity than usual, and even I could see that what I had produced was mesmerizingly beautiful.” The old man rises with difficulty from his desk and takes his latest volume from where it lies in front of him to hand to the priest. He moves slower today, using his stick for support rather than effect.

"I find that my scenes from everyday life along the canals and in the streets have a timeless quality. The students drinking in the Campo dei Tolentini seated on the steps down to the canal edge, their feet inches from the lapping water, their conversation noisy and full of youthful gaiety."

The priest follows his progress as he turns the pages displaying each exquisite drawing completed in the most meticulous detail. What is different about each is not the fact that they are so beautiful but that they are depicting a Venice of the past. The priest says nothing and allows the old man to continue,

"The well-dressed coffee drinkers of Florian in Piazza San Marco relaxing around small tables, smoking and listening to the musicians playing on the raised dais between the columns. The weather was unusually warm and the sun bathed the square in a comforting glow. I engaged in conversation with a group of dapper, old men who had just emerged from Santa Maria della Salute having attended mass, their conversation witty, eloquent and enlightening, my inclusion seemingly natural and welcomed.

New friends surrounded me, but loneliness inhabited me. It was as if a part of me was missing. It made me melancholy and pensive as I sought, but could not find, some indefinable comfort from this placid interlude."

The old man sat lower in his upright chair and is deep in thought. The young priest continues to flick through the pages until he comes to the clean page to denote the end of the day.

"The city has taken on a peaceful calm that I had not noticed over the last few days. Perhaps this is because it is the first full working day after the start of Carnival. I expect everyone is exhausted from the festivities of the weekend, grateful for a period of recuperation. I felt that the carnival was passing me by as I toured the streets and alleys. The previously daunting prospect of the Ball became less of a challenge and more of a captivating expectation."

The priest is momentarily confused. Carnival ended many weeks ago and the old man has obviously lost his sense of time. He has seamlessly slipped back into the telling of his tale, his confession, without appearing to be aware of the fact. The priest is troubled by the change in the old man but tries to concentrate, no longer merely listening to a reminiscence but reverting to his role as the recipient of a confession.

"As requested, the other evening, I attended Maurizio after my dinner." Again, the old man faltered, as if trying to remember a detail or fact. "I went to that little trattoria at the end of that narrow street of tall houses. You know, near your church." The priest did not know which restaurant he was referring to but nodded as if he did to keep the story on track.

Each building seemed to be occupied by families who talked volubly as they gathered together for their evening meal. Even in the chill of the evening, the windows were slightly ajar to let the cooking smells waft into the cavern between the high facades. These combining aromas stirred the taste buds and sharpened the appetite of anyone passing. For my part, I greedily ate a plate of soft egg pasta served with a creamy sauce, fegato alla salvia (slightly pink) and a selection of cheeses the like of which I had never tasted before. The owner diligently looked after me despite the number of other diners and he recommended a wine that complimented all that I ate. The finale was a strong black espresso served with a complimentary amaretto. My attentive host effusively bade me goodnight upon my departure and I contentedly wandered back to the hotel, my brain pleasantly suffused with alcohol and tiredness.

Maurizio was still on duty, and even at this late hour he continued to diligently serve the needs of his guests. He told me that he had spoken again to his brother, Vincenzo, and that I was to go to La Fenice in the morning where I would be given a tour of the theatre. Following this, Vincenzo would then provide me with my costume for the ball on Friday night. I noted all his instructions and asked him if he had had any luck locating the Galleria D'Abrinzi. He apologised profusely for not having done so, that he had been very busy but assured me that he would definitely let me know if it still existed. As if by way of compensation he provided a list of other galleries that I could visit the next day, but I forgot the names as soon as I had left him for my bed.

However, true to his word, when I descended in the morning to the front hall from breakfast, Maurizio stopped me. With a beam of satisfaction, he proudly announced that he had found the location of the gallery.

"But it has long since closed, Signore. In fact, it is a piece of Venetian history that even I was unaware."

"When did it close, Maurizio? Recently?"

He laughed loudly, and then realised that I was unaware of the knowledge that he possessed. He took a piece of the hotel stationary on which was written some brief notes and handed it to me.

"No, Signore. The gallery has not been there since the late 19th century. It is not surprising that you could not find it. The buildings were demolished and new ones put up in their place."

I took the piece of paper on which he had scribbled the address and the dates. I saw that it was the same deserted quay that I had visited previously. I popped the paper into my pocket having thanked him for his trouble and thought nothing further about it.

"Now, Signore, you must get going to La Fenice if you are not to be late for my brother." I looked at my watch and saw that the time had moved on. I thanked Maurizio once again and took up my bag and stick and hurried from the hotel.

La Fenice beckoned, and a costume fitting for the Grand Ball. I really had no idea why I had let Maurizio talk me into such an event – but then I remembered that it was not he who had cast the die. My Voice had done that for me.

I twisted my way along the back streets, crossing the narrow Rios that eventually led to the Gran Teatro La Fenice. As I approached along a path beside a small canal, I saw before me the rear loading dock and the water entrance named after Maria Callas. A group of stagehands were talking and smoking, possibly waiting for a barge to arrive, such as the one I had seen the other day. They were seated beneath a glazed canopy that was supported by gilded, delicately scrolled, cast-iron brackets, each with a gold phoenix at its centre.

Walking on, I passed the stage door to one side of the theatre and emerged into the modest Campo San Fantin. The steps up to the columned entrance supporting the delicate balcony above gave a strong sense of arrival. It must have been a spectacular event when it was opened in 1792 to an expectant Venetian society. Now it was none the less impressive, but the surrounding properties had a tired, down at heel feeling to them, which possibly enhanced the splendour of their theatrical neighbour.

Beneath the balcony, in the centre of the supporting columns was a large golden phoenix, rising from the flames, and from which the theatre took its name. Above the balcony were two statues within curved niches depicting tragedy and dance and above them the masks of Comedy and Tragedy. Either side of the steps stood ornate lamp standards, against one of which a group of Somali street vendors was standing with their battered suitcases containing goods of dubious provenance awaiting a gullible public.

It was just before 9.30am and I mounted the steps and entered the great doors into the main foyer. Smart middle-aged ladies were bustling around preparing for the day's visitors and I approached the main desk to announce my arrival. I hoped that they would know who I was coming to see as I realised that I had no surname for Maurizio or his brother, Vincenzo. A rather fierce looking woman with ash coloured hair stood behind the desk. She lifted her eyes to look over a pair of severe, designer glasses that were balanced precariously on the end of her nose.

"Si? What can I do for you?" Impatience and intolerance bounced from every syllable.

"Buon giorno, Signora." I replied affably, seeing no reason to omit the usual courtesies that I had witnessed from everyone I had met – until perhaps this moment. "Come sta?"

My fluent Italian surprised her, and any apparent hostility evaporated. She smiled sweetly and reciprocated the courteous formalities. Then, politely and somewhat formally, she asked whether I had come to see anyone in particular or if I merely intended to take a tour of the theatre, in which case I was too early?

"Both, I hope. I am here to see Vincenzo who is kindly going to give me a private tour."

Her demeanour softened still further at the mention of Vincenzo's name.

"Ah, you are Signor Farthing?"

I lifted my hat in response, and she picked up the telephone hidden beneath her desk. Briefly she informed someone that the English gentleman had arrived. She replaced the handset and asked me to wait for Vincenzo in the inner foyer.

I used the time to study the décor and layout of the foyer which was divided into two mirror images lit by a central, dramatic candelabrum. Identical versions were hung over the half landings to the two flights of stairs that ascended to the upper floors. Marble columns with scrolled capitals supported decoratively detailed cornices were reflected in the highly polished marble floor. The walls were a light russet pink with decorative plaster panels and delicate wall lights. The sense of opulence and history was almost overpowering. As I was to learn later from Vincenzo, this was the only part of the building that had survived not one, but two fires, one on the night of 13th December 1836 and the other on 29th January 1996. La Fenice was truly the Phoenix that had risen not once, but twice from the flames.

A small man with a mane of thick, long, greying hair pulled back into a ponytail tripped lightly down the stairs. He was dressed in an immaculately tailored suit over a crisp white shirt with an open neck collar that exposed a darkly tanned upper chest. His highly polished loafers were worn without socks and competed with the sheen from the floor. Upon reaching the foyer the man glided silently across the surface. He appeared considerably younger than Maurizio and had the easy movement and the lithe build of a dancer as he approached with a ready smile and bright intelligent eyes. His hand was outstretched as he greeted me like a long-lost friend, grasping my own hand in both of his and shaking it vigorously.

"Signor Farthing, what an honour and pleasure to meet you. My brother has told me a great deal about you. He has also shown me the remarkable portrait you have created of him. Anyone with such a passion in the execution of the arts is always welcome in Venice."

He spoke swiftly and softly but with the confident enthusiasm of someone who is also a master of his craft. I felt very flattered at his praise and, in those days, somewhat unusually for me, I did not seek to moderate his compliments through unnecessary or ungrateful modesty.

"It is most kind of you to spare me your time. I am also grateful to you for providing me with a suitable costume for the masked ball to which your brother has so kindly made arrangements for me to attend." The sentence sounded very formal, almost archaic and I found myself bowing slightly as I spoke. He accepted my thanks with his own nod of the head.

"You are most welcome. In the short time that we have been acquainted I am satisfied that your stature and bearing is wholly suitable for what I have in mind for you." He paced around me as he spoke and surveyed me with a discerning and practiced eye. "Your height and slim build are perfect for the Bauta. This is a very traditional mask and the accompanying ensemble will be carried well by you." He paused to observe my own attire and nodded with approval. "It is pleasing to see someone who dresses so well and with such panache, particularly, if I may say so, from England. It is rare that a tourist should complement the beauty of our fair city with a level of sartorial elegance such as you have displayed. I thank you and hope that I will be able to maintain your own high standards."

Once again, I thanked this dynamo of a man, but he dismissed my gratitude with a wave of his hand to usher me towards the stairs.

"Before we retire to my studio, if it would please you, I would be delighted to give you a brief conducted tour of the theatre which is the greatest in the world. But, as you will appreciate, I am probably slightly biased in my view?" His eyebrows rose in self-mocking shock and then he broke into a rippling and surprisingly deep guffaw.

I have been to a number of theatres both in London and elsewhere, but La Fenice is unique and the most glorious example of an extravagant Rococo style. I had to keep reminding myself that this master class of decorative construction was not undertaken in the mid seventeenth century but completed in the late 1990s. The main 'house' with the most exquisite ceiling, galleries and ornate Royal Box was a feast for the eyes. As we entered one of the private boxes the senses were rewarded still further by the sound of an orchestra and a solitary female singer rehearsing a striking aria. I smiled in rapt appreciation and Vincenzo just grinned with pride. We sat quietly for some minutes listening to the clear notes that rose from the stage.

I could have stayed for considerably longer but was aware that Vincenzo was becoming slightly fidgety and clearly had other things to do. We left the box and he swiftly completed his tour before leading me down a staircase that took us to the back of house.

"I would have liked to allow you to stay longer, Signore, but I must return to my work. I could see that you were emotionally moved by Katarina's rehearsal. Are you a keen opera-goer?" Before I could reply he hurried on, "I would be very honoured if you would accept a complimentary ticket for this evening. Sadly, I cannot attend but you would be very welcome to take my place. Being Carnival at present it is a slightly more formal occasion?"

"I am afraid that I did not bring any evening wear with me. I was not anticipating attending anything of this nature during my trip."

"Do not concern yourself. When I refer to formal, I was meaning 'Carnival formal'. Everyone will be wearing their costumes and so the Bauta will be perfect for both the opera and your ball on Friday."

"Well if you think that is acceptable, I would be delighted to attend."

I thanked him yet again and he waved his hand theatrically to dismiss my effusiveness.

"It is a small exchange for the wonderful drawing that you gave to my brother. Now, let me explain. Tonight is the last performance during Carnival of 'La Traviata' and so it is special. You could not possibly come to Venice and miss the Opera that had its premiere on this stage."

"I am very honoured, that sounds wonderful."

Satisfied, he turned, and I followed in his wake as we proceeded along secret corridors hidden from the average tourist - or opera lover.

He chatted amicably all the way and I had little need of response, his conversation being as fast as his pace. I scurried along behind him and listened to his reminiscences of the people he had dressed and those he had socialised with, interspersed with many statistics and historical details about the theatre. La Fenice was his life and he had dedicated himself to the part that he played within it. He was proud of its role within the city, but personally humble and self-deprecating as to his contribution to the place. During his long career he had dressed the cast and stars of hundreds of productions that had enthralled audiences from all over the world.

Vincenzo had taken over the position from his father and Maurizio had initially worked alongside him. However, when the theatre was burned down in 1996 there was little work for the costumiers and so Maurizio had left to find another job and had never returned. Vincenzo continued from a small studio around the corner until the theatre had been restored to its former glory and then he returned as the head costumier. He casually informed me that he also had a passion for ballroom dancing. I asked if he would like to give me a crash course and, laughing, he stated that it would be impossible. The only advice he could give me was to relax and allow the music to enter my body and to take over my soul. This did little to quell my anxiety, but it would have to do.

His office cum studio was efficiently organised and spotlessly tidy so that he knew where everything was when he needed it. Racks of rolled material, clear work desks with modern state-of-the-art machinery and all the tools of his trade were readily to hand.

A mannequin stood to one side of his main workbench dressed in black with a startlingly white mask beneath a black Tricorn hat. A long flowing cloak hung to the floor and a lace hood was lying loosely across one shoulder. He saw me looking admiringly at the costume,

"I think that you will look magnificent in the Bauta, Signore. Shall we try it for size?" He picked off a loose thread from the costume as I started to remove my jacket, but he raised his two hands to stop me.

"No need, Signore. This is designed to wear over your evening dress. You will find the material very light and not at all oppressive. This was the mask and costume worn and made famous by Signor Casanova." He winked conspiratorially as gradually the elements of the costume were assembled on my body. After a close inspection as to the fit and hang, Vincenzo announced that he would like to do a couple of minor alterations to ensure that it fitted perfectly. As far as I could see it was already perfect, but I could not argue with the maestro.

"If you are looking to have some lunch then I can recommend an excellent little restaurant nearby. In the meantime, I shall arrange for the work to be done this afternoon."

"Do you not need time for this evening's performance?"

"My dear Giacomo," he stopped at his informality, "May I call you Giacomo? It seems that I know you so well."

"Of course." It seemed only natural to me too, and anyway, I preferred the use of the Italian version of my name.

"My dear Giacomo, if we are not prepared already for this evening's performance, it is too late. Everything has been done and we merely await the arrival later of the performers for their make-up and dressing."

I felt slightly embarrassed that I had implied that he was ill prepared.

"Might I suggest a small restaurant close by? Mainly local gondoliers and artisans frequent it, tourists rarely visit. But I am sure you will be made welcome; you have the air of a Venetian. The owners are an old family that has satisfied the hunger of the local residents for many centuries."

"That sounds wonderful. Would you be free to join me? To buy you lunch would be the least I could do to repay your kindness."

"I am sorry that I cannot join you. However, do tell them that I have sent you. I am sure that they will look after you and that you will eat well."

Vincenzo gave me brief directions and stated that he would arrange for my costume to be delivered to my hotel in time for me to change for this evening's performance.

"I trust that you will have an enjoyable evening and do not worry about returning the costume as Maurizio will bring everything back to me after the masked ball."

I thanked him fulsomely for his kindness and he guided me back to the stage door on the side street that I had passed earlier that morning. Vincenzo shook my hand, wished me a successful visit and pirouetted back through the open door disappearing from sight with a breezy wave of his hand.

After a couple of abortive attempts, I eventually found the restaurant on a narrow quay by a bridge across a small canal that ran alongside. A painted, wooden sign on a wrought iron bracket hung above the door confirmed the name provided by Vincenzo. Unlike most of the tourist establishments, this had no plastic covered menu outside, and the windows gave no indication as to what lay within. I entered through one of the two narrow, glazed, timber doors into a room that was dark when compared with the bright light outside. My eyes gradually acclimatised, and I saw that a bar ran down one side and the floor was of bare boards. The place was busy with tables occupied by customers of all ages, shapes and sizes. The conversation was boisterous, and my arrival was ignored save for a woman who came from behind the bar and asked if she could be of assistance. I informed her that Vincenzo had sent me (I still did not know his surname, but it was of little consequence as he was clearly well known to her). On my asking for a table for one, she looked dubiously around the crowded room and then approached a small table that had a solitary individual enjoying his lunch. The man had just raised his full fork to his mouth when she peremptorily picked up his plate together with his wine glass and moved him to join a larger table occupied by two older men sipping an aperitif. No one complained or argued, no one begrudged the stranger his right to sit and enjoy a meal. I mumbled an apology to the dispossessed diner who was unperturbed and had already returned to his plate of food.

The small table at the front of the restaurant had the window behind it, which provided good light and gave me a clear view down the full length of the room. A white linen, not paper, tablecloth was dappled with colour from the stained glass behind me. The location was perfect for me to observe and draw over a leisurely lunch.

I ordered from the simple, short menu which offered a more varied selection of local delights than the voluminous menus found in the more popular visitor locations. Here there were no pages of brightly coloured photographs (in case anyone did not know what a Spaghetti Bolognese looked like) of unappetisingly stereotypical meals. Unrequested, a small jug of local red wine and one of water were silently delivered to my table. I poured myself a glass of each, took an appreciative mouthful of the wine and began to sketch. No one cared or took any notice of the industrious, well-dressed gentleman in the corner enjoying his lunch while scribbling into a thick journal. This was a city of artists and writers for whom the isolation and disinterest of the surrounding populous was a gift to creative endeavour.

The meal was all that Vincenzo had promised and the clientele proved rich material for my book.

I rested over a cup of deliciously bitter espresso coffee and remembered the scrap of paper that Maurizio had given me just before I left the hotel for La Fenice. I found it scrunched up in my pocket where I had hastily deposited it. The address that was scribbled on it, I was sure, was the same desolate wharf that I had visited already, but I could not recall how I had got there or where it was in relation to where I was now seated. I took my map from my bag and spread it out on the small table. Using the index, I eventually found the street in the Dorsoduro and saw that it was but a modest walk away. I decided to return to identify the precise building, as I could not remember from my general perusal of the area which of the decrepit structures was the long obsolete gallery.

Crossing the arched timber Ponte dell' Accademia I looked again upon the comparatively bland façade of the Galleria dell' Accademia that seemed out of place in the splendour of the neighbouring baroque facades. Simplicity suited the former residents of the monastery and church that now housed a vast collection of Venetian paintings that I had viewed yesterday, or was it the previous day? I had begun to lose track of time.

Another five to ten minutes of brisk walking found me back at the entrance to the dank alley that led to the even dourer quay. I took a deep breath and the hint of a putrid wind blew down the alley into my face as I bent forward to view the approach. My stick tapped onto the damp, slippery stones that corrugated the floor, the sound absorbed by the eroded brickwork of the arched walls and ceiling.

The forbidding buildings hung over the putrid water, each looking even more forlorn than on my previous visit. I edged my way down the terrace checking for any evidence of a number on either the doors or their surrounds. Eventually I stood before a solid oak door with wrought iron fittings and a broken borrowed light over. It sat in the shadow of the scaffolding that had been in place for many years, the pudlock clips and joints corroded and the bolts unyielding to any scaffolder's spanner.

I approached the door with a slight sense of trepidation and tried the ancient latch. The rusting metal was cold to the touch and, perhaps to my relief, unyielding. If I had gained access, I would have had to duck my head to enter. I tried to look over the door through the borrowed light but, despite it being designed to accommodate a population of lesser stature, the frame and opaque glass was too high. As a modern gallery it lacked any adequate window to display the artists' wares and those windows that existed had been boarded up. I tried to peer through the gaps between the slats of wood, but the interior was too dark to give any idea of the layout of the accommodation.

I stood back on the edge of the quay and, taking care not to get too close to the black water, looked up at the building and its lacework of scaffolding that obscured much of its detailing. There were three floors above street level, the upper windows being larger than those on the lower floor. This would have provided excellent natural light into their interiors. I looked around and above the high, dilapidated wall that bounded the canal on the opposite side and ran the full length of the quay, locking in the foul water at its far end. The analogy of a cesspool was not unreasonable when you studied the filth that floated on the surface of the water. It did not need detailed consideration, as some of the detritus was unmistakeable. I thought that modern Venice did not suffer from the deposition of raw sewerage, but I was clearly wrong.

Over the wall, in the distance, I spotted a tower with a pitched roof and the sun softly illuminated the left side as it departed for the evening. I surmised that this meant the windows on the front of the buildings benefitted from North light, much favoured by artists and painters as being of the purest. As the light continued to fade the far end of the street darkened and became uninviting once again. The blackness crept towards me and the temperature dropped until I shuddered and felt that it was time for me to go. The buildings embraced the darkness, sucking it into their heart through the gaping windows and an eerie silence weighed heavily upon the air. The sound of my footsteps, the click of my cane on the damp, uneven stone sets were deadened, absorbed by the surrounding brickwork while my breath gathered around me in increasingly thick clouds of exhaled vapour. My breathing quickened along with my pace and the hairs on the back of my hand and neck lifted in inexplicable fear. As I retreated, the alley through which I had entered this malevolent street was nowhere to be seen. I was trapped within a seemingly deadly grip and the dusk had swiftly passed into night. No light from surrounding buildings or streets invaded this deep recess. I maintained my position against the front wall of the building and felt my way to where I was sure the alley existed. My body temperature had dropped but sweat was on my forehead, a silent breeze wafted a stagnant smell of stale water and effluent into my nostrils and I gagged slightly, coughing to clear the foul stench. The lapping of the thick polluted water became louder and I was sure the level was rising to slowly and insidiously creep across the surface towards where I stood. I could not allow myself to become transfixed with fear. I had to move on.

I continued my increasingly frantic search for the exit, my sense of panic barely controlled. The thick water continued its advance, rolling with a high meniscus as if it were cold molten lava. Like a blind man, I used my stick to tap along the wall, the light having finally deserted this wretched place. The alley could not have disappeared, chased away by the enveloping dark. It had to be somewhere. I continued to fumble along the wall; lichen and droplets of condensed water ran off my fingers. I was sure that I felt the stinking, glutinous water clutch at my shoes as each step became heavier, more leaden, than the previous one. I could not have missed the alley, and if I had, I could not return, as the clawing water would surely engulf me.

Panic started to overcome me as I imagined that the passage had been sealed, trapping me in this god-forsaken quagmire. Then, suddenly, I felt a hard, stone quoin and a void in the brickwork. With enormous relief I saw the warm light beckoning to me from the far end of the malodorous alley.

A bell sounded softly in the distance, slowly tolling a mournful requiem that echoed around the abandoned district, muffled by its obscurity. I do not know why, but as I departed that hellish place, I cast an eye back into the blackness. To my surprise I saw a reflection high on the opposite wall of a yellow flickering light. Whether it was from the derelict buildings or beyond was unknown to me and I had no desire to return and find out.

With an enormous sense of relief, I hastily followed the welcoming light to make my escape.

"Priest. Fetch me some water. My mouth is dry."

The priest walks through the door from where the old man has previously appeared with drinks. There is an inner dressing room with a full range of cupboards and drawers that he imagines houses the older man's considerable wardrobe of clothes. To one side is a bathroom and to the other a small, but spotless kitchenette. He finds a glass, and from the compact refrigerator takes a fresh bottle of water. Upon his return to the room, he sees the old man sitting at his desk with his eyes closed.

He pours out the water and places the glass within reach of the old man. There is no movement and the priest leans a little closer, wondering if the man is asleep. His breathing is very shallow and catches now and again. Suddenly his eyes open wide,

"I'm not dead…yet," he snaps. The priest jumps away and stands across from the desk. The old man grabs the glass with a shaky hand to take a long drink, rivulets of water escaping down the deep creases in the skin either side of his mouth. He puts down the glass, muttering as he does so and takes out his handkerchief to mop away the moisture.

"Shall I continue?"

"Please do."

XVII
The Opera

When I got back to the sanctuary of my warm room at the hotel, I found my evening attire and costume for the opera and masked ball carefully placed in the antiquated wardrobe. The door had swung open, or was left open, and the full-length mirror attached to the inside of the door reflected my arrival. I was relieved to have returned to the comforts of this house, which now dispelled the groundless, but none the less fearful, memories of that repugnant quay. I had no desire to return there although, strangely, I felt that the place sustained a draw that I was powerless to resist.

I placed my bag on the bed and rang down for some tea. Involuntarily, I turned to face the wardrobe mirror and cautiously rubbed my hand over my previously battered and bruised face. The pain and the discolouration that had been the outward evidence of the assault had all but disappeared. A couple of pale lines in the skin above my eyebrow evidenced the fading scars. My newly acquired beard was in need of a trim but had grown well and I liked the changed face that looked back at me.

A soft knock on the door announced the arrival of my tea. A young waitress I had not seen before placed the tray on a side table. She had long curling black tresses, clear dark eyes and a flawless complexion. She was tall and her legs slim, the calves well defined and strong. Her dress was a pinafore style, the hem above the knees but not to the extent that it would shock her grandmother. She smiled sweetly as she left, giving the mere hint of an old-fashioned curtsy. I would have liked her to stay a while, as she would have made a superb life model with her taut body and long limbs. However, although my intentions were purely artistic, to ask her to do so might have been misconstrued. I did not want a repeat of the embarrassment and misunderstanding experienced over lunch in the restaurant a couple of days ago.

I poured the tea and settled back into the chair that gave the view over the canal and a horizon of jumbled rooftops. I closed my eyes and breathed deeply to relax the tension of the day and dozed for a few tranquil minutes. I heard Vivaldi music drift from somewhere beyond the confines of my room and I slipped into a contented and strangely comforting dream that stimulated and refreshed. A dream that was incapable of being recalled when I awoke a few minutes later. I believe that short, deep periods of sleep are more beneficial than long light ones and certainly I found myself revitalised and ready for the evening's entertainment. I knew that my slumber had been short as the tea in my cup had not lost all of its heat and that which remained in the pot was of sufficient temperature to provide me with a passably refreshing second cup.

The next hour was taken with my preparations for the evening, including a careful shave and trim of my beard. A lengthy, hot shower to wash both my hair and body removed any clinging remnants from the ghastly quay and cleared the memory from my mind. I banished the fear as being foolish and unfounded. I applied cologne to myself, not something that I did at home, but it was in my bathroom and it seemed appropriate for the evening ahead. The smell was pleasant, and it invigorated my skin as it gently entered the open pores. As I combed my hair, I noticed that it had grown longer than I would have found acceptable at home, it not having been cut since before Christmas. However, it seemed to be very much in keeping with my current bearing and my environs.

Tonight, I was to attend the finest opera house in Venice, if not the World, dressed by a costumier of international renown. I felt that this new paradigm was as natural as my previous existence was anathema. My assertiveness in both my art and my social bearing should have surprised me, as should my increasingly fluent Italian. Such things did not happen to people like me, but they had, and I had accepted the changes with uncharacteristic equanimity. Where this was all leading, I did not know. My future was predestined, and I embraced the experience. I was willing to allow myself to float along with the current of Venetian life that was swirling around me.

I, Giacomo Farthing; artist, traveller and convert to all things Venetian.

I descended the staircase into the main hall of the hotel, my silver topped cane that now always accompanied me connecting with each stone step. My newly acquired eveningwear accentuated my height and slim build, the long cloak protecting me from the chill night air and accommodated my sketchbook without any visible stretching or tension. I carried the tricorn hat in my left hand as I felt it inappropriate to wear it in the hotel. A couple of my fellow guests stopped and exchanged comment between one another as I passed, deferentially bowing their heads in approval. I smiled as Maurizio approached with his hands outstretched. I stood in front of him and he looked me up and down as if to check that I had not inadvertently transgressed some point of Italian couturiers' etiquette. I knew that everything was perfect, as I had taken a considerable degree of time and care when dressing. After his initial careful scrutiny, he announced that I carried the fashion like a true Italian. This was high praise for an Italian to give an Englishman.

"I have your brother to thank for that. It fits me perfectly"

"Ah, yes, maybe. But they are mere pieces of cloth until filled by the man."

We laughed and I turned towards the main entrance of the hotel. Maurizio stayed my departure and held me by the elbow.

"Signor Farthing, may I offer you an aperitif before your departure?"

There was time and I accepted his offer and accompanied him towards the bar. A number of guests were standing in the entrance to the small room, drinking prior to going for dinner. They parted as I entered, and Maurizio announced to the assembled company that I was attending the opera. A couple of those present asked where and what I was to see, and I politely replied as Maurizio poured a stiff malt whisky into a cut glass tumbler. I remained the centre of attention for a while until the crowd announced that they had to leave for their booking at a restaurant that Maurizio had recommended. They wished me a good evening as they departed, and the room was suddenly empty. I finished my drink and Maurizio came out from behind his bar to escort me from the premises.

"I hope you do not mind but I have taken the liberty of arranging transport that is more appropriate to your evening."

He led me away from the bar towards the doors that faced onto the Grand Canal. Through the float glass I saw a gondolier standing against the timber pontoon, the lights at either end of his gondola bobbing up and down with the rhythmic swell of the water. The lights from the hotel reflected on the smooth black surfaces, the rich upholstery and gilding, fresh and clean as if only applied yesterday.

I turned to face my friend; his eyes were bright with excitement at the surprise he had prepared for me. My obvious delight at the prospect of arriving at La Fenice in such style filled him with pride. I would never be able to repay this kind, gentle, man. I was not an emotional sort of person; English public schools did not encourage such feelings amongst boys of my generation, but here in Italy men were more attuned to their emotions. It seemed a very natural thing for me to show my appreciation by enveloping Maurizio in a hug and for him to reciprocate with a number of hearty slaps on my back. No words were exchanged, and no words were necessary.

As we parted, I carefully placed my mask over my face and pushed it against it. Miraculously it fixed itself to the contours and felt solid. Catching sight of myself in the reflection from the glass doors, I stopped and surveyed my new urbane persona. I was excited at the prospect of promenading on the streets of Venice. I remembered as a small child constantly looking down at my feet when my parents had bought me new shoes, to see what they looked like. Now I found myself casting sideways glances at my reflection in windows and mirrors, getting a new boost of confidence on each occasion. I stood more erect, my stride was long and confident; James was no more, replaced by the suave and talented Giacomo. I stepped into the gondola and sat with my cloak wrapped around me, the Bauta mask hiding my true identity from the world but announcing the new. Not James Farthing, but Giacomo Favretto, citizen of Venice, artist and cognoscente.

The gondolier silently moved us across the water away from the pontoon, onward to La Fenice.

A few tourists pointed and took photographs of the solitary traveller in his private gondola. They tarried on their way back to their hotels, apartments or hostels to watch our progress as we sedately slid past vaporetto, last minute shoppers or those hurrying towards bars and restaurants.

I cannot recall our route to the theatre save that we took many narrow canals and passed under a multitude of arched stone bridges crowded with numerous onlookers. Once in Rio de Fenice we passed under a final vaulted bridge and berthed expertly against the water entrance to the theatre. Vincenzo had told me that it was rare that this entrance was used but it was to be used this evening as a special occasion. I felt privileged that I was able to witness and participate in this event and I suspect this had more to do with collusion between the two brothers, than my ill-deserved and illusory celebrity status. There was a small crowd who had watched our arrival and as I was assisted onto dry land, I heard the digital clicks of mobile phones taking pictures. I turned to thank my gondolier, who removed his boater and bowed low.

"Signore, I shall be waiting here after the performance and will return you to your lodgings." I returned his gracious bow and followed the small gaggle of other members of the audience who had taken advantage of the opening of the water entrance.

In the foyer we joined the main throng of fellow opera lovers. Everyone appeared to have entered into the spirit of the evening. The costumes around me complemented the opulence of our surroundings with an elegance that I felt was so missing in our modern world. In London, I would have felt uncomfortable at being among such overt displays of affluence and power, but here my confidence was bolstered by the expense, style and quality of my own attire. As I looked around me the 21st century faded into the background and I was transported into the late 19th century. Masks prevailed, as did long cloaks, lace, velvet and crinoline. What flesh was exposed was delicately dusted and blemishes, such as there were, had been camouflaged beneath expertly applied cosmetics.

I found myself bowing with increasing extravagance to reciprocate the acknowledgement of gentlemen and their ladies, my cane flashing its silver top in the flickering lights.

Candles? Each chandelier was festooned with pure, white candles, all lit and all evaporating at the same speed to give a consistency of height that was uncanny. When I had visited the opera house to meet Maurizio's brother, I had failed to notice this detail. Looking beyond the open entrance doors, the flickering yellow illumination cast wild shadows around the small square in front of the theatre. Ladies observed proceedings from behind their half masks, lips quivering in playful smiles and eyes flashing within the deepened sockets of their masks.

All was surreal.

All was mystical.

I appeared to be in the centre of a scene that was itself like something out of an opera. I expected the characters to burst into vigorous song at any moment. As if on cue, a light mist wafted across the square from the canal and dusted the crowd as they flowed up the steps beneath the portico, a burble of polite conversation accompanying their progress.

Tonight, I was to experience a performance of Verdi's "La Traviata", premiered in this very theatre in 1853, the same year that Ruskin published his "Stones of Venice". At that time Venice was part of the Austrian empire and I had read that at the end of the performance the audience, with cries of "Viva Verdi", threw red, white and green flowers onto the stage – each representing a colour on the Italian tricolore. Whether the story was true or not, I was not sure, but I liked the idea of such an artistic act of defiance. What was known about the premier on 6th

March was that the portrayal of the heroine, Violetta, and the hero, Alberto, was not met with unanimous approbation. In fact, there was jeering and booing in the first act, primarily because the soprano was considered to be overweight and too old (at 38) to be a convincing courtesan dying of consumption.

After presenting my ticket I was directed to a private box on the second floor, which was long and narrow, set at a slight angle to the stage. I could see the imposing but slightly over-ornate Royal box just to my left with its red velvet furnishings and expansive quantities of gold gilding. My box gave a panorama of both the stage and the magnificent interior of the theatre that seemed even more resplendent than when I had seen it briefly with Vincenzo. The ever-increasing crowd brought an excitement and anticipation to the space as they took their seats. A buzz of expectant voices soared up into the faux, painted, domed ceiling, thence to be ricocheted back towards its source.

Removing my cloak, I hung it on a hook by the entrance. I was unsure whether I should remove my mask but decided to maintain the charade until the lights dimmed for the performance. The four delicate wooden seats at the front of the box appeared too fragile to take the weight of an adult.

Being the first, I confidently took the front seat and I wondered if there was anyone else going to join me. I examined my fellow patrons as they settled themselves into their places. There were two levels of boxes beneath me and I could quite clearly see into a number of them. This was the cream of Venetian society and I was interested to note that almost everyone was masked. The variety of designs and colours was extraordinary, from full-face masks such as my own to delicate ones that merely disguised the upper part of the face from recognition. A couple that I noticed were virgin white with diamanté gems and a plume of feathers rising from the crown – totally inappropriate to the venue and I pitied anyone seated behind these peacocks.

The temptation was too great for me and I swiftly returned to my cloak and retrieved the sketchbook from its inner pocket. It was so full of extraneous pages and drawings that the leather cover was stretched and bowed. I had had to obtain a new, broad, red ribbon from a small shop close to the hotel to hold it all together.

Just below and to my left, beyond the Royal Box, I had a clear view of a box that was occupied by a solitary figure dressed in black. She had the air of a grand-dame; her gown high necked, surmounted with a diamond-encrusted choker and accompanied by matching bracelet and earrings. Her hair was of pure white set high upon her head, which served to exaggerate her long, porcelain white neck. The intricate, lace covered black mask hid the upper half of her face, but even from the distance at which I observed her I could see that while her skin was lined, her complexion was soft and clear. Strong hands were laid lightly on her lap, two brilliant diamond rings twinkling in the light from the huge gilt and bronze chandelier that hung from the painted ceiling. She was sitting in the upright chair without any hint of a slouch so prevalent amongst the aged. Her features were refined and, even in her latter years, she retained the elegant beauty that, in her youth, must have triggered a vigorous level of competition amongst the young men of Venice.

As we waited for the performance, I became engrossed in the elderly lady as I proceeded to add her portrait to my gallery. The inability to see her eyes behind the mask was a challenge for me and I found that I had to start the drawing on a number of occasions to overcome the absence of my usual focal point. Her mask camouflaged the facial proportions and tricked me into a number of false starts. Gradually the pencil produced a passable likeness but before I could add any detail the lights dimmed, and the overture started. I reluctantly placed the book on the floor by my feet and took a final look in her direction.

Her stare was straight towards me, daring me to continue. I could now see directly through the eyeholes of her mask. It was to my considerable consternation that the eyes that held me in their gaze were steely cold. They seemed to cut through the stiffness of my mask and expose my true identity to her. Those eyes were unblinking and forcefully held my own to the extent that I was unable to draw them away. I remained motionless until the full dimming of the lights finally restored my failing sense of anonymity.

I concentrated on the dark green velvet curtain across the stage covered with its hundreds of gilt leather flowers. As it rose and the light spilled out across the auditorium, I risked a quick glance in her direction and my confidence ebbed still further. She continued her visual assault upon my person with those glaring gimlet eyes. Her accusatory glare challenged me to remove my mask – but I could not. I hastily returned my attention to the stage, brutally aware of her presence, willing me to look in her direction again.

On stage Alfredo was confirming his love for Violetta in a pure tenor voice. Eventually, I courageously stole a quick look at my nemesis and was relieved to see that she was intently watching the players on the stage. Now she was apparently oblivious to my presence, which enabled me to remove my mask and enjoy the remainder of the first act in peace and comfort.

I was transported into Verdi's world by the quality of the performance and all too quickly the interval arrived. I clapped enthusiastically as the curtain slowly descended, while off stage Alfredo's voice retreated as he departed from his true love's salon in Paris. Almost without thinking, I looked over to the grand-dame's box but could not see her. I ran my eye along the row of boxes in case I had mistaken her location but all, save hers, were full of appreciative opera fans. I was slightly surprised that any aficionado of opera would depart early from such an exquisite performance but concluded that she had perhaps retired to the foyer bar or elsewhere to avoid the rush. The prospect of a cool glass of prosecco was appealing and I decided that I would join the throng. I replaced my mask and picked up my folio to return it to the pocket of my cloak, which had dried from the damp mist that had engulfed the square and my gondola when I arrived.

It was only then that I noticed that a small table had been set to the rear of the box, by the entrance, on which stood an ice bucket, a bottle of prosecco, a solitary flute and a small plate of canapes. A small envelope addressed to 'Giacomo – The Artist' was standing against the glass. I opened it and, removing the stiff card within, read the handwritten message.

"I hope that you enjoy your evening."

It was unsigned and I studied the reverse side of the card for any clue as to who had sent it. I assumed that it was from Maurizio and/or Vincenzo. I felt like a VIP as I poured the chilled prosecco into the flute.

It was then that I realised that the Bauta was still on my face, although I had to admit that it fitted so perfectly that I was unaware of its presence. While I was told that my mask was designed to accommodate both drinking and eating without its removal, I was not wholly convinced. Initially I seemed to be inept at the skills required. After a couple of dribbling attempts, I removed it and placed it on the table, hoping that I was not transgressing any formal etiquettes. I sipped the chilled liquor and stood to the rear of my box looking out into the majesty of the theatre. The auditorium had emptied somewhat as patrons took refreshment and, as usual; I started to review the faces of those who remained. I automatically felt for the folio and placed it on my chair, but it slipped and fell to the floor, opening at the last sketch I had commenced. The grand dame glared up at me, and the drawing of her eyes seemed to be more complete than I recalled. It had been difficult to capture them behind the mask and from such a distance, but here they were in clear detail, maintaining the piercing stare that had so disconcerted me earlier. I was sure that I had not achieved that degree of detail but dismissed the point as unimportant. The speed at which I could now work had greatly improved since my arrival in Venice. I seemed to have given her eyes a defiant appearance, but I also thought I detected a hint of uncertain recognition. That point at which you see someone and wonder whether you know them or not but are reluctant to make an approach or enquiry in fear of making a fool of yourself. The grand dame was too resilient to have such trepidation or to concern herself with the judgement of others. I stooped, retrieved the book from where it had fallen and sat looking into those eyes. The more I looked, the more I felt a stab of familiarity in the shape of her face and the unexpected clarity of her eyes within the holes of her mask. Idly, I flicked back over the many pages of sketches that I had created during my trip. The people in street cafes, the facades of medieval buildings and the many elegantly arched bridges that spanned the canals – all were put to paper for future reminders of this mystical trip. The girl at the restaurant appeared before me and I physically jumped as I saw her eyes.

I immediately turned back to the most recent piece of work depicting the elderly woman, and then flicked between each drawing.

There was no mistaking the similarity between the physiological compositions of the two sets of eyes. The only variation between them was the length of life that each had experienced and which I had managed to capture and reflect in their depths. One set was young, happy and carefree - in the fullness of life. The other, while still sharp and alert, were greyer, rheumy, determined but also somewhat world-weary. I worried again whether my sketching was repeating a structure of the eyes such that the true character was being lost, each face a pastiche of others. If that were the case, then the repetition would be evidence elsewhere in my folio. But no, as I scanned back through past work, I saw a wide variety of different eyes. None matched those of the young woman who had bewitched me in the restaurant, or the grand dame who had so haunted my arrival in this box.

However, I had to defer any further consideration of the dilemma because the lights had started to dim, and the orchestra announced the recommencement of the performance. Once again, I put the folio down at my feet. As I straightened in my seat, I noticed that the grand dame had retaken her place in her lonely box. To my annoyance, she was staring straight at me, however her demeanour had changed. The animosity had been replaced with a look of bewildering recognition, the eyes enquiring for an answer to a question that I could not fathom. I realised that she could now see my face, my having removed my mask, and she clearly thought that she knew me. As I returned her gaze, she did not break eye contact and we held each other in a state of uncertainty. Eventually my nerve gave first, and I broke an invisible bond that had formed between us during those few fleeting seconds. I knew from that moment that there was something she wished to ask me but was unable to do so because she felt a degree of mistrust or insecurity. For my part, I did not know whether to pity her or despise her for ruining my evening. For all her elegance and grace, her behaviour was verging upon intimidation and any sympathy that initially I might have felt for this despondent, elderly lady waned, to be replaced by exasperation at her effrontery.

It was impossible for me to relax and enjoy the performance on the stage because I was constantly aware of her unwavering attention to me. Her body did not move, and her eyes were unblinking. She appeared to be trying to reach a conclusion, a decision as to whether I was who she thought I was. I tried to re-engage with the story being played out on stage but, even without looking, I knew that her gaze had not faltered and was still upon me. It was as if she were calling to me from across the void between our boxes. I imagined, briefly, that I heard, underlying the music filling the theatre, a softly spoken plea for me to recognise her, to come to her, to assist her. Within my head her voice mingled with that of Violetta singing of her grief at having agreed to Giorgio's request for her to surrender her love for Alfredo. The two sounds in a harmonious duet, the sound rising amidst the warm air and dust motes that caught in the spotlights across the auditorium.

I became increasingly restless and irritated at the intrusion until I could stand it no longer. I suddenly rose from my chair and walked out of my box into the corridor. In consequence of the uninvited attention that this witch was foisting upon my person, I knew that I had to confront her and that necessitated my having to find and attend at her box. I descended the flight of stairs to the corridor in which I thought she was located. Counting down the doors, I came to where I calculated she was seated. I inhaled deeply in preparation for the confrontation and took hold of the brass handle of the door into her box. To my surprise, it did not yield and remained steadfastly locked. I tried to turn it in the opposite direction but still the door refused to open. I pushed and then pulled the door, not understanding why it would not grant me access. As I continued to struggle with the lock a uniformed usher appeared at my shoulder and quietly asked if he could be of assistance. Feeling slightly awkward, I explained that I had seen an acquaintance and wanted to have a word with her.

"Not in this box, Signore." I let go of the handle and stepped back to look him in the face.

"What do you mean?"

"This is a private box and has not been occupied for this performance."

I stood confused and then replied somewhat sharply that it had to be occupied as I had seen the lady who was in it.

"You must be mistaken, Signore. There are many boxes and perhaps you have miscalculated which she was in. It is easily done." I detected that the usher was beginning to patronise me, which did nothing for my already irritated state of mind.

"I do not think so. She was sitting alone in this box. I am sure it was this one."

"That is impossible, Signore." His use of the word Signore was becoming less convincing as a mark of respect, but I ignored it for the moment.

"Why impossible?" I snapped.

"Because all the boxes on this level are full," he conclusively stated, as if that was the end of the discussion. He saw my disbelief and re-emphasised his point.

"All full, save for this one which, I can assure you, has not been occupied this evening." This final statement was his 'coup de grace' and he had clearly satisfied himself that I was defeated. He shrugged his shoulders in supplication and extended his hand as if to guide me back to my own seat.

"That is not possible. I saw her with my own eyes, and she was sitting in this box." My voice had risen, and I noticed that another couple of ushers had appeared and were standing off, as if waiting to assist their colleague with this irrational member of the audience. I was not to be dissuaded so easily.

"Do you have a key to this door?"

"Of course." The Signore had been dropped and his voice had taken on an alertness that demonstrated a preparedness for action, if it should prove necessary.

"Open it!" I countered his impudence with a level of authority that surprised both him and me, but it worked. With sullen resignation he removed a master key that was attached to his trousers by a silver chain and silently unlocked the door. He gently pushed it away from him and gave me a withering look of contemptuous triumph.

To my consternation the box was indeed empty. Not only was the grand dame not seated to the front of the space but also it had been relieved of all of its furniture. I brushed past the usher to fully enter the box to confirm what I was seeing. The usher followed in my wake and in an insistent whisper asking me to leave.

"But this is impossible. I saw her! I know I did! She was staring at me." I was perplexed and my confidence had wavered. Almost speaking to myself rather than the usher I continued,

"She was not a mirage, not a figment of my imagination!"

My voice had reached a volume that summoned shushing from those members of the audience in my immediate vicinity. My noisy protestations were causing a disruption to their enjoyment.

I could not explain what I was witnessing and, somewhat as an afterthought, I looked up at my own box.

There, standing where I had been seated was the silhouette of what had to be the woman.

"Look! There!" I pointed up to my box.

"Please! Be quiet!" an unseen person snapped.

I pulled the usher into my vantage point and hissed for him to look up at my…… Shamefaced, I saw that the silhouette had gone. The usher gently took me by the elbow, and I did as was requested of me and left the box. I took one last look over my shoulder to reaffirm the unassailable facts before me. As I emerged, deflated, I noticed that the supporting ushers had moved into more strategic locations should they be needed. Rather like the waiters in the restaurant where I had tried (in their eyes) to pick up the young female diner, these ushers smirked and whispered one to the other. Dazed and confused, I felt that I had to try to defuse an inexplicable situation.

"I really don't understand it, but I apologise. I was obviously mistaken." The usher bowed his head imperceptibly in his own unapologetic acceptance of my seemingly weak and slightly unconvincing defence. He offered to escort me back to my own box, not as an act of courtesy but more by way of a requirement to ensure that I did not cause any more trouble and, in his words,

"To perhaps appreciate what remains of the performance?"

I am sure that the remainder of the opera was superb, but it was lost on me as I struggled to understand what I had experienced and the ignominy that had befallen me at the hand of the apparition. At the end of the performance I left La Fenice with a sense of dazed incomprehension. The intoxicating self-assurance that I had experienced when I had arrived had all but evaporated and now the anonymity afforded by my mask and attire was more than welcome. My gondolier was as good as his word and was waiting diligently at the prearranged pick up point. He enquired after my enjoyment of the performance and my response was tersely polite, discouraging any further conversation. He took the hint and we travelled back to the hotel in a pensive, if not sullen, silence.

It seems sacrilege to admit that I can remember little, if anything, of the return journey save that the night air was cold and the sky overcast, devoid of stars. The buildings fronting the canal were dark and few lights shone from the many windows overlooking our progress. I was grateful for my warming cloak and remained seated with my back to the toiling matelot guiding my craft across the inky, dark waters. I was impatient to return to the haven of the hotel.

Thankfully the reception was deserted. I scurried to my room and discarded the costume. Sitting at the small desk overlooking the dark swirling waters of the Grand Canal below, I cross-examined my memory as to the reality of the events that had occurred. Had I, or had I not, seen the grand dame? Was it a shadow created by the spotlights that played upon the stage and reflected back into the auditorium? Neither seemed likely as before me I had the evidence in the form of the partially completed drawing.

But how had I completed the eyes behind the mask? I could hardly see them in the low lighting of the theatre, let alone draft a likeness to this detail and complexity. And what of the similarity between the two women, the faces of whom I compared as I flicked between the relevant pages in my sketchbook? The young woman in the restaurant and the Grand Dame – they appeared as one in the same - merely divided by years and experiences. Could they be related, was one the granddaughter of the other? They were decades apart in age but so aligned in appearance. I continued to turn back through the pages; slowly scanning the copious completed and partially completed drawings that filled each one. Slowly my trip aimlessly passed me by in reverse order - some hasty line drawings of passengers in the airport, on the train home and finally at the Monkeychops Club reception.

And there she was!

My breath caught in my throat and I felt my heart palpitate to the extent that I wondered if I was suffering the onset of a heart attack. I took some slow, deep breaths and poured a glass of water to moisten my dry mouth. When I felt settled once again, I looked back down at the page. It was her – the eyes unmistakeable, glistening and untroubled. The Contessa Wolfhertz, seated in my drawing and looking slightly thoughtful, was clearly identifiable as the second epoch in the life of this face that was increasingly haunting me.

While I accept that the Contessa had made a strong impression on me, as had the young woman in the restaurant, surely not to the extent that I had fallen foul of deceiving my eyes and not drawing what was before me? I could not bring myself to accept that I would have allowed the characteristics to become unified within these three drawings.

Sleep eluded me for hours. I sat in the chair or lay awake on my bed looking up at the ceiling of my room wrestling with this conundrum. Eventually, I gave up the notion of sleep and opened up my iPad and searched for the Contessa on the Internet. The only prominent reference was to two paintings done in the sixteenth century by Veronese of the Countess Livia da Porto, one with her daughter and the other as a family group with her husband and son. The likeness between my Countess and the one depicted in the painting was non-existent. The only bond between the two was that it was felt that the paintings had been executed in Venice. I could find no other relevant reference to the woman who I seem to have seen in three different eras of her life.

Surely, I thought, someone of her standing must have a social history of some kind?

I jadedly returned to the crumpled bed and lay against the pile of pillows, staring disconcertedly out of my window without focussing on anything in particular. The faces of the three women alternately floated before me, reflected in the rolled glass panes as if they lay next to me. At times they seemed to be teasing me, in others happy and contented and finally displaying a pitiful expression of desperate need, of comfort, of help. However, it was impossible for me to fathom out from their alternating countenances whether they were the same woman or three doppelgängers. The Contessa - the young woman - the grand-dame - the young woman - the grand-dame, the Contessa again – who were they and why was I the apparent subject of their curiosity? Questions and precious few answers continued to circulate in my weary thoughts until eventually I drifted off into an uncomfortable and fitful sleep.

The old man has emptied his glass and the priest gets up to refill it. The recounting of this part of the story is tiring the old man and the priest is concerned that he may have allowed him to continue for too long.

"Am I mad, Priest?"

The priest pretends not to have heard the question as he takes another bottle of water from the refrigerator.

"No more water! There is a bottle of malt whisky next to the olive oil."

The priest closes the 'fridge door and, locating the liquor, he pours a modest measure into the bottom of the glass.

"Get yourself one." Not a request but a command. The Priest pours himself a smaller measure into a clean glass and takes them through to the living room. The old man looks disconsolately at the inadequate measure in the glass that is put before him.

There is silence in the room as each man contemplates his drink and sips the fiery liquid. The Priest reflects on what he has heard and reminds himself to return to the Internet when he gets back to his lodgings. The Priest had looked up the San Cassiano hotel but had not had time to go there prior to his trip to Florence. He placed this on his mental 'to do list'.

The old man is thinking back to the events that he has just described, running over the details to ensure that he has not missed anything of importance. Finally, he reverts to the present and asks,

"What were you doing in Florence?"

The Priest is taken aback by the sudden question.

"An errand for my Bishop," and then added, "Nothing of importance."

"No?" The old man does not sound convinced but does not pursue the point.

"Are you coming tomorrow?"

"If I have time." The priest has planned to examine some of the details of the old man's story.

"Make time."

The room descends into silence once more.

XVIII
Question of Faith

The San Cassiano Hotel, or Casa Favretto, is located close to the fish market and the Priest decides to make a diversion after he has obtained his regular weekly purchases. The entrance from Calle della Rosa is much as the old man has described. The reception area also reflects his reminiscence although the Priest does not find the surroundings quite as lavish as the old man had recalled.

There is no one on the front desk and the Priest wanders down the hall towards the water door. Sure enough, on his right is the small bar and out on the pontoon a couple are enjoying the view over a cup of coffee. A voice from behind him asks,

"Can I help you?"

The Priest turns to see a fresh faced, young man in a smart suit. At the sight of the priest's clerical collar the hotel employee becomes more deferential,

"Ah, Father, I did not realise."

"I am sorry to disturb you, but I was wondering if Maurizio, the concierge, is around?"

The young man pulls at his earlobe and shakes his head slowly from side to side.

"There is no concierge called Maurizio here," he pauses and then, keen to please the Priest, he adds, "but I only arrived this season, so this Maurizio might have worked here before I came. What's his surname?"

"I am afraid I don't know. Is there anyone who works here who might know him?"

"Not at the moment, but I can ask the owners. They are away at present, but if you care to come back in a day or so then I shall be happy to see if I can assist, Father."

Accepting that this was a temporary dead end, he thanks the man and leaves the hotel.

The walk to La Fenice is well known to him and he briskly covers the ground, unsure whether he is on a fool's errand or not.

The foyer to the theatre is busy with the first tours being organised. The Priest approaches the desk in front of the queue. A French woman starts to complain to her companion about queue jumping but relents when she realises the young man's calling.

"I shall be but a minute, forgive me," he reassures her fluently.

"Yes, Father. What can I do for you?"

He answers the woman behind the counter,

"Who is the head costumier here at present?"

The woman is surprised at the random question and gives a name that is not recognised by the Priest.

"When did Vincenzo leave?"

"Vincenzo, Father? I don't know any Vincenzo." She turns and speaks to a colleague just behind her who confirms that he is also unaware of any Vincenzo working at La Fenice as a costumier.

"Maybe he is at one of the other theatres, Father?" she helpfully suggests.

"I am sorry. I must be mistaken."

As he walks to the ferry home, the Priest begins to consider whether the old man's story is a complete fabrication. He has looked on the Internet for the Contessa and found nothing of assistance. At the suggestion of his Bishop, he had travelled to Florence to consult with a friend who he knew from his university days and had subsequently specialised in psychiatry. The behaviour of the old man was consistent with his friend's diagnosis of him being a psychotic.

"It is important that you do not seek to deny or argue as to the veracity of what the patient is recounting. Similarly, try not to apportion or suggest blame in respect to any actions that he might claim to have seen or perpetrated."

This gave some comfort to the Priest who began to acknowledge that perhaps the killing by the old man of his attacker was not a real event. That the original attack had occurred he had established from the newspaper article that he had found on the Internet. Further searches had not unearthed a report on the murder, although there seemed to be daily reports of stabbings in the UK press.

That Giacomo Favretto existed in the late 18th century was an unequivocal fact and the drawings that Giacomo Farthing had executed whilst in Venice were undoubtedly heavily influenced by the former artist's style and subject matter. There was no denying that his Giacomo was a very talented artist, but this was the only tenuous link to any of the story having substance to it.

Satisfied that he had a better understanding of the old man and his affliction, he felt a sense of relief. While not being any kind of an expert on psychoses, at least there was a reasonably rational explanation to what he was witnessing - except for one point.

He had heard the Voice.

XIX
The Ballroom

"*Why do you perpetuate your conversations with that meddling Priest*?"

"I speak with him to cleanse my mind. To seek some sort of absolution."

"*Absolution? Absolution! What do you require of absolution?*"

"From you and your intrusions. From your malevolence."

"*Malevolence? Frankly your ingratitude is galling. I grant to you talents that have increased your abilities to a level consistent with the great Favretto. Is that not what you demanded of me in exchange for the small task I sought from you?*"

"I was a pawn in your scheme since you discovered me following the death of my family."

"*Oh, but I found you before that little episode.*"

"What do you mean?"

"*Think well about your continued relationship with this Priest. He is not to your advantage. I will not be confronted by him or any of his kind.*"

The old man is mumbling in his sleep, wrapped in a blanket on the balcony. The Priest cannot decipher his words but clearly the old man is upset, agitated. He wonders if he should wake him or whether he might leave him a moment in an effort to catch some clue as to the subject of his dream. The movement ceases and the reclining body appears to be in repose.

The Priest is seated across the balcony, the wind whipping around him, ruffling the old man's white hair and flapping at the loose edges of his blanket.

"How long have you been here, Priest?" The old man does not move, but one eye is open beneath a bushy raise eyebrow. He fixes the Priest in his sight and watches for any hint that he had spoken in his sleep.

"Not long."

The old man shuffles up his recliner and sits slightly more upright, placing the blanket around the lower half of his body.

"Lift the back of this thing so that I can look out over the lagoon."

The Priest moves to the back of the recliner and lifts the section that is supporting the old man's back until it clicks and locks into place.

"I have put something on my desk for you to look at, to judge for yourself." The Priest gets out of his chair and walks through the double doors to the desk. There is a large sheet of plain paper concealing the surface of the desk and he lifts it gently to reveal three portraits lying next to one another, each in a separate plastic envelope, each carefully removed from the sketchbook.

The Priest studies the triptych and admits to himself that the three faces did bear a remarkable resemblance to one another. But is this so surprising if the old man is a psychotic? The images of the three ages of the same woman are in his mind and he has merely transferred them to physical form through his art. That does not mean that they are flesh and blood, or that they have haunted the old man. Haunting was not something the Priest believes in, mysterious beings that live beyond death. Then the irony hits him and he chuckled to himself. His belief in the story of Jesus was different. Totally different – wasn't it?

"What's so funny?"

"Nothing."

"Why are you laughing then, or was it a snigger?"

"It was neither." The Priest changes the subject, "These are very good."

"Never mind the quality. Are they, in your opinion, the same woman?"

"They certainly look to be so."

"That's what I thought at the time. So you can understand my bewilderment when I viewed them all in my room after the opera?"

"I can certainly see why you thought that they were the same person. Though the different eras defy explanation." The Priest looks closer at the backgrounds to each portrait; the detailing being so intricate that even the old man could not have completed them on site but must have worked on them after the initial sketch. "Did you see any of them again?"

The Contessa was the key to unlocking the puzzle because, however inadequate, I knew the most about her. I had a name and from the enthusiasm she expressed about places she knew in Venice, it would seem reasonable that she had, or still did, live here. I decided that I should consult Maurizio as the source of all local knowledge. The Contessa had spoken of Venice as if she was a resident, or at least a regular visitor. He might be able to shed some light on my riddle.

From behind his bar Maurizio shrugged his shoulders and looked blankly at me.

"Many visitors, both of common and noble birth inhabit this city but I have never heard of this lady. Naturally, I shall make some enquiries but there is only a vague possibility that I can find one person out of millions." He took a scruffy pad from beneath the bar and scribbled a note by way of a reminder.

"Thank you", I replied, ready to leave him to his duties. It was then that I remembered the other place, apart from the Galleria d'Abrinzi, that the Contessa had mentioned when we met at the Club.

"Oh, Maurizio, she also mentioned that she swam at Rima's floating baths in the summer."

Maurizio looked at me in disbelief and then laughed with a deep uncontrolled guffaw.

"Not unless she is over a hundred years old!"

"What do you mean?"

"Your Contessa could not possibly have gone swimming there. The baths used to be taken to Murano each winter and dismantled before being rebuilt for the next season. But that has not happened since 1905. She must have been referring to somewhere else, perhaps The Lido? She could not have possibly meant Rima's baths."

But I knew that I had not mistaken the name, because the Contessa had mentioned them twice. Once when she told me she swam there and secondly when she told me that they would not be available for me to swim in at this time of year.

How could the Contessa have confused the baths with The Lido? She seemed so sure.

Maurizio looked at me with unease, "Are you feeling well, Signore? You seem a little," he hesitated to find the appropriate word, "distracted?"

"No, I'm fine. I didn't sleep well last night – strange dreams. I suspect it was all the excitement of the opera last night that left my head buzzing."

"Si, Signore. That is often the experience of visitors to La Fenice. It over stimulates the senses and extends the imagination beyond the normal limits of day to day life." We stood in an uncomfortable silence, each on our own side of the bar. Then, as if to change the subject, he asked suddenly,

"Do you have all you need for the masked ball tonight?" Not waiting for my reply, he continued, "It will be a great event and all the tickets have been sold. They are commanding a considerable price in the City."

I saw a possible escape from my dilemma,

"Are they? I would not want to deprive anyone from going who really wanted to and needed a ticket. As I explained, I don't usually go to balls and I am a terrible dancer."

A flicker of disappointment, or possibly disapproval, passed across Maurizio's face and his eyes darkened infinitesimally.

"No, Signore. You have a ticket and you must go." His voice adopted a harsh, insistent tone; "You would regret it afterwards if you did not attend."

I spread my hands in defeat and accepted the inevitable. I would have to attend, if only to satisfy the two brothers who had gone to so much trouble to prepare me. Upon reflection, I acknowledged that my attempt to extricate myself from the ball had shown a degree of ingratitude that was unacceptable.

"Well, thank you again. I'm greatly looking forward to it." I lied while hoping that I sounded sincere. It seemed to satisfy Maurizio who reverted to his usual amiable countenance.

"And in the meantime, Signore," he tapped his finger on the note he had written on his pad, "I will attempt to find your elusive Contessa."

My day passed pleasantly enough, but I could not concentrate on my surroundings and found myself yet again wandering aimlessly around the City, my thoughts constantly returning to the empty box at La Fenice, the young woman at the restaurant, the Contessa and their respective portraits that now resided in my room. It was as if they were with me in person, but incapable of conversation or explanation. The sights around me were, no doubt, wonderful but they did not tarry in my memory for long. The streets became indistinguishable one from the other, the canals mere channels of limpid water conveying their predominantly human cargoes hither and thither. The buildings were just edifices of containment, standing in defiance of the elements. My sketchbook remained unopened wherever I sat, and my pencils unwanted in their tin. I was preoccupied by my innermost thoughts and so can give little detail of what occurred save to say that I returned to the hotel at around five o'clock as the sun disappeared from the city. My deliberations swung like a pendulum between my confusion over the three women and apprehension over my attendance at the ball that evening. Both were distractions and as the time for the latter grew closer, my nervousness increased.

While I was confident about the quality and the anonymity afforded by my costume, I was still very reticent about my presence at a gathering for which I had little natural aptitude. I did not want to be shown up as merely a figure of amusement for the assembled company. As the hour for the start of the ball approached, I realised that I could no longer put off my preparation and started to preen myself. Self-assurance was going to have to be achieved through the power of the costume that had served me so well at the Opera the previous evening. Was that really only yesterday? Time seemed to have lost its structure and was more ethereal rather than having any composition aligned to reality.

Slowly and carefully, I put on each part of my costume. Once again, I experienced a gradual metamorphosis. The self-assurance and strength of character that I had found in the days following my arrival in Venice returned. I rediscovered Giacomo as I stared at the man in the gesso mirror.

By the grace of the Bauta it was impossible to recognise me, as I had discovered at La Fenice. The mask had a prominent chin that over sailed my mouth, and despite my rather inadequate efforts at the opera, did allow me to eat and drink without its removal. No ribbon or elastic was present to secure it in place. Magically the fit was such that once in place it remained. The tricorn hat had decorative braid work to its edges, and the satin and macramé lace capelet, or zendale, provided a further line of defence for my self-crafted reputation by concealing any part of my face not hidden by the mask. As Casanova proved, the costume guaranteed complete anonymity, thereby allowing the wearer to commit transgressions that would destroy the reputation of any upright gentlemen…or refined lady.

Vincenzo had provided a dress shirt as an afterthought, which was slightly too flouncy for my taste, having a lace ruff down the front and at the cuffs. No doubt it complied and complemented the fashion I imagined was prevalent at any formal 19th century masked ball.

My cloak was made of a light material that had protected me surprisingly well, considering its minimal weight, against the chill wind of the canal last night, but also did not cause me to overheat, even when in the warmth of La Fenice. It allowed my skin to breath so that I remained comfortable throughout the evening. I lifted it down from its hanger and wrapped it around my shoulders, clipping the clasp together to hold it in place. All this seemed so familiar but, bearing in mind that I had only worn it the once, should not have been so. Admittedly, I was not wholly unaccustomed to a cloak as I used one at home quite regularly. While I had always purchased clothes of quality, and probably spent too much of my hard-earned salary on them, the materials and cut of these outfits were above even my demanding standards.

While vanity is not one of my overt sins, I had to admit that I looked wonderful. As I twirled on my toes the scarlet satin lining of my cloak flashed in the bright lights of my room. I lifted the finely crafted lace and satin zendale capelet out of its box. This was the part of the costume that I was most nervous about as it shrouded my head and hung down across my shoulders to around stomach level. It was of no weight at all and at least it toned-down the ruff on my shirt, which was still visible beneath the fine black lacework. My head was covered in black satin and I appeared to be a combination of a nun and an ageing thug in a hoodie. My moustache had developed a slight flick at the ends without the addition of any wax. The beard had matured into a natural embellishment to the slightly rakish face that now stared back at me. I appraised the version of myself that was now before me. A crooked smile and emerging arrogance did not seem to accord with the person that I had so recently left behind in England. Now it sat comfortably with the character that seemed to have subsumed me in this city of dreams.

The final elements to my attire were the Bauta mask followed by the tri-corn hat. I very cautiously placed the mask over my face. The eyeholes provided a good level of peripheral vision, but the room somehow looked different, the lighting became subdued, less well-lit and softer in hue. Despite this, the drapes to the windows, the decoration to the walls and the furniture were fresher, the colours more vibrant. This was slightly disconcerting, not least because all was restored to apparent normality upon my removing the mask. When I interchanged between the mask being on and off this strange phenomenon was repeated. The room was transformed as if my surroundings had regressed into a bygone era and returned again.

I carefully arranged the zendale around the edges of the mask to eliminate any prospect of my being recognised. This was unlikely as I hardly recognised myself. Slowly, I promenaded around my room in my new regalia and watched the shadows glide across the ceiling and walls. A stranger once again stood before me, reflected in the full-length, ornately carved and gilded mirror that hung on the wardrobe door - erect, self-assured and haughty - a man of potency in both thought and deed. No hint remained of the former resident of this bodily shell, removed from his shallow existence and replaced by Giacomo – for, as tradition dictated, this was the character that I had assumed for the evening. I treasured the fact that the two names, James and Giacomo, were synonymous but I was keen to assume the character of Giacomo Favretto who had become my alter ego and whose work I had come to so admire. Why should I not play the role of the talented young artist about whom so relatively little was known?

My right hand rested lightly on the silver top of my polished ebony cane - the transfiguration was complete. Signor Favretto bowed his head slightly in my direction to acknowledge his own reincarnation.

Before I left, I decided that some Dutch courage was required in the form of a malt whisky sharpener. It would enable me to check once more that the practicalities behind the design of the Bauta were correct. Would I be able to eat and drink without its removal? I retrieved a half bottle of whisky that I had packed in my bag but not opened. The pale amber malt slid down my throat and burned in my belly. It was nectar. I relaxed a little more as no liquid escaped from the sides of my mouth and I became reasonably satisfied at my proficiency in taking advantage of the design.

The time had arrived for me to present the phoenix that is Giacomo Favretto to the world. I wondered if another tot might help but dismissed the idea. Instead I placed my sketchbook and some pencils into the pocket of my cloak.

The corridor outside my room was silent and devoid of any other residents. A temporarily erected sign on an easel by the stairs directed me to the rear of the building where I found a lift that previously I did not realise existed. The double concertina-trellis doors slid apart smoothly on well-oiled tracks and with surprisingly little effort or noise. I entered the panelled and mirrored interior, the brass work freshly polished and gleaming. The sweet smell of a pungent perfume filled the small space, presumably from the previous occupants. The legend 'Ballroom' was engraved on a brass plate below the top-most ivory button, and I pushed it. The lift juddered into motion and it rose upwards, passing the floor with the breakfast room and then onward to what I concluded must be a fourth floor. This had not been visible to me upon my arrival from the opposite side of the Grand Canal.

Most ballrooms of my infrequent acquaintance, mainly when attending business dinners in large London hotels, were located in the basement of the premises. I surmised that in a waterlogged city such as Venice this would be impractical, if not impossible. To place such accommodation at roof level would have the added advantage of providing a spectacular view of the surrounding city. However, when the lift quivered to a halt and a uniformed servant slid back the lift gates, the scale of what I was to find was to prove to be beyond my wildest imagination.

The Ballroom was of such enormity that it must have spanned the whole of the hotel and then beyond over neighbouring buildings. In front of the lift was an open foyer with fluted stone columns supporting a barrel-vaulted ceiling, with gilded angels floating from a deep reticulated stone cornice. Within the bed of the ceiling was a painted fresco representing an imagined heaven of clouds, stars and astrological forms the like of which would be unrecognisable to any present-day astronomer. To the centre of the ceiling was a gold cupola that rose to an indeterminable height, presenting to the observer below a clear star-spangled sky. Beneath the cupola stood a huge polished copper pool in which cavorted a group of shimmering silver nymphs, not statues but real bodies, silently moving, water gushing from jugs held under their arms or above their heads. Water lilies danced upon the disturbed surface of the sparkling crystal water.

Two statuesque Blackamoors towered over the guests and stood sentinel either side of an ornately carved, oak screen with large glazed panels and full height, glazed double doors that opened into the main body of the ballroom. Set in recesses between delicate columns supporting the cupola, were Chinese pots that stood over six feet in height. Light washed upwards from the interior of each one to throw the cornice and frescos into relief. The floor glistened with polished marble tiles set in a chequerboard pattern and the small number of guests in the space stood like chess pieces awaiting an instruction to move. They all faced me as if they had been awaiting my arrival and I relished the unexpected attention.

All my fellow attendees were dressed in period costumes with the obligatory masks. As I moved across the floor, they discrctely bowed in greeting and I returned their welcome in a similar manner. The beautifully decorated masks worn by the women did not entirely cover their faces, allowing their mouths to flicker and pout coquettishly, while their eyes mischievously sparkled from within their disguise.

I was unsure if I had stepped back in time or time had caught up with me. Whichever was the reality, it had succeeded in totally immersing me in the 19th century world of Giacomo Favretto. A member of staff, dressed in a brightly coloured satin frock coat, his head beset with a lightly powdered wig, advanced to offer me prosecco served in cut glass flutes balanced on a silver tray. His mask was more modest than most in both design and size which gave him, in my eye, the look of a rather camp Wild West bandit.

I gratefully took the proffered flute and crossed the hallway, sipping the chilled liquid as I went. I passed beneath the lifeless stare of the two static Blackamoors and entered another realm, another world. This space also had a vaulted ceiling supported by an avenue of columns, similar to those in the foyer, which extended down the full length of the room on either side. Beyond the columns were mysterious colonnades, illuminated, but with a subdued light that cloaked any indiscrete assignation or liaison. To the right I looked out over the Grand Canal with Cannaregio beyond, while to the left the view was of the rooftops of San Polo and San Marco. Extravagant Murano glass chandeliers lit the main portion of the ballroom casting further dark shadows into the secret alcoves behind the columns where small groups of guests were talking or admiring the vistas.

The polished parquet floor was of intricately designed circular patterns that had a remarkable similarity to the crop circles seen in rural England, the expanse providing sufficient space for the designs to be repeated on a number of occasions across its length and breadth. There were gilded chairs and tables each of which was set for between six and eight guests, all carefully spaced so as not to overcrowd the diners or restrict the appreciation of the architectural and decorative splendour of the room. The tables were set far enough apart to move freely around the vast room, and simultaneously maintain privacy one from the other. Each one was laden with glittering glassware of varying sizes while serried ranks of highly polished cutlery were all placed with precision. The plates and bowls were delicate, brightly patterned porcelain in vivid colours, islands of contrast to the sea of starched white tablecloths. At the end of the room was a slightly raised stage behind which was a semi-circular wall of verdant vegetation broken at regular intervals by statues of lithe young nymphs. These living statues had made their escape from the water feature in the foyer; they effortlessly changed their poses at regular intervals and then froze for the admiration of the onlookers. A moving life class that I ached to capture, but it would have been inappropriate to commit these beautiful young bodies to my sketchbook.

A tail-coated orchestra occupied a tangle of chairs and music stands on the stage and were softly playing, somewhat inevitably, Verdi. The sound swelling and subsiding against the conversation, every so often a short burst of laughter from one or other of the groups briefly overwhelmed the music.

Intermingled with the guests were jugglers, fire-eaters, magicians, acrobats and clowns, all in costume, who sought to enthral and amaze. The impression was of a peripatetic circus where the audience were part of the performance and the distinction between player and guest misted.

Members of staff were discretely stationed beside each table waiting to serve the partygoers or directing guests towards whatever it was they searched for or desired. The tables encircled the centre of the room, which was almost devoid of anyone other than the performers. A thin hedge of enthralled guests formed the boundary to the display. Other guests wandered along the colonnades or milled around the edges, mesmerised by the scale of both the entertainment and the room, tentative to approach the tables too early. I entered the colonnade to the right of the main ballroom and looked out from one of the many French windows that opened onto a narrow balcony. The sun left one final angry smudge of red that stained some heavy, isolated clouds hanging over the pantile roofed horizon. As my eyes rose to the zenith, the last vestiges of the fire retreated and left an inky black sky studded with millions of sparkling diamond stars. No artist could recreate such a display. The 21st century light pollution had been banished and the air that ruffled the light curtains either side of the doors was warm and balmy, totally at odds with the time of the year.

I stood in awe of nature and its acceptance of its juxtaposition with the built environment of Venice, nestled in comfortable harmony beneath this awesome, incomparable eternal ceiling.

A gavel cracked several times against a hard wood block in the main body of the room breaking my admiration of my natural and man-made surroundings. We were informed that dinner was about to be served. Table plans were located in the four corners of the room, but I had not noticed these upon my arrival. I felt that the use of a seating plan seemed to negate the concept of anonymity until I saw the myriad of characters identified on the various tables. Each alter ego was noted and allocated a seat, some of their choosing and some, such as my own, apparently allocated at random. The master of ceremonies reminded us that throughout the evening there was no requirement for anyone to divulge his or her true identity from beneath his or her mask and Signor Favretto had no intention of doing so.

I strode over to the nearest easel displaying the seating plan and noticed that the other guests moved deferentially out of my way, some perpetuating the imperceptible bow of acknowledgement while others made discrete whispered comments to their partners behind bejewelled hands. I was unconcerned as I was sure that my costume gave no hint as to my real identity. In deference to this formal politeness, I reciprocated in respect for the conventions about which I apparently still knew little.

However, if anyone had been able to see behind my Bauta they would have detected not a look of perplexity, but one of amusement. This was not in any form of disrespect for those around me, but an uncontrolled sense of bliss that I found myself experiencing. I was in an unfamiliar environment that would, in London, have left me feeling awkward and instilled within me a strong desire to absent myself from the whole proceedings. This was not what had taken hold of me now – I relished the prospects that the evening held and almost had to restrain a sense of over confidence that might be seen as arrogant to those whom I would meet. The apparent notoriety that surrounded me was a powerful stimulant that was enhanced by the prosecco from the empty flute that I placed on a passing tray in exchange for a full one.

A staff member stood by the easel to assist those who could not find their place. I looked down the list of names and each one was of a fictitious character or a character long since departed from this world. I was not surprised to find my own name, Giacomo Favretto, and knew that there would not be two of us in attendance. A waiter took a step forward to position himself at my side. He bowed more extravagantly and lower than my fellow guests, or than was absolutely necessary.

"Signor Favretto," I was not sure if this was a question as to my assumed identity or a statement of recognition. Perhaps his overly low bow enabled him to glimpse beneath the Bauta, but even then, surely, he could have no idea as to which pseudonym I had decided to adopt. He continued before I could respond,

"You are on Table 13, Signore. This way, please, Signore."

As I followed in the footsteps of the servant the phalanx of guests who were crowded around the seating plan remained silent and shuffled back to form a corridor in the direction of my table. I was shown to my seat, which had its back to the colonnade from which I had just emerged. I overlooked the dance floor, beyond which was the opposite colonnade now emptying of guests and performers. I thanked my escort who bowed again, turned and left me alone at my table.

I stood behind my chair, having carefully placed my cane beneath it, awaiting the arrival of the five others to be seated at my table. I had not had time to study who my fellow guests were, but it would have served me little as they would all be pseudonyms. It was a strange sensation to stand in this room and to have removed neither hat nor cloak. But I was not alone in that all the men maintained their full attire. I remember studying a number of paintings of similar gatherings during one of my many visits to various galleries, each image depicting the varied attire that was now before me as historically correct.

Gradually all the other tables filled up and the conversation rose in volume as place names were found and introductions made. Similarly, my table began to be occupied and the first to arrive was a heavily built man of late middle age wearing a somewhat faded red smoking jacket, crisp white evening shirt and hand tied bowtie. His trousers were of a military style, tight like a cavalry officer with a red satin stripe down the outside edge that joined a loop that hooked under the instep of highly polished boots. All that was missing were a pair of shiny spurs, but I guessed that he had decided that such an addition would not be appropriate to this occasion. His mask was simple and unadorned as befitted a man who did not seem at ease in his disguise, preferring his real identity to any attempt at anonymity. It extended to slightly below his nose, but this could not hide the pencil thin moustache that in turn sought to disguise a buckled hair lip.

In his wake an elegantly statuesque woman accompanied him, a dramatic contrast to his fustiness, in that she wore a simple, expensive and well-fitting gown that flowed around her and accentuated her fulsome hour-glass figure. The extravagant mask that she had chosen, obviously with great care and attention, concealed the upper part of her face and had a plume of brilliant white feathers that rose from its crown. Otherwise it was simply decorated with small jewels, the large voids giving a clear view of her green eyes that sparkled beneath the disguise. It was these stars of delight that I instantly recognised, and my excitement heightened when she spoke,

"Signor..." she paused with a sense of anticipation, as if to recall my name, "Favretto? What a joy to meet you again. I am so delighted that you took my advice and have returned to our beloved Venice." Her consort carefully looked me up and down with what appeared to be a degree of contempt. He made no move to formally introduce either himself or his lady.

"May I call you Giacomo? It is so much less formal, and, after all, tonight is a night for informality – is it not?"

She extended a lavishly ringed hand towards me and I gently took it as I bowed and, uncharacteristically for me, kissed it. Her skin was soft and cool to the touch. The bejewelled rings were those that I had seen at the opera, but then on a more aged hand than the one now beneath my lips. I was astounded, but I should not have been, as now I knew that my presence in Venice was expected, if not pre-ordained.

Our eyes met. I had never been more certain that I faced the Contessa. The Contessa of the reception, the one at our chance meeting in the Firepit, the one who had told me about the gallery and the Rima baths. I hesitated for too long and although she appeared not to notice, she turned to her partner, who was unimpressed with my apparent acquaintance, if not familiarity, with his wife.

"Giacomo Favretto, may I present my husband, The Conte de Wolfherz?" She stood back slightly, "He has eschewed the ignominy of hiding his identity."

The Count clearly absorbed the blow of her lightly veiled disapproval at his inability, or unwillingness, to enter into the spirit of the evening. But clearly, the sharp barb had pricked his pride.

"Signore," His voice was clipped and to my delight he exposed his Germanic credentials with a sharp click of his heels. "Perhaps for the purposes of this farcical evening you should refer to me as Wolfhertz," and he bowed stiffly.

"I am delighted to meet you, Wolfhertz."

"Conte de Wolfhertz, if you please?" he replied curtly.

Corrected, I bowed my head a second time somewhat insolently to one side and duly acknowledged his title,

"Conte."

I turned to his wife, who immediately detected that I was unsure as to how I should address her and how much of our earlier meetings should be acknowledged. I felt that her enthusiastic greeting had been made in haste and had revealed more than she had subsequently wished to in the presence of her husband. From his rather cool demeanour towards me, it was clear that he already was suspicious of the fact that the Contessa apparently knew this stranger.

"And you may call me Violetta," she suggested.

I instantly remembered the courtesan heroine from La Traviata and smiled as I bowed and took her hand and kissed it gently a second time.

"Violetta, a very appropriate name. I had the pleasure of seeing you at La Fenice the other evening." It was pure pantomime until she responded,

"Oh, I know."

I was caught unawares and tried to hide my surprise on hearing the revelation that implied she was also present. I caught sight of the Conte out of the corner of my eye as he turned with a snort and, with overt contempt, observed the scene around him.

"My husband hates these balls," Violetta confided. "He only comes to ensure that I am not left alone to entertain myself. Don't worry; we'll have time to talk later." She rested her hand lightly on my arm and gave it a gently squeeze, "Generally he indulges me in respect to my…" she hesitates and flashing her eyes conspiratorially, "interests. But I must be careful."

"What did she mean by that?" The Priest asks.

"At the time I had no idea, but I rather enjoyed the notion of intrigue with this flawless woman."

The old man comes into the room from the balcony as the heat from the afternoon sun dissipated and the wind calmed. His steps are unsteady and, unusually, he uses his cane for support.

"Close the doors, it is getting cold in here. And turn the lights on, I can't see much."

The priest does as requested and takes his seat at the old man's desk with the three portraits still lying in front of him. He flicks his attention from one to the other.

The old man flops onto the Chesterfield and balances his cane against the arm of the sofa, within easy reach.

"You said your table accommodated six people, who else was there?" The Priest is studying the drawing of the Contessa de Wolfhertz.

"At that point there was only Violetta and the Conte, oh, and me of course. Are you intending to interrupt again?"

"My apologies. Please proceed."

XX
The Ball

"I think we should be seated," the Conte brusquely announced and sat in his place. I moved to the back of Violetta's chair and held it out for her. She took her place and I sat down beside her. Three seats remained to be filled. One was directly opposite me, and one was to my left. The final seat was on the far side of Violetta; leaving the Conte separated from us. He seemed somewhat self-conscious in his isolation.

As I looked around to locate our missing guests, a member of staff moved unseen behind me and gently touched my shoulder to warn me of his presence. I turned to see that an elderly woman was accompanying him. She lightly held his arm with scrawny, bejewelled fingers, an affectation of support that in reality was unnecessary. She moved easily and despite her age, appeared strong and well able to take her seat unaided. Her deportment was imperious, and she walked with a tall, ebony stick topped with an ivory finial. She was dressed in black from head to toe, her mask of damask that covered her face from nose to forehead. A veil of black lace shrouded her white hair and she appeared as if in mourning rather than attending a frivolous ball. She was escorted to the seat next to the Conte, who stood to welcome her, but she ignored him. He sat again and looked dejected.

I was far from dejected, more perplexed.

La Fenice!

It had to be. It was the Grand-Dame from the theatre.

I tried to catch her eye, but she was concentrating on Violetta who in turn was returning her gaze with an unemotional expression. I asked Violetta to excuse me for a minute and walked round to the old woman. As I stood above her, she slowly raised her eyes to face me. It was as if I was looking at the portrait again.

"Signora, we have not been introduced."

"Contessa, Signor Favretto. Not Signora." Her voice was acidly indifferent.

"I apologise Contessa. We are honoured to have two Contessas at our table tonight. I am…"

"I know who you are, Signor Favretto. I wasn't sure, but I know now."

I was waved dismissively away and so I retreated back to my seat. No one seemed to have taken any notice of the exchange, no one save for the Conte. He looked pensive but I was unperturbed by the abruptness of the older Contessa. I was not going to let her ruin another evening for me.

The orchestra quietly played on and the conversation ebbed and flowed as the final stragglers found their seats. I was in such an animated discourse with Violetta as to the glories that I had experienced during my stay in Venice, that I had not noticed the arrival of the young woman who remained standing silently next to me. She listened politely until Violetta drew my attention to the new arrival by placing her hand on my arm to silence me. I twisted in my seat to apologise to the new member of our little band and as I politely started to get up from my chair, I froze. Whether my mouth actually fell open or not I cannot be sure. If it had not, then it was a miracle. Standing before me was the young woman who I had seen at the canal-side restaurant whose drawing of me now was secreted in my room. My astonishment was either unseen or ignored as I slowly completed the effort of rising to my feet. With a stammer, I started to introduce myself but was again interrupted by a silken voice,

"I know who you are, Signore. I have admired your work and I am honoured to have the opportunity to sit at your table."

"Then you have the advantage of me," I replied. "Who are you?"

"Tonight, you may call me Cocola."

The other guests made no attempt to introduce themselves to her. It was as if they already knew each other and that I was the newcomer in their midst.

Cocola's eyes, so familiar in shape and hue, demurely dipped behind her mask as she offered her hand. I took it in mine and noticed that it was unadorned with any jewellery. I brought her soft skin to brush against my lips. A shiver of excitement raised the hairs on the back of my neck. Why had the old habit of kissing a lady's hand in greeting died out? It was the sensuality of such a simple act that impressed itself upon me. I suppose modern sensitivities would not condone such stereotyping of the sexes.

She slid her hand from mine and, as I held out her chair, she sank effortlessly into the seat and placed her hands demurely in her lap.

She wore a figure-hugging gown that was cut low, but not revealingly so, and it radiated sophistication. The single piece of jewellery that adorned her was a simple and unassuming necklace of pearls that had been selected with great care to complement her gown perfectly. There was no wedding ring, and no circle of un-tanned skin where a wedding ring might once have been. Inadvertently, I looked down at my own finger and saw that my ring was missing, but the faded skin witnessed my unknowing deceit.

Where was my ring?

When had I removed it and why?

I self-consciously, and possibly too hastily, concealed my hand beneath the tablecloth.

As if coming to my rescue at such an embarrassing moment, a tall, well built, man arrived at the seat opposite me. His clothes were well tailored, his shoes polished to a sheen and his half mask black, with a red surround to the eye holes – and two stumpy horns emanating from the top of his forehead. His short dark beard and moustache was tightly clipped and lay well with his mask.

He opened his large hands seeking our forgiveness and smiled a most beguiling smile that captivated the ladies and befriended me; the Conte viewed the stranger with suspicion. My misgivings only arose when I heard his Voice.

"Conte, Contessas, Signore, and Signorina," He gave a brief bow to each as he addressed them in turn. *"Please forgive me for my tardiness. I have no excuse but that I had affairs of State to attend to before I could enjoy this evening."*

I gasped and simultaneously pushed my chair back as if expecting a confrontation. My hand moved involuntarily towards my stick. Violetta and Cocola looked at me with brief alarm before returning their attention to the urbane arrival. There was a silence; I was incapable of uttering any sound. It was the Conte, possibly intimidated by the self-importance of our final guest and, no doubt, determined to reestablish his own high status at the table, who broke the impasse.

"And who are you, Signore, to be concerned with affairs of state?"

The Voice smiled patronisingly down at the Conte de Wolfhertz, taking full advantage of the fact that he stood while his interrogator remained seated. Any minor command that the Conte felt he might have regained was swiftly exorcised.

The Voice slowly cast his eyes around the table, as if evaluating each of his fellow guests. His response was directed to the Conte but was inclusive of all present.

"It appears that I am Diablo." An elegant hand pointed to his mask. *"I believe my disguise reflects that traditional character, and so I shall happily adopt this persona. As to my affairs, I fear that those are not for me to divulge."* De Wolfhertz visibly bridled at the comment, his exclusion from such matters incomprehensible to him.

"Rest assured, one day all of you will know my business. Until that time, I am delighted to make your acquaintance, albeit perhaps prematurely for some."

The Voice had been an acquaintance of my mind for some considerable time. This man was the personification of that Voice, the architect of my evolving persona that increasingly dominated my future. As he settled himself next to the elderly Contessa, I shook my head attempting to regain my grip on reality. Was this a figment of my delusional imagination? Apparently, dressed in all his finery, he was the embodiment of that delusion.

Diablo engaged the elderly Contessa in light conversation. She laughed a rippling sound, aware that the other women at the table were watching, some enviously craving the attention of this mysterious guest, while I merely watched from within a cocoon of contemplation. The sound of his softly spoken voice was unmistakable – the same huskily, resonant tone that imbued in me a sense of discomfort every time it impinged upon my consciousness. However, somehow it also injected into me a feeling of encouragement, boosting my self-reliance and poise that had so lacked in my former existence. I had never anticipated that my Voice might appear to me in a physical form.

I studied what was visible of his facial features. The smooth sun-tanned skin clipped black beard, the perfect teeth and the winning smile, his general features were perfect but unremarkable. He had one of those faces that, in my experience, would be very difficult to commit to paper. It was too perfect in proportion and form. As I contemplated the challenge, the two women between whom I was seated were briefly ignored.

Becoming aware that he was still the centre of everyone's attention, he looked around the table again, taking care to achieve full eye contact with each person in turn. I followed the passage of his gaze across the assembled company. I wondered if we were all pawns in a game to which only he knew the rules. I could not decide whether the presence of Diablo was a comfort or a threat.

Gradually the conversation around the table returned and so the impact on me of the presence of Diablo diminished. The only person who did not fully immerse himself in the conviviality was the Conte, who drank copiously while simultaneously maintaining an overtly watchful eye on his wife. She was impervious to his attention and I became increasingly immersed in the pleasurable company of both Violetta and Cocola. Each was witty, charming and regaled me with numerous tales about

Venice and its characters. I found that my usual reserve dissipated, and my delightful companions laughed and confided in me as if we had all known each other for many years.

Once or twice I stole a look across the table and on each occasion Diablo seemed to detect when I was doing so. He returned my glance with a reassuring smile, much as an uncle might to a favourite nephew. It was as if he was a mentor giving approval to the maturing behavior of a young acolyte, albeit that I was at least twice his age.

As the meal progressed and the wine flowed, it seemed that my conversations were becoming the focus of attention at the table and I held the whole company in the palm of my hand. Even the Conte unwittingly smiled at a couple of my stories. My self-deprecation remained prevalent but appeared to charm the ladies and relax the Conte. Diablo just sat with an amused look on his face. The noise from our table rose as we all became more animated.

During a brief respite in my banter, Diablo gave a description of the origins of the masked ball and the use of masks. He spoke with authority, as if he had witnessed many of these Carnivals over the decades.

"Many noble ladies found the mask an excellent excuse to demonstrate their feminine

whiles. In some cases, they chose to satisfy any unrequited desires that their own husbands were unwilling or unable to satisfy." Cocola feigned shock at his revelation as he continued with his dissertation.

The old Contessa nodded, as the discourse appeared to invoke memories of happier times, perhaps with her husband, perhaps with another. Similarly, I noticed that Cocola and Violetta exchanged a knowing look, bound by a secret that only they shared. They laughed when they saw I was watching them, Violetta placing a long finger gently against her lips. I wanted to be a party to their exchange but was clearly excluded for the time being. I retreated and resumed my part in the general conversation.

Meanwhile, the Conte was beginning to look bored while continuing to imbibe liberally.

Our glasses were regularly topped up and plate after delicious plate of exquisite food was consumed with relish. The noise in the high-ceilinged room became louder and louder as the inebriation of the partygoers became more amplified and, as a result, everyone became more self-assured as to the quality of their own wit and self-perceived attractiveness to their fellow guests. Knees met beneath tables and furtive contact was achieved in seemingly innocent actions – the passing of a cruet, the filling of a glass, the whisper of a lascivious secret, breath upon a soft earlobe, the touch of a hoary hand upon temptingly naked flesh.

Here was Venice in all its visceral glory. I had to adapt my usual mores to accommodate an easier approach to the relationships between men and women. This was a more enjoyable and less prescriptive approach that enabled flirtation and idle musing without recrimination. What might have been, or what might be possible, was the elixir that electrified the atmosphere. If my family could see me now, they would be horrified. But if my family were alive, then I would not be in Venice, here at this surreal occasion. I sighed at the thought and, as if aware of my brief period of melancholy, Diablo incorporated me back into the conversation, seeking further details of the highlights of my life in Venice.

All through the meal the orchestra had continued to softly play but on completion of the final dish they struck up with more gusto. The dance floor at the centre of the room became a melee of twirling bodies – some dancing formally and others in a more esoteric manner. This was the point of the evening that I had previously dreaded.

I wondered if I could make a sly exit from the room or find a quiet corner to sketch the revelries of others. There was a momentary pause in the conversation – the women expectant and the men self-consciously silent. Violetta suddenly stood up and announced that as obviously none of the men at this table were going to initiate an invitation to dance, she would have to do so.

"Giacomo, you would not decline my invitation to dance?"

She held out her hand for my acceptance and I immediately lost my newfound composure.

"I cannot dance. I have two left feet and a complete lack of any sense of timing."

Diablo looked across the table and laughingly denounced my protestations, stating that with the right partner anyone could dance. The Conte glared threateningly at me, daring me to take up the challenge that had been thrown down by his wife.

Hesitation gave way to a defiant acceptance. The Conte grimaced and gripped his glass to the point just before it might shatter.

I took her outstretched hand and we entered the fray on the dance floor. Somewhat to my surprise, I found that the alcohol and Violetta's undoubted gracefulness, combined with the regular rhythm from the orchestra, was such that my feet did not flounder, and we moved smoothly around the floor. Our bodies floated between the other couples as we were engulfed within the dancing mass, invisible from our table - and the searing eyes of the Conte.

I found the whole experience exhilarating and, when the first dance came to an end, I was not at all reticent about suggesting that we remain for a second attempt. Violetta looked at me from within her mask and smiled warmly. Surely, I had known this woman for considerably longer than just this evening and a fleeting conversation at the MonkeyChop Club? It was also the point at which I realized that I still had tight hold of her hand – and she had hold of mine. I had no desire to release her and, when the music recommenced, we once again enfolded each other and danced in silence.

I could feel her body against mine as we twirled and glided around the floor. I focused on the rich fabric of her gown. I know nothing of the art of the seamstress, but the gown appeared to my eye to be of an earlier era, hand finished and expensive. In fact, as I looked around, all the costumes had the same characteristics.

Her embrace tightened infinitesimally as if she detected that my concentration had wavered from her presence. I imagined her heart beating in time with mine. We had an undefined empathy between us – responsiveness in our every move that accentuated my sense of a previous familiarity. She lifted her head from my shoulder and looked directly into my eyes. Her breath was slightly laboured from our exertions as it drifted over my chin. Our progress slowed to a languorous shuffle. I thought for one fleeting moment that she was going to kiss me and wondered what I would do. Somewhat surprisingly, the design of my mask did not seem to cater for this particular eventuality!

We slowed almost to a halt. Her lips were slightly open, and I thought they quivered in expectation.

The music stopped, people clapped, and the spell was broken.

"I need refreshment," she said decisively and, breaking my hold, led me further away from our table to a small bar set up in the opposite colonnade. The French windows remained open and the air was warm as the draught billowed the light lace curtains into the room. Despite it being February, the breeze held a fragrance of jasmine in its warmth that was out of step with the season. The lights that shone from the distant windows beyond the narrow balcony were a flickering yellow. The canal had gondolas moving to and fro, lanterns swinging from metal poles. The whole scene was lit as if it were a film set, not real, yet of its time.

In my mind, none of this seemed to be odd or out of place. I accepted the surroundings as well as the company as perfectly normal. Nothing was out of place; all was as planned.

We both took glasses of prosecco from the wide selection of drinks that adorned the table and walked over to one of the open doors. Standing in close proximity, sipping our drinks, each of us was deep in our own individual thoughts. Violetta leant back and supported herself against my chest; wisps of her hair were softly blown against my cheek and she spoke quietly but with some intensity.

"My husband is such a possessive man, my love." I was not expecting either the urgency or level of intimacy of her address and I wondered if I had missed something on the dance floor. She continued in almost a whisper, "We must be careful. I cannot afford to upset him."

Now somewhat alarmed that I might be misreading the events that were unfolding, I replied,

"I certainly have no intention of upsetting him." It struck me that the Conte was not someone who would take to being cuckolded with equanimity. Why had I used the word 'cuckold', one meeting and two dances did not constitute such a conclusion.

She continued before I could say another word.

"He already suspects. He watches me all the time. I cannot move. I cannot work. Every time I attempt to come to your studio, he is questioning me. That is why I have not been for so long. He is not an unreasonable man and has made no excessive demands upon me since we married, but equally his pride will not permit him to be publicly made a fool of."

I was confused and began to suspect that my disguise had been too effective and that she had assumed me to be someone I was not. The reference to a studio, my studio, sounded so natural but deep inside I knew that it was a deception out of my control.

I attempted to stop her before she revealed some secret that she would regret. "Violetta, I think you have made a mistake."

"No! Never! I love what I do for you." Her voice was emotional but uncertain, unsure whether to expose her own true feelings. She remained looking out of the window,

"So, what are we to do now that I find that I have fallen in love with you, Giacomo?" She turned and faced me, tears in her eyes. "I have modeled for you for two decades. Ever since the first day we met I have admired you. You have drawn and painted me with such intimacy, I feel that the transition from artist and model to lovers was natural…preordained, inevitable."

Her eyes darted over my shoulder and instantly became alarmed. I felt the presence of someone as a shadow was cast against the curtain in front of me. Violetta took a step back, sharply retreating from her proximity to me and I turned to find the Conte. His mask could not camouflage his mood and he stepped between us, completely ignoring my presence and facing his wife.

His bulk was such that I could not hear what his deep, rasping whisper intoned to Violetta. Her previous poise was immediately deflated, and she passed by me without looking in my direction. I started to object but was silenced by a flash of real fury from the Conte.

"Signore, do not presume to do more than you have done already."

His eyes were cold and steely, his fists clenched tight by his side and his body tensed in readiness should I have the temerity to intervene. The rush of adrenalin in his body had dilated the pupils of his masked eyes. He was in fight or flight mode and there was no evidence that the latter was going to prevail. I started to mouth a response but was silenced.

"Should we ever meet again, Signor Favretto, and I do not think that wise, then you had better come prepared."

I looked at him, assessing the warning without truly understanding the meaning. He held my gaze until it was clear that I was not going to defy him. Only then did he turn on his heels and, satisfied that I had resolved not to attack on his departure, his large hand roughly took Violetta's arm as he guided her away from me. I remained where they had left me. My hand was shaking as I took a large draught of my prosecco.

Already having been an unwitting victim of violence, I had no desire to repeat the experience. My stick lay beneath the table and anyway, I had no appetite to physically resist the might of the Conte, for the Contessa's sake as well as my own.

I reflected briefly on the bizarre conversation and resolved to avoid any further socializing with either Violetta or her husband. However, I had no need to concern myself on that account as they had already departed by the time I nervously returned to my table. Seated implacably was the old lady. She observed me knowingly as I approached the table. It was as if she was aware of the unpleasant exchange between the Conte and me but chose to make no mention of it.

There was an overwhelming sense that I should join her and speak to her, as she seemed to have been deserted. Besides, there were questions from La Fenice that remained unanswered. At that moment the orchestra completed another tune and the remaining members of our party were returning exhausted. The moment was lost. Cocola returned with Diablo. She was flushed and breathless from her exertions and sank onto her seat.

"Where are the Conte and Contessa?" she asked, looking around the room.

"I believe they had to leave early," Diablo replied. I wondered how he knew and whether he also was conscious of the exchange that had occurred between us. Jokingly I tried to reassure the table that it was probably my appalling dancing that had caused the Contessa to depart, but this was brushed away with hoots of derision.

Diablo stood by his chair and when the merriment subsided, somberly announced,

"I clearly cannot compete with the footwork of Signor Giacomo and so must also take my leave of you all. I know that we shall meet again, but in the meantime, I wish all of you a very good night"

"Really?" Cocola asked with obvious disappointment. "Must you go so early?"

"I am afraid so; wheels are turning, and I cannot progress my work while continuing to partake in this celebration. I leave you in good hands. Signor Giacomo has proved that he is fleet of foot and is more than my match." Turning to me, he added, *"You will take care of this charming young lady in my absence, will you not?"*

Diablo looked directly at me and my soul flinched again. It was not a request but a clear directive. The old lady watched keenly but with no display of emotion.

"It would be an honour and a pleasure," I rather pompously replied.

Cocola laughed and placed a slender hand on my arm,

"Then I am delighted."

Diablo moved around the table and took the hand of the elderly Contessa and kissed it delicately.

"I hope that you will forgive me for my early departure, but I need to attend to arrangements that I believe you will find acceptable."

She smiled up at him, looked across at Cocola and then me before she mouthed a silent 'thank you' to Diablo. He softly patted her shoulder and the old lady placed a hand over his momentarily.

As he passed me, he touched my arm and led me out of the earshot of the others,

"Enjoy the remainder of the evening. Let your heart rule your head, for you have a role to play in this pageant." Before I could respond to yet another riddle he added, with a shrug of his shoulders, *"I have provided the purpose and the means. I can do no more."*

He moved silently into the crowd and disappeared before I had digested what he had said. I remained standing, searching for his back, desperate to understand what was to befall me. What task had been set?

"Come, let us all have a drink and then we can take to the floor once again." Cocola excitedly suggested. We drank, the Contessa listened as the young woman talked, sipping a clear liqueur from a delicate glass. I allowed my mind to wrestle with all that had occurred, little knowing that the events of this evening had not yet concluded.

Cocola imaginatively regaled us with tales both fictional and factual that were interwoven around our assumed characters, each far removed from our real lives. The game, for I assumed it to be a game, was challenging but enjoyable. The old Contessa said little, observing, absorbing but making no contribution. We learnt nothing material from each other and the fantasy world in which we temporarily existed became more and more exotic by the moment. After a while we had exhausted our inventiveness.

"Now, Signor Giacomo," Cocola taunted, "let's dance and you can show me some of your fancy footwork."

"I shall try to live up to the reputation that has been imposed upon me," I replied. Turning to the old woman, I politely asked if she would excuse us for a while.

"Certainly, I am only sorry that this decrepit body is no longer able to take advantage of your undoubted talents." She smiled sweetly, if not entirely convincingly.

A thin, angular man with hungry, darting eyes stumbled behind my chair and apologized as my chair legs caused my sketchbook and pencils to skitter into the passage between the tables. My cloak slipped from where I had placed it across the chair back and lay crumpled on the floor by them. I bent down and picked everything up, assuring him that no harm had been done. He apologized again and watched as I slid the book and pencil tin into the inside pocket of the cloak and folded it onto the seat of my chair. He went and sat in the chair next to the Contessa who seemed to know him, and they entered into an animated conversation.

I followed Cocola towards the dance floor. As I looked back, I saw that the Contessa and the man appeared to be retaining an interest in my chair. I thought it strange but gave the matter little further thought as the young woman pulled me onto the dancefloor.

It was with some relief that I discovered that my dancing skills had not deserted me. In fact, after the initial dance with Cocola, I found myself rarely without a partner, or a glass from which to drink. The room became hotter and the dancing more feverish. Eventually, I had to take a break from my exertions, and I returned to the bar in the colonnade for a refreshing drink. The party was now in full swing and for some all inhibitions seem to have been thrown to the wind.

I took the glass of cool, still water and wandered along the darkly lit colonnade. The lighting appeared to be more subdued than it was when I had entered the ballroom. All very natural with dimmer switches and electric lighting – but no such technology had been used. Now I noticed that all the chandeliers and wall lights were flickering candle flames. I was sure that I would have noticed if the lighting had been reliant upon candlepower. Clearly, I had been so over awed by the elegance and scale of the room that this fact had failed to register. Perhaps such a detail was so natural that it was dismissed as such.

Some couples had retired to the darker recesses and were deep in secretive conversation. A few had abandoned themselves to passionate embraces, which resulted in a removal of the more restrictive masking from their flushed faces. I presumed that these were amorous individuals who had the freedom of choice and were not restricted by the vows of marriage or chastity. I smiled to myself and leant against one of the columns to view the dancing of others.

After a short while, I realized that Cocola was leaning against the other side of my column. I was not sure if this was by intent or accident, but she casually slid round the curved stone to stand at my side.

"You are too popular this evening, Signor Giacomo. You seem to have no time for me. Have I offended you?" She gently pushed against my shoulder as if to emphasise that her comment was made in jest.

"How do I get any time with you?" she enquired.

I smiled down at her. Mindful of the confusion I had experienced with Violetta and the Conte, I responded cautiously.

"You too are a magnet for the young men who eagerly compete for your company."

"We have danced but once. Was I too clumsy for you?"

"Not at all. Was I too slow for you?"

She thought for a moment as if summoning up courage to suddenly change the subject.

"Did you take my drawing from the restaurant?"

I immediately recalled her as the girl who sat at the table where I had lunch a couple of days ago. No longer dressed in jeans and jumper, her hair piled up on her head, she looked completely different. I felt guilty and flustered. My response was pathetically unconvincing as I tried to regain some composure.

"Which drawing? Have we met?"

"Not met but we know each other. You have drawn me, and I have reciprocated. Now we are even." Still I could not quite believe that this was the person who had produced the exquisite sketch that now sat in my portfolio.

"Where did you learn to draw like that?"

She looked perplexed.

"What I mean is that it shows considerable ability?"

"Why, thank you, Signore. That is high praise from Giacomo Favretto. I have watched you and learnt."

"Really?"

"You have taught me well."

She slipped her arm in mine and guided me over to a side table that had been vacated by a middle-aged couple who had taken to the dance floor. We sat next to each other on one side of the table; our knees almost touching, and heads close so that I could hear her voice above the revelry all around us.

"Mmmm. Ok, role play is over. Tell me, where did you study?"

"I am a student at the Accademia, but the fees are high, and I have to support myself as best I can. Hence you see me in numerous galleries around the city."

"Your work?" I asked, impressed. She threw her head back and laughed.

"No! My body – I am a life model in my spare time." She waited for me to react, but I was silent.

"Do you disapprove?"

"No, not at all." I did not want to appear unworldly, nor to compromise myself for the second time that night. I was sensing that this conversation was proceeding along a dangerous path. Cocola cocked her head and gave me a coy sideways glance,

"But I suspect you knew that already."

I responded rather too quickly, "No, No. How could I possibly?"

She smiled and then clapped her hands together excitedly

"I should model for you. I think you would enjoy it. I know that I would."

I was flustered and blushed beneath my mask, which thankfully was hidden from her sight.

"I find the experience of being studied in detail highly erotic. The artist transferring a soft line onto the canvas, the stroke of the brush to render the skin, moving across every bodily curve, hollow and mound. His brushes stroke me, I am swathed in his exertion to recreate my likeness, melding the thick, wet paint across my opaque skin and caressing my soft hair that kisses my neck and oscillates down my naked back. The final result provides a proprietorial sensuality for the artist and the relinquishing of part of my being as the model. The physical disciplines are intense, I have to remain stationary but alert, visually forceful yet without any sign of strain or fatigue. Truth be known, the life model is a true artist in their own right, and you must admire their dedication, as well as their form." She watches my reaction to her description of her work, a winsome curl to the edge of her mouth.

If she was indeed the girl from the restaurant, then there was no doubt that Cocola had been a desirable subject to draw and even to paint. I was unable to detect whether her offer was serious or a tease. I was cautious as I was in danger of reverting to the foolish old man that she had seen in the restaurant.

She was witty, beguiling, attractive and her gown exemplified her physical attributes. She was young and I was, in her eyes, old. Any liaison, even here in Venice, would be a mistake. It would undoubtedly end in disaster for us both. Surely, I had experienced enough uncertainty and misunderstanding with the Conte and Contessa earlier in the evening not to compound my mistakes.

"What are you doing tomorrow night?" The excited child in her had returned. She took hold of my hands as if to restrict any notion I had of escape. Such a notion was distant from my thoughts, but I did feel that this young girl's warmth towards a man old enough to be her father – possibly even her grandfather - was not entirely appropriate.

"I do not think I am..." I struggled for a convincing response.

"You cannot hibernate in your room during Carnivale! Come with me to a party – well, more of a gathering of friends?" I knew that this was not right.

"Please?" she implored.

Her child-like insistence was as innocent as it was dangerous. I struggled with my innermost caution and firmly decided that this was a step too far.

"I would enjoy that very much."

I whirled around expecting to find Diablo standing behind me, but he was nowhere to be seen.

My voice had not forsaken me in my hour of temptation. Yet again, I had uttered decisive words against my best intentions, against what I had concluded was the sensible course of action.

Cocola flinched at my sudden movement. I involuntarily shook my head as if to dislodge the interloper. Cocola regarded me with concern,

"Are you alright?"

"Yes…Yes. I am sorry." How was I to explain the unexplainable.

"I thought I felt someone behind me," I lied. The response did little to console her and she stood up and rested a hand on my shoulder as I sought to rise.

"Stay there. Let me get you some more water." I watched her as she sashayed across the floor to the bar and brought back fresh glasses and a full jug of water. I drank to refresh myself and to banish any chance of my fainting. Cocola watched me with continued apprehension as my shock gradually faded and I recovered some of my poise.

"I am sorry about that. I don't know what came over me." Had the last few minutes been a fantasy, a figment of my febrile mind that would evaporate into reality? I was quickly grounded of any such flight of fancy.

"Was the prospect of coming out with me so awful?"

We laughed together, but for different reasons. She took my hand and, turning it so my palm was uppermost, she scribbled an address on it in biro.

"Come to this address tomorrow evening, any time after 7:00pm."

She dropped the pen on the table and released my hand. I reluctantly thanked her without reference to exactly what she had written.

"What is your real name?" I asked.

She laughed again and waggled her finger from side to side in front of me. "You know the rules. If you want to reveal that part of me, you will have to come tomorrow evening." She rose, leaving me spellbound.

"I must go," She suddenly announced and skipped away, giving me a last look over her shoulder. She was like a thrilled child who had been promised a long-awaited treat.

My question as to her identity remained unanswered.

I felt unconscionably tired and was not going to bother to return to my table until I remembered that my cane and cloak were there. I found it crumpled on one of the seats and gathered it up together with my stick that remained where I had placed it under my seat. There was no one at the table, my fellow guests having either left or mingled elsewhere. The waiters were clearing the debris that had accumulated on it and so I retraced my steps across the dance floor to the side table where my water glass stood. Some of those still on the dance floor proffered a greeting as I passed, but I felt too tired to acknowledge them.

I sat alone at the table sipping my water, contemplating the strange events of the evening. I had enjoyed my alter ego, the role play and concluded that there was a strong attraction in being feted and admired.

I adopted the role of observer of human frailties as the evening drew to an end. New unions had been created, some possibly even consummated. I watched discretely as a couple engaged in a passionate embrace. She sat facing her partner, on his lap, her legs either side of his waist, her gown riding high on her thighs. He was nuzzled deep into her neck and her body was arched back in ecstasy. He caressed with both his hands her naked back and shoulders, exposed by the cut of her gown. They were by no means alone in these overt expressions of ardour. It was to be witnessed in many, if not all the various nooks and crannies of the colonnade. It was becoming more of a bacchanalian orgy than a refined ball.

The elderly Contessa, who I had assumed had left the party for her bed, silently seated herself in the chair that had been vacated by Cocola. She muttered her disgust and disapproval of such behavior declaring it to be wholly unbecoming of her beautiful Venice. She spoke in English but with a rough Italian accent, a coarseness that ill matched her look and refined mannerisms. Her face was still masked. I could see through the lace veil that her skin was like porcelain and completely unblemished save for the creases of age. This was a woman who had lived through trials and tribulations to defeat all but the toughest of adversaries through sheer strength of character.

Her black silk gown was traditional in design and fitted her slight frame perfectly. She raised her hand in a majestic gesture before she spoke,

"Signore, if you would be so kind? I need some fresh air to dispel the sight - and the smell - of these less than discrete displays of overt passion that are, to me, both distasteful and, sadly, now unattainable. I have no need to witness what surrounds us in such abundance."

I instantly stood in blind deference to her request and took her hand. It was thin but her grip was vice-like. With the aid of her tall stick, she rose effortlessly to her feet. I took her arm out of politeness rather than necessity. She led me through the colonnade to a French window at the far end, beyond which was one of the narrow balconies overlooking the Grand Canal.

We stood and both took some deep breaths of the fresh night air that, as the hours wore on, had become refreshingly cooler. The sky was cloudless and the stars that had bejeweled it earlier had rotated to new positions. A solitary, late night gondolier ferried two interlocked passengers along the canal, its bow cutting and distorting the reflection of the moonlight in the water.

Her voice was thin but displayed a persuasive authority that would silence anyone who sought to interrupt or doubt her. The fact that I had to lean forward to hear this noble, old lady meant that she commanded my complete attention and, by so doing, instilled a sense of social inferiority in me.

"You were not accompanied at the Opera. Why?" My surprise at her unexpected question must have been palpable to her. She paid no heed and fixed me with pale green-blue eyes that were rheumy but retained a harshness that was as ferocious as her grip.

She implicitly knew that I had recognized her as the woman in the box at La Fenice, the one who had mysteriously disappeared. She impatiently awaited my response.

"I am in Venice alone."

She silently considered this answer.

"Not entirely alone."

"What do you mean?"

"The man at our table tonight, Diablo. He seemed to be well versed in your life. And your loss."

I stood against the balustrade for support, speechless, unable to respond. She continued,

"You appear to be chosen for his attention."

“I am sorry, but I am not sure that I understand.”

“He is a mentor, is he not? A catalyst in life.”

“But I don’t know him,” I protested, “I’d never met him before this evening.”

The Contessa turns on me, those gimlet eyes displaying a look if disbelief.

“The loss of your family. What do you put that down to? Perfidy? Probably. An error of judgment? Maybe. Bad luck? No. Your destiny was not one of happenstance. It was preordained. Planned with precision.”

I was dumbfounded. How had this crone come to know of the tragedy that had befallen me and plagued my life over the years? Like my Voice, like Diablo, this woman spoke in riddles the answer to which I was unable to grasp. What was this sorceress trying to tell me?

She continued to hold my attention with her piercing eyes, unblinking, as her impatience grew at either my lack of response or my lack of understanding. I began to feel irritated at her persistence through silence. I pulled my head away from the proximity to her that I had adopted in order to hear her clearly. She was delving deeper into my past than I was prepared to permit, observing my every emotion as if the papier-mâché skin of my mask was connected by muscle and sinew to the synapses in my brain, exposing my reactions to her every word. Once she had observed my own weaknesses, she disdainfully dismissed any sentiments that did not conform to, and accord with, her own particular standards of behavior. Eventually, I began to piece together the implications of her words and I did not enjoy the experience.

"My wife died in an accident." I spoke flatly, all emotions omitted from the simple sentence.

"Is that what he told you?"

I felt my heart falter at the concealed accusation. The Bauka did nothing to hide me from her penetrating stare. I do not know if she was judging me, but I turned away from her to look out over the rooftops. We stood in a tense silence and I wondered why this haughty crone had chosen to speak to me or draw me onto this despicable balcony. I felt unable to leave her company, held by some inexplicable force of nature. Her quavering voice continued, whether affected by sympathy or anger I could not deduce.

"You have been granted an abundance of favours, and you have embraced each and every one. The sights, the smells and our people all intoxicate you. This is a freedom that has little future. All the while, we have remained imprisoned within our own forsaken circumstances. We too await a release from the injustices of the past. We have awaited your arrival for many years."

I was becoming exasperated by her hectoring tone, she hinted at things of which she could not possibly have any knowledge. I felt that there was no requirement for me to justify myself to her and I was of a mind to immediately leave when she spoke again, her voice softer, less bullying.

"I am like you. I too once knew love. Mine was a love that was snatched away prematurely from my embrace, to be replaced by a desiccated and decayed existence, all within the bands of matrimony." She looked up at me with an expression of wistful regret. "It is a lonely vigil that I have kept in hope rather than expectation." She looked reflectively out of the window, "For my epoch it is too late." Her body seemed to slump, lose its poise as if the thought sapped her strength. She continued to stare across the vista. The gondolier below disappeared into an unlit side waterway, the wash from his boat silently slapping the mooring poles that stretched upwards towards the sky from the dark, clawing water.

I should have expressed some words of comfort to this drained soul, but my mind was unwilling to summon any crumbs of sympathy. She had invaded my privacy in some obtuse way and allowed the once deeply submerged thoughts of my own loss and sorrow to be reignited. She had banished the exhilaration of the extraordinary evening that had swept me up into a euphoria that now had evaporated. She was my adversary, capturing the excitement of the moment and dispatching it to a wasteland that was reality.

"Signor Favretto, you have fallen in love with more than just this city, as I did in my youth. We only hope that your presence here heralds better fortune for us who await an alternative, and long overdue, finale."

For the third time that evening, a woman of little genuine acquaintance, but with a fulsome familiarity, had treated me as a confidante but spoken to me in riddles. Riddles that in my current surreal state of mind appeared to question events that were unknown to me and made little sense in the real world.

Was she a fortune-teller, a seer or a witch?

I could not decide whether her intent was benevolent or malevolent. All three of these women had an incomprehensible bond that I could not untangle. They manifested themselves as one in the same bodily form, separated by years, each having a different countenance dependent upon what stage of their lives that they had reached. Normally, in my safe world, I would have put the ramblings of this delirious old woman down either to alcohol or senility. But I was unable to do this; something stopped me from dismissing it all as nonsense.

As I was offering no response to her tête-à-tête, she gave a sharp cough and held out her blue veined hand for my attention.

"It seems that revelation has not been realized, but I hope the judgment of others is well placed. Personally, I am not so sure, but we shall see. I shall leave you to your thoughts, Signore."

I bowed in silent response and she floated away from me. After some five paces, she twisted to fix me again with her piercing eyes,

"Do not disappoint us, Signore."

Her arrival was no less unexpected than her departure into the gloom, her form enveloped and dispersed into the dark, shifting shadows that wavered between the columns from the dwindling stragglers who lingered to the bitter end.

The air on the balcony was now cold and an involuntary shiver ran through my body. I returned to the relative warmth of the ballroom musing the whole time over the conversation that had just occurred. I felt as if I was a passer-by who had witnessed the encounter rather than having been a participant. The conversation was obtuse and left me wondering if I had missed elements of her discourse due to the almost inaudible voice that she had employed. Was this on purpose, a ruse to get me to overly concentrate on a construction of words and phrases that made no sense to me? Had I lost my understanding of my native tongue, for she definitely spoke to me in a heavily accented English – or had she? Which was my native tongue as both languages seemed to be as natural to me as if I had been brought up in the streets that surrounded me. Had I assumed meanings where such meanings did not exist?

It is said that placing food in a narrow-necked jar can trap monkeys. They push their hand through the restricted opening and as they take hold of the bait, they find it impossible to extract their tightly clasped fist from the jar. I was the monkey; my hand was deep within the slender necked jar that was this enfolding Venetian mystery. My fingers were closed tightly around the newly enhanced talents that guided my creative hand, talents that sought to govern my future, my existence. I was trapped and powerless to understand what was necessary to secure my freedom.

To find freedom was to let go.

But I held fast.

XXI
The Garret

The Priest had left the old man late the other evening. He had listened, fascinated, the detail with which the story was told made it hard to believe that this was the imaginings of a sick old man. His health seemed to be failing him and increasingly he was looking every one of his ninety plus years. He had made no mention of the Voice, apart from in his story and its materialization at the Ball as Diablo.

As time passed, the memory of having heard the Voice himself receded, the Priest now satisfied that he was mistaken, and it was merely the old man's own voice that had become hoarse. He had returned to the Hotel Cassiano and was unsurprised to be told that no-one was aware of any Maurizio having ever worked there. He decides to consult his friend in Florence once again and calls him before going back to see the old man later in the morning.

"I can find nothing factual to corroborate the old man's story."

"As I told you when we met, these delusions will be very real to him, the hallucinations, the voices."

The Priest interrupts his friend,

"He only has one voice. Initially quite benign but from his story, that voice is perhaps more malevolent than he initially thought."

"All perfectly usual for this condition. Do you know if he has misused drugs or alcohol, or has had specific stresses or anxiety during his life?"

"Yes to the latter, but I do not know about drugs or alcohol, although he does enjoy a drink. His whole family was wiped out in a terrible motor accident about fifteen years ago, and around ten years ago he was the victim of a brutal attack. I have managed to verify both these events as being true."

"Well, I think we are dealing with a fairly typical case of psychosis. What are you going to do?"

The priest thinks for a moment.

"I have been hearing his story as a confession, although not in any formal way."

"In that case, I would allow him to continue. It may be that this will have a cathartic effect and give him respite from thoughts that have been bottled up in his mind. I still suggest that you do not upset him by seeking to correct any of his story where you know the facts to be uncertain."

There is a pause in the conversation as the Priest assimilates what he has been told.

"I have made some enquiries about some of the characters that he has mentioned but can find no record of them. I have not told him of my enquiries."

"I would not do so," the friend advises. "How is he physically?"

"When I first met him after I came here, he was remarkably resilient and certainly neither acted nor was as physically infirmed as I would have expected for a man of his considerable age. However, he has been deteriorating over the last week or so and does now look less well."

"Mmm. And the Voice that comes to him now, does he still tell you that he hears it?"

"He has not mentioned it recently."

"OK. I am not sure that I can help you much more at the moment, but you know where I am and don't hesitate to call if I can help."

"Thanks, Paolo."

The friend hangs up and the Priest feels more comfortable. He collects the box that he bought earlier that morning and leaves to go to see the old man.

"I've bought you some pastries."

The old man is lying in his bed and looks rumpled and frail. His hair is wild, and a couple of days stubble is visible above his usually well-groomed beard and moustache.

"Thank you, my boy." This is the first time the old man has not just referred to him as 'Priest'.

"You are welcome, Giacomo." It is the first time that the Priest has felt sufficiently comfortable to use the old man's first name. Giacomo looks sideways from his pillow at the young man and smiles.

"Do we have these with coffee, or shall we have something a little stronger?"

"I don't mind. What would you like?"

"Let's push the boat out and have some Prosecco. There's a bottle in the fridge." The old man pulls himself up from his lying position and with the control, raises the back of his bed so that he can sit in more comfort.

"I kept you rather late the other evening. I assume you got home OK?" He raises his voice so that the Priest can hear him. The Priest replies, after the pop of a cork,

"Don't worry. I rather enjoy walking the streets at night. It is peaceful and I can think." He appears with two flutes filled with Prosecco. The box that the Priest brought is on the desk and he goes to get a plate and then places the pastries on it for the old man to choose.

"They look delicious." The old man takes the largest and bites into it, crumbs falling all around his sheets.

"What have you been thinking about?"

"You, funnily enough. Or your story, at least."

"What is there to think about? Do you think it is the babblings of a mad man?" He takes another bite and swigs from his glass before bursting into a fit of coughing as the two catch in his throat. The Priest relieves him of his glass and gets a towel to clean him up.

The old man waves him away,

"Don't fuss me," he splutters between coughs and gradually regains his composure. "Old age is a bugger."

"You always seem very spritely to me." The priest hopes the flattery will appease the old man. "A great example for someone your age."

"It comes and goes. Depends who is with me." The old man brushes the crumbs from his sheets onto the floor.

"What do you mean?" asks the priest.

"I have better days when he is here."

"He?"

"My Voice."

"Is he here now?"

"Obviously not – look at me."

The Priest hears these words and feels sympathy for the old man who is considerably weaker than on the other occasions when he has come to see him.

"Have you heard your Voice recently?"

The old man wonders if the Priest is humoring him, but when he looks into his face there is a compassion that is worthy of his calling. He decides that the question is honestly, well meant

"Not for a while. You seem to unsettle him!" He chuckles and takes up his glass again. "Any more cakes? And a bit more Prosecco wouldn't go amiss."

"You'll get me into trouble and we'll end up with hangovers!" The Priest chides.

"Not as bad as the hangover I had after that Ball. Oh God, but what a hangover!"

The unseasonably warm weather had broken, and dark grey clouds scurried overhead. Waspish flurries of rain blew along the Grand Canal like a curtain of mist, droplets rattling against my window. The water was leaden below my room, accentuated by the grey of the sky and seemed to have taken on a glutinous viscosity as it lazily lapped against the quaysides and jetties.

My head was similar. Thick, heavy and reverberating to a throbbing that echoed around the eggshell skull encompassing my alcohol-damaged brain. My throat was dry and somewhere behind my furry teeth was a thick, flaccid tongue that seemed to be stuck to the roof of my mouth. The pounding fought to break through the fragile shell, pushing out against my swollen eyeballs, pressurized and protruding from their sockets, in danger of imminent expulsion. The viciously blinding light that invaded my room through the window was such that I saw bright blue and red flashes when I turned my head with any speed. Bile involuntarily filled the back of my throat.

I leant against the cill to the window, the initial swell of dizziness on standing upright had almost overcome me but then, slowly and progressively this subsided. Being vertical was infinitely preferable to lying down. I staggered to the small refrigerator on top of which lay the opened half bottle of malt whisky that was the initial cause of my current state of malaise. I slowly bent down, groaning as the blood rushed back into the shrunken and desiccated brain, and blindly grabbed at a bottle of water. I eagerly gulped down the chilled liquid and the dramatic change in temperature stung the back of my throat to add to my catalogue of self-inflicted pain. In my haste to rehydrate, slivers of cold water slipped between my lips and ran down the side of my mouth to splash onto my bare feet and the carpet upon which they were precariously rested.

The second bottle I drank at a slightly slower pace as I tried to recall the events of the previous evening. Initially my recollections were a jumble of dashed images mixed with fragments of disjointed conversation. The dread with which I had approached the party had not materialized and I seem to have embraced the whole affair with remarkable and uncharacteristic enthusiasm. Dancing, laughing, drinking, talking, drinking, dancing, laughing and drinking - at some point I must have eaten – but the exact order of events was still a jumbled mist.

More water.

The bottles of still water had been consumed and so I resorted to sparkling, the taste of saltiness being surprisingly welcome.

The people and events partially reassemble themselves in my abused brain. The people who sat around the dinner table had been exuberant and noisy; the young women flirtatious and frivolous to an extent that I would have found intimidating in England. My conversation appeared to have been seen as witty, any innocent, reciprocated flirtation recognized for what it was, rather than the unhealthy attentions of a lecherous old man.

I danced with many women last night but the Contessa, the girl from the restaurant (her name temporarily escaped my befuddled brain) and the old crone were the only ones who remained with any true clarity. In fact, they had dominated my night, swimming in and out of my dreams, melding into a single infatuation.

I gently lowered my aching body onto the bed, my taut muscles, unaccustomed to dancing, stretching and grating as they loosened their unyielding grip.

And what of the men? One man. His face immediately materialized in my mind's eye; the apparent embodiment of my Voice.

That bloody Voice.

Diablo, who had brought my Voice to the table, and who had encouraged me throughout the evening to challenge everything that had previously been the behavioral tenets of my life? The person that I was, or had been - summarily dismissed, banished without any overt objection on my part. In fact, I had embraced the role, the anonymity, and the excitement of the game.

Was my Voice real or an illusion? Had he sat before me at that dinner table, engaged us all in conversation and cast his reassurance upon my burgeoning confidence?

And the possessive Count, he had definitely been there. As had the delectable Contessa, his wife, my Violetta, such an incongruous coupling. And why had he become so aggressive? What had I done to cause his displeasure? The effort of recall was exhausting. The whole thing seemed like one of those vivid dreams the threads of which, upon waking, were impossible to reassemble with any accuracy. What was real and what had become mingled with the visions that had filled my night?

Perhaps it was not worth the effort and I should have just accepted that an interesting evening had occurred and move on with my day.

After having consumed all the bottles of water in the refrigerator, I was physically feeling slightly better. However, I remained somewhat disorientated and clumsy in my attempts to shave. Several trickles of blood from careless nicks mixed with the remains of the foam and I wiped the vestiges from my face with the towel.

I noticed some feint writing on my palm, and I read the address together with a time that decorated the heel of my thumb. Cocola's invitation was remembered and, for reasons that I cannot rationalize, I copied it down on the small notepad by my bed. Then I removed the appointment from my hand forever.

Gradually I dressed and prepared to make my way to breakfast. Out of habit, I looked around for my folio of sketches, for that was what my sketchbook now resembled given all the additions that I had slipped between the pages.

But where was it?

To my increasing alarm it was nowhere to be found. I thought that I had put it into the pocket of my cloak, but that proved negative. I started a slow and methodical search, but as alternatives for its concealment reduced, my hunt became more frenetic. Surely, I could not have lost it? Perhaps I had not taken it to the ball? I could not readily recall. I rarely went anywhere without it, so it seemed most unlikely. It was my comfort blanket, a foil to my solitude in the cafés or bars.

I decided I must speak to Maurizio to see if anyone had handed it in and, if not, I would return to my room and proceed to turn it upside down. I took my key from where I had thrown it down on the bedside table. It caught on the small folded piece of paper that held the address and fluttered to the floor. I picked it up and looked at the shaky writing that was on it.

I did not recognize the address and would have to look it up in my guidebook. I was still not sure if I would go to her party - but there again, I had promised to do so, albeit under the influence of a surfeit of alcohol…and, no doubt, with the compulsion of Diablo. And she seemed so childishly delighted that I had agreed to go. How could I deny her? How could I deny myself?

The entrance hall to the hotel was crowded with guests coming and going about their business. Umbrellas were unfurled and flapping, luggage was being loaded onto trolleys for carriage to a waiting flotilla of water taxis. The hotel seemed to be disgorging all of its guests following the ball. I moved through this organized mayhem towards the concierge's desk, disconnected from the migration. There was no sign of Maurizio and I assumed that he was busy shunting cases and trunks into the impatient boats. In fact, as I looked around, the staff in general appeared new to me. Clearly a different shift had taken over, probably relieving the previous members of staff who would have been exhausted after the late ending of the previous night's festivities.

A harassed young man was behind the desk usually so diligently occupied by Maurizio. He was speaking in slow deliberate and heavily accented

English to a large American woman whose flowery trousers seemed to be cut ridiculously short of her thick ankles. Her trainers were a vivid day-glow pink and silver. Varicose veined and blue hued skin poked out from hem to ankle while an overly tight blouse fought to retain the rolls of flesh that looked for a means of escape. The vision did nothing to assist my feeling of nausea. I could not be bothered to wait and listen to her whining complaints and reluctantly I concluded that now was not the time to make enquiries about my lost property.

In the meantime, I decided that the simplest thing for me to do would be to return to the ballroom to see if my sketchbook had been picked up and put to one side.

I entered the lift behind the stairs and pressed the button for the top floor. Slowly it ascended and eventually bumped to a halt. I could see that the area beyond was dark and deserted. I slid open the concertina doors that squealed as they grated in their runners. Cautiously, I edged my way forward into the gloom.

I cast my hand over the wall to the left and then to the right of the frame to the lift gates until I found a light switch. It felt gritty and stiff to turn on, but with a sharp click, a number of bare bulbs hanging from the ceiling glowed dimly upon a wholly unexpected sight. I stood transfixed, perplexed and bewildered. This was not the ballroom that I had entered some twelve hours before.

My heart pounded and I felt a wave of lightheadedness pass through me as I surveyed the space. Steadying myself on my cane, I closed my eyes and waited for the feeling to pass, sure that when I opened them again the original ballroom would be restored.

I was to be disappointed.

Perhaps once it might have appeared to be a similar style of room but now it was covered in dust and cobwebs, clearly unused for decades. The proportions were much smaller than I recalled and, as I stumbled forward, the former elegance and scale became apparent only through the auspices of a deftly applied but peeling trompe d'oeil to the walls. The spectacular entrance, the colonnades and the high French windows with the stunning views over the adjoining canals to the rooftops beyond were merely faded one dimensional representations of reality applied to the timber lining that formed the walls to this modest garret. The high vaulted ceiling and its cupola were figments of the decorator's florid imagination, and a skillful use of perspective. The corners were now inhabited by generations of spiders, moths and flies.

I wandered across the small floor space and felt the thump of my hangover intensify as my blood parched brain tried to come to terms with the images that were before me. This was a hollow duplicate that defied the logic of the events that I had witnessed and been a party to the previous night. Here was a room in which I had been one of a hundred or so people who were wined, dined and entertained. But the space before me would struggle to accommodate a quarter of that number - standing up – close together. Certainly, the painted walls and ceiling gave a representation of the ballroom in which I had danced with the Contessa and Cocola. I walked the short distance to the end of the room. The colonnades and French windows mirrored where I had spoken with the elderly crone and stood breathing in the fresh night air, but this morning the reality was pictorial and not physical. The air smelt stagnant with damp and age, not the remnants of a celebration.

Befuddled, I returned to the lift, which had remained with its metal shutter gates open, the weak light falling across the detritus that littered the floor. This was not a place of merrymaking but one of desolation and dilapidation. I studied the brass control panel with its ivory buttons indicating each floor visited on its limited vertical trajectory. This was the uppermost storey, there was no other. In a state of bafflement, I hesitantly re-entered the car and pressed the button to return to my room.

On the journey down I fought a sense of panic. Perspiration covered my cold skin and my legs weakened under the weight of my body. I thought I was going to feint and held onto the side of the lift car. My mind raced and all manner of thoughts scurried across the surface of my imagination, none managing to get a toehold on consciousness. My heart was thumping in my chest and I seriously wondered if I was to die in this miserable lift car, arriving as reception as a crumpled heap on the floor. I took a deep breath and sought to control my inner self. Slowly my mind calmed itself and some strength returned to my legs. The lift juddered to a halt and I weakly opened the grille and stumbled out towards my room.

A trolley loaded with clean sheets and towels was parked part way down my corridor and I squeezed passed it, desperate to get to my room before I collapsed. The familiar surroundings of my floor and the daily activity of restocking and cleaning of the rooms comforted me, returned me to some semblance of reality after the unexplained disappearance of the ballroom. I rather hoped that my room had been dealt with as my hangover was re-establishing its control upon both my head and stomach. My legs tentatively supported me; my feet shuffled my body forward.

Upon entering my room, I saw with some relief that the bed was neatly made, and the fridge restocked with fresh water, which I happily consumed to slake my recurring thirst. The bed looked soft and inviting and a short nap beckoned to take me to lunchtime when, hopefully I might have some relief from the swirling, foggy images that filled my disorientated head.

It was only as I prepared to collapse onto the bed that I noticed a carefully wrapped parcel laying on the counterpane. The paper was a rich red with a thick gold ribbon tied around it, finished in an extravagant bow. I picked up the package and turned it over in my hands but there was no label or hint as to where it might have come from or who might have delivered it to my room. Regardless, I knew from the weight and dimensions that it was my sketchbook. Someone must have found it and, knowing that it was mine, returned it to me via reception. No doubt the chambermaid had been asked to deliver it when she made up my room.

I carefully opened the package and was relieved to find that it was all intact. I had feared that someone might have flicked through it and taken some of my carefully retained mementos that I had slipped between the pages. However, this was clearly not the case, as it appeared as thick and untidy as it had been when I had last seen it. Somewhat comforted that this particular mystery was solved, I lay on my bed and I took a closer look at the wrapping and ribbon that I had meticulously folded. It had a fibrous, handmade texture and I suspected it was expensive due to its undoubted quality. Such paper was not uncommon in the shops in Venice and the heavy silk ribbon seemed to be of a similar quality. Whoever had found and wrapped my book was clearly someone who had exceptional taste, matched with a deep pocket. I would keep the paper, together with the ribbon, as it was a large sheet and appealed to the environmentalist in me – as well as to my frugal side.

I lay back against the gently yielding pillows, closed my eyes and wished for my headache to ease and the constriction in the back of my throat to relax its grip. The mystery of the ballroom preyed on my mind but was eased by the relief at the recovery of my sketchbook. I clutched it to my chest in a possessive embrace and in some semblance of contentment I drifted off into a deep sleep.

I awoke with a start and the light through the window was a sulphurous yellow reflected from the clouds that had sunk lower over the city. I had clearly slept far longer than I had expected. The crushing headache had eased, but my stomach felt hollow and in need of food. A half-drunk bottle of water sat on the bedside table and I took a long swig to clear my mouth, which still felt dry.

Lifting myself against the mound of pillows and cushions that were piled against the headboard I could once again see the ever-present Grand Canal from my bed. Activity was muted and a hint of diesel fumes wafted through my slightly open window. The noise from the water traffic had subsided and provided a tranquillity that had been so absent during the previous days of my trip. The view was constant, and my room provided a sense of familiarity, it was comfortable, almost homely.

I pulled the sketchbook towards me and opened it to start to flip through the pages to remind myself of the events of the past few days. I reflected as I scanned the drawings that my remaining time in Venice was limited and I needed to use what was left to the full.

The pages of faces, people and architectural features passed before my eyes and it was only when I reached the young woman in the restaurant that I noticed anything amiss. I had continued to work on the drawing of her after the event, as I often did in spare moments. I had placed the table in the foreground but had no recollection of doing any of the background. I could recall a dark passage to the side of the causeway, with an ugly corroded metal grill barring the way into it. If I were to complete the drawing, I would have undoubtedly massaged the background to represent something more appealing than the disagreeable metalwork.

But now my drawing was not incomplete.

The grille was in place and behind it stood a bearded young man who had wild, hateful eyes, his arm thrust through the grills as if he was trying to touch the girl. I stared at the page and initially thought that someone had tampered with the drawing – perhaps as a joke. If so, I was angry as I was strongly proprietorial about any of my work. I knew that my style and drawing technique is quite idiosyncratic and so there was no doubt in my mind that the strokes of the pencil were mine - or had been exceedingly well duplicated. Just beneath the drawing was some indistinct writing that appeared to be in black Indian ink and, if I was not mistaken, was executed with a crude pen or even a quill. There was a name, an address – a house in Campo San Silvestro in the San Polo district - and a time and date – tonight at 8.00pm. Beneath this was a baroque solitary L in a unique style that I recognised. I looked around and found the plastic folder containing the drawing Cocola had completed of me and extracted the sheet - the same L was beneath the picture I held in my slightly shaking hand.

Both the writing and the address rang a bell with me – I had seen this before but could not recall when or where. Then, as if a lightning bolt had cracked across my febrile memory, it occurred to me. I hastily leant across the bed and retrieved the scrap of paper that had fallen to the floor earlier that morning. The script was the same – except I had written this note.

Returning to look at my drawing of the young woman, still I had no recollection of having completed the work. However, there was no doubt in my mind that the marks that formed the added elements to the drawing were mine. The execution of the drawing was fantastic, and the tones picked out the decrepitude of the metal work, the darkness of the sinister passage and the haunting facial expression of the man. The lines had been dextrously applied, thin and precise. This was not the work of an amateur but of an adept and competent artist – but was I that artist? Had I completed this piece and just forgotten?

I continued my methodical review of the other

drawings with a sense of purpose that I could not explain. Almost immediately the pages opened at another, what I had known to be, incomplete drawing of the elderly Contessa, before she had disappeared from her box at La Fenice.

I had returned to this drawing on a number of occasions as I had wondered if I could complete her features from memory. This had proved elusive and so merely the unmasked portion of her face around and including the eyes had remained. I was almost reconciled to what I would find.

Her face was complete – and in completion I saw before me the elderly woman who had spoken to me at the ball last night. The missing features of her face below the mask had been added and the finest detail of the veil was also complete. The quality of the work was equally exquisite, each decorative feature of the lace defined and recorded.

Again, adept additions had been made to the drawing that seemed to be trying to illustrate a tale that was incomprehensible to me. Standing behind the Contessa was a portly but elegant man with a grey whiskered face and blazing black eyes. Initially I saw his hands as resting gently on her shoulders, but on closer examination it was clear from the creases skilfully drawn into the older woman's skin, that these hands were exerting pressure that was not consistent with affection, but possession. From his clothing this was a man of means, a man of authority who was not to be dallied with as he had made clear to me last night. The Conte de Wolfherz was easily recognisable despite the fulsome whiskers and the added years that had been applied to his portrait. The thickening of the body from decades of good living, the fleshy jowls that had puffed up his facial features, the hair-lip and the bucolic complexion did nothing to disguise the spiteful nature of this ageing character.

As before, there was the same delicate writing below that gave the address of the gallery that I had tried to visit yesterday and discovered to be nothing more than a menacing backwater. The date was today, and the time written as 11.15pm. The single L was engraved at the base of the page.

These embellishments to my sketches redoubled my uneasiness but I could find no rational explanation apart from an elaborate hoax or joke.

Who would bother?

Cocola?

I did not doubt that she had the expertise, and the mischievous nature.

But what purpose was such a hoax to serve?

I turned between the two completed drawings and wondered what was to be made of the text beneath each. Clearly, these were invitations, but would I keep the appointments that were so carefully written onto these pages? Certainly, the first was confirming the note written on my hand by Cocola last night. I knew that my curiosity was far too exercised not to appear. As for the later appointment, I was unsure. I detested, if not feared, the barren backwater and I had no great desire to revisit it, particularly not in the dead of night. But would I ever resolve this puzzle without following this particular clue?

Time had slipped inexorably by as I struggled to make sense of the conundrum that had been placed before me. It was long past four in the afternoon when I realised that I had failed to return my costumes to Maurizio for delivery to his brother. I left the intractable mystery on my bed and looked in the wardrobe for the costumes, but they had gone. Maurizio must have removed them, possibly while I was asleep, and returned everything to his brother. But I had not seen Maurizio on duty earlier. Perhaps he had asked someone to do it for him. I would have to write a note later to thank him and his brother for their kindness.

I collected together my sketchbook and tin of pencils. The heavy rain continued and, as I looked for my raincoat, I remembered that I had left it at home. No matter, I was confident that the hotel would be able to furnish me with some suitable wet weather gear. I had resolved to walk to the first address and see what I might find there. If nothing, then I would ignore the second appointment and put the whole thing down to a prank in poor taste. If I ever saw Cocola again then I would tell her that I was not amused by her idea of a joke – or was I just jealous of her skill and not her audacity at completing my sketches?

I decided to walk down the stairs to reception, perhaps because I had lost faith in the lift that had seemed to conspire with Cocola to play their tricks on me.

Now the entrance hall to the hotel was deserted and the large wooden doors to the outside had been closed against the weather. The reception desk was empty, and I looked for any sign of an umbrella or coat that I could borrow. I wandered down towards the bar and found an unfamiliar face was stationed in Maurizio's place. I approached him and asked if he had an umbrella. He silently shrugged his shoulders and walked past me into the hall. He approached a door opposite the reception desk and disappeared through it, eventually to emerge with a heavy waxed cape that he trusted would do the job. It had a voluminous pocket inside the lining and so fitted my purpose, if not my frame, admirably. As an afterthought, he proffered me a well-worn, wide brimmed hat that looked decidedly old fashioned, but again would keep the rain at bay.

Dressed in yet another set of unfamiliar clothing, I took hold of my trusty cane, which was the only outward evidence that I was the person within the enveloping cape, the brim of the hat hanging low to cast my face in a sombre shadow. I was about to depart when the young man called out to me as he emerged from the back room again with a tall pair of boots.

"The acqua è alta, Signore. The tide is very high, and you will need these if you are to walk about." I took the boots and tried them on for size. They were slightly large but would be adequate. I looked up to thank him but too late, he had disappeared from sight.

XI
Revelation

Venice managed to retain its beauty and mysticism whatever the weather and could be appreciated even under the veil of my hangover. I walked out of the courtyard into streets that had become shallow canals. Water slopped everywhere and I could no longer make out the edge to the Rio di San Cassiano. Raindrops disturbed the still surface of the water, creating expanding rings that overlapped and merged as they dissolved into the shallows.

I seemed to have the city to myself.

Looking down towards the Grand Canal, the gondoliers were absent as were the tourists who had obviously chosen alternative pursuits that were out of the rain. The heavy clouds were scurrying across the sky and appeared darker than those of the morning, the rain harder and more set in. I crossed the Rio and entered the Campo San Cassan, a small square that contained the high, stuccoed façade of Palazzo Muti-Baglioni. The arched entrance to the palace, with its carved gargoyle on the keystone, was off the dark narrow Calle Baglioni. I noticed that the lamps were dimly flickering an eerie yellow light into the canyon between the tall buildings. The water lying all around reflected their phosphorescent glow onto the decaying brickwork of the walls. There was a smell that reminded me of tallow, or was it turpentine? Upon closer inspection I could see that each lamp appeared to be fuelled by oil causing smoky black deposits to be lifted into the damp evening air. The neon that I was used to had disappeared.

The maze of alleys became meaner and the houses were quiet and watchful as I passed beneath their closed windows. The small shops that I had seen previously selling food, books and musical instruments now were all shut up, impromptu floodgates of timber or bags of sand positioned across thresholds against the rising tide. No lights shone from their vacant windows. On one occasion I turned down a dead end, but resisted venturing far fearful of missing a set of worn steps and falling into the uninviting water beyond. My voluminous cape and boots would surely drag me down and to an untimely death. Retracing my steps, I became more and more disorientated but found no one to put me back on the right track. The passageways were deserted and the amount of lighting to some of these paths was only just sufficient to see my way.

I continued to tread warily through the wet

alleys and passages until finally I crossed a small stone bridge that rose out of the surrounding water and passed over what I recognised as the Rio San Aponal. A curving alley led me to the back of the church, which fronted onto the Campo Sant'Aponal. I walked around the tall building and admired the façade with its white finials that were visible behind the wispy flurries of rain carried past on the gusts of wind, which had accompanied my progress.

The round well in the centre of the square stood proud of the water that surrounded it. There was a small group of women standing by it gossiping. When they saw me they collected their ewers and meandered off into the shadows or disappeared into gloomy doorways. The hems of their long dresses dragged through the floodwater and each wore a shawl wrapped around her shoulders against the wind. In all my wanderings, this was the first well that I had seen that was not capped off. I had understood that they were no longer in public use but here these women still collected water for their everyday use as was done decades ago. I wandered over and looked down, but there was nothing to be seen, just an inky black hole.

I continued out of the square along yet another narrow alley that led me into the larger Campo San Silvestro, the obligatory church to my left dominating the square. The houses around the Campo were unassuming save for one to the centre of the far side that had high arched windows and a delicate first floor balcony.

A hunched figure entered the square from a side street to my right and furtively sloshed his way through the water to one of the doorways in which I noticed a woman was standing. There was a brief exchange of words and they both retired inside. As they did so, another younger girl took her place. She looked idly over in my direction and smiled an invitation. I suddenly realised why and busied myself looking for the number of the house that was the subject of my quest. I was relieved to discover that it was on the other side to the brothel, the girl continuing to offer her services to me with an encouraging flick of her head towards the entrance, her skirt pulled to one side to reveal her thigh.

I shook my head and walked towards the panelled, double doors to the house where I believed the party was being held. I realised that, apart from the women at the well and the business being conducted across the square, I had not passed a single person for the entire duration of my walk. Even allowing for the flooding, it was strange to not have seen anyone.

Subdued lighting shone from inside the

building and I could hear the muffled sound of animated conversation from the first floor where a window was slightly open, and curls of cigarette smoke drifted out. I hesitantly approached the door; unsure as to whether I really wanted to enter or would rather slink away. Something moved me forward and, as I raised my hand to pull an old-fashioned bell pull, a young man flung one of the doors open. He was dressed in not dissimilar attire to my own. He looked at me in apparent surprise and silently stood aside making an expansive sweeping gesture for me to enter, which I did. I thanked him, but he just swept past me as if disdainful of the fact that I had taken his welcome as serious and well meant.

From the waterlogged stone flagged hallway, a curved staircase led upwards and the noise increased. An unseen door slammed on an upper floor and I looked up through the bannisters to where the party was in full swing. I took the steps like an automaton, wondering what on earth I was doing here but apparently powerless to stop myself, attracted to the sound of merriment like a moth to a flame.

I knew that it was unlikely that there would be any familiar faces for me to recognise. Cocola might be there, but at that moment I was not feeling very well disposed towards her. The door to the apartment was ajar and I cautiously pushed it open. A wall of noise, smoke and heat hit me. People were everywhere and it was not easy even to enter over the threshold into the throng. Nobody seemed to notice my initial arrival. I removed my cape and hat and hung them on a row of hooks that was already groaning under the weight of other similarly wet weather gear. The collection of garments emitted a damp odour and dripped onto the wooden floor. A rivulet of water joined an ever-expanding puddle that had formed beneath the steaming clothing and was making its escape down a crack between the floorboards. Against the opposite wall was an array of house shoes, or slippers, and as I removed my boots, I assumed that these were for the use of guests.

Carefully I took my folio of sketches from the pocket of my sodden cape and held it tight to my body thankful that the rain had not penetrated the waxed material onto the pages. Those standing closest perfunctorily turned to see who the new arrival was. I held fast to my cane and looked around at my fellow guests and wondered whether I had gate crashed a fancy-dress party. Everyone was dressed in clothing that seemed too well made for mere dressing-up costumes and the quality of the material and accoutrements too lavish. It was as if I had entered a film set for a late nineteenth century costume drama. Ladies in stylish gowns, hair coiffured with cascading ringlets, sipped from delicate champagne glasses, the bubbles bursting into the air. The men wore coloured waistcoats decorated in braid and frock coats that were highly tailored. Breeches were tight fitting and shoes buckled. It was a fantastical scene and I was captivated with the atmosphere.

A small, thickset man standing by me, his pudgy fingers holding a goblet of red wine, was looking intently at me as if he was not sure if I was expected or another gate-crasher. In the circumstances, I wanted to dispel any such suspicions and asked him if my host was around, albeit that I did not know exactly who that might be. Fortunately, the man did not ask me to name our host and, to my relief, he turned from me to call over to a slim, grey haired figure talking to another tall man who had his back to me. What I presumed to be my host immediately apologised to his other guest and advanced through the melee of bodies, plucking a spare glass from a passing tray. He had a broad grin on his face and was also dressed for the evening to match the general tone of the other guests. I began to feel rather dishevelled in comparison.

This thin, angular man with the flurry of grey hair and quick darting eyes was known to me, or rather we had spoken briefly at the Ball last night, when he had apologised for dislodging my cape and then gone on to confer with the old Contessa. He gave me an effusive welcome and thrust a glass of champagne into my hand while dextrously holding a half full bottle and his own glass in his other hand. I accepted it graciously and immediately, to my surprise, he sought to guide me by the elbow through the throng to what I presume was a study that was off to one side of the main room. I was slightly alarmed at this unexpected welcome and glanced back briefly into the body of the party. I could see the man to whom he had previously been speaking standing alone, his imposing height exceeding that of those around him. He slowly turned to face in my direction. He was immediately recognisable, even without his mask.

Diablo looked at me from across the room and raised his glass in salutation as my host closed the door behind me. A rush of heat surged through my body, beads of perspiration breaking out on my upper lip.

"Signore, I am grateful that you have found time to come and honour my humble gathering with your presence." He ushered me into one of the two low, velvet-upholstered chairs that sat either side of a carved marble fireplace, the fire slowly dying as the last embers glowed dully in the grate. I sat as bidden and placed my cane on the floor by my feet.

"I am the one to be grateful for the generous invitation I received, albeit that the invitation was second hand and delivered in a somewhat unconventional manner," I replied, looking at my clean palm and then thinking of the note in my sketchbook. My host laughed but took no further notice of the comment and proceeded to gush forth about how he had seen a few of my drawings and how much he had admired what he had seen. I had to interrupt his flow to achieve clarity about what I was hearing.

"I am afraid you have the better of me, Signore," I said. "You seem to know who I am but, as we have not been introduced, I am at a disadvantage."

"Ah, my apologies. How remiss of me. Of course, I must rectify my error immediately." He stood, formally bowed, "I am Alberto Abrinzi." The introduction completed, he sank back into his chair

I automatically raised my eyebrows in surprise at the mention of his name.

"Forgive me, but are you anything to do with the Galleria d'Abrinzi?"

Signor Abrinzi rose again from his chair and hopped from foot to foot in excitement at my having instantly recognised his standing within Venetian society.

"Yes, yes, yes. I am the proprietor of Gallery D'Abrinzi, is it known to you?"

"Well, yes, but I had been told that the gallery was no more, closed many years ago."

This time Abrinzi's brow had furrowed as I continued,

"I have tried to locate your gallery, but I could not find it. I only found a derelict backwater which would surely not be where you would have an establishment?"

He still looked puzzled. He filled his glass from the bottle and topped up mine at the same time.

"I am not sure that you have the right address, Signore, but I would be delighted if you would visit to see what I am exhibiting at present." He sat again and leant forward to hand me an embossed card with the name and the address of his gallery.

"Perhaps you would like me to exhibit some of your work?"

I was flattered but equally confounded as to how he knew anything of my drawing ability. I asked him and he rather shamefacedly admitted that he had not seen much of my work, but what he had seen he greatly admired. He looked expectantly at the sketchbook that I still held close.

I remained somewhat confused, but over the last few days this trip was proving to be increasingly mystifying in the twists and turns that its course was taking. Rather than fight against the apparently inevitable, I had surrendered myself to its tortuous route, not appearing to have any control.

"I am very flattered and obviously I would like to consider your kind offer, if I may?"

"Of course." He returned his beady eyes to my sketchbook. "But I see that you have brought a considerable volume of work with you tonight." He eyed the folio in anticipation as yet again he topped up my glass.

"I assure you, Signore, that from the small selection that has been made available to me, I detect a rare talent that deserves to be exposed to the populace." His form of speech was strangely flowery and archaic to my more contemporary ear. The mane of grey hair flowed to either side of his head from a central parting. It cascaded over his collar and he swept his fingers backwards through it to keep it from flopping into his eyes as his enthusiasm became more pronounced.

Eventually, unable to contain his curiosity any longer, he extended his hand forward to take my book for inspection. I handed it over watching him all the while, more curious than hesitant. He gently turned the pages, carefully ensuring that none of the extraneous bits of paper were dislodged or fell from their position. As he proceeded, he alternately blew and sucked air between his teeth, some barely audible but all apparently appreciative of what he saw. This continued until he gently removed the plastic envelope containing Cocola's drawing of me that I had picked up from the restaurant.

How was that there? I felt a mixture of shock and guilt. I was sure that I had safely stowed it in the safe in my room. My guilt was followed by a spark of fear as to how I could explain the presence of this masterpiece. His face flushed and his eyes sparkled. He shot a look in my direction, which I interpreted as accusatory. Did he know that I had taken the drawing from the restaurant? He lifted the sheet with great delicacy, turning it cautiously over and over in his hands as if it was a piece of brittle Murano glass.

"Where did you get this, Signore?"

I was not sure how to respond and so tried to pass it off dismissively as something that I had picked up in Venice. All absolutely true, of course. He observed me very closely as if trying to reach a decision as to the authenticity of my reply and the honesty of my character. After a few seconds, he lowered his avaricious eyes back to the drawing and squinted closely at the signature.

"Signore, I think that this drawing of yours could be worth a great deal. If I am right, it is a rare piece from a series of drawings done by a very talented but unknown young artist who we believed worked with or was a pupil of Favretto."

Slightly stunned, I held out my hand for its return, but he was reluctant to do so as he said he wanted to continue to look through my work. I hoped that his unwillingness was a product of cultural advancement rather than financial gain. At my request, he carefully replaced the sheet back into the folio, but he continued to look covetously at it leaving the book open on his lap.

"Who is the drawing of?" I asked.

"Why, Giacomo Favretto of course".

I started and wondered whether he was looking at the same picture that I recalled. I still considered the drawing to be of me and not Favretto. As if he detected my conceit he laughed and any previous tension between us was broken and I slid back into my chair.

"I know what you are thinking, Signore, and I will admit to you that you do have a striking resemblance to Signor Favretto. Of course, he sadly died of typhoid at the tender age of 38, but if he had lived, he might well have looked a lot like you."

I chose not to admit that I had thought the drawing was of me. Nor was I going to be so foolish as to disclose the fact that I had witnessed its creation at the restaurant. Or had I? I thought that I had seen Cocola draw it, but perhaps I was wrong. Maybe she had brought the drawing with her and had left it on the table. But why? And if it were as valuable as Abrinzi seemed to be implying, then surely no one would be so careless.

"I have obviously surprised you. May I?" He rose to refill my glass.

I held it up and let him take it from me, as I needed time to think. He upended the bottle and a last couple of drops of liquid splashed into the bottom of the flute. Placing the empty bottle in a brass bin, he walked across the study to get a fresh one from the adjoining room. As he opened the door, I enquired,

"Is Cocola here? It was she who suggested that I should come tonight."

Abrinzi gave no appearance of having heard my question against the barrage of noise from the adjoining room and disappeared momentarily, to then return with a full bottle. He filled my glass.

"Cocola, is she here?" I repeated.

"Cocola? I don't think I know your Cocola.

She invited you here tonight?"

"Yes. She was on my table at the Ball last night. You were there and might have noticed her before you spoke to the elderly Contessa."

He looked at me with champagne filled eyes that displayed his bemusement and shook his head.

"I am sorry, Signore, you are mistaken." His words were slightly slurred, "I was at no Ball last night but here in my apartment. Perhaps this gentleman you refer to was masked? This can cause no end of confusion and probably misled you. To a degree, that is the idea."

Undaunted, I decide to take another line of enquiry,

"Your gallery was mentioned as being one of the places that I should visit. In London the Contessa de Wolfhertz ...." I paused as his mouth curled with a knowing grin.

"Ah, now that is a name that I do recognise."

I sipped my drink in relief at someone finally knowing the Contessa.

"'Contessa', eh? Well, by aspiration more than birth," he chuckled with undisclosed amusement.

"What do you mean, 'by aspiration more than birth'?"

He crossed the study and closed the partly open door to eliminate the noise from the adjoining room that had become a distraction to the relative quiet of his study.

"My friend, your 'Contessa'", he emphasised the word to belittle her apparent status, "was no more than an ambitious courtesan who lived - and loved - to the full. She came to Venice penniless from the rural hinterland. Initially, like many other young women of limited means who were attracted to the opportunities that this city had to offer, she made a living by modelling for artists. However, her ambitions were far greater than merely displaying her, albeit attractive, body for impoverished painters. She did not restrict herself to just modelling. It is rumoured that she had rooms in this very square, Campo San Silvestro, which in those days was a poor district where the ladies of the night plied their trade. The church itself has had a variety of uses including a mill, a poorhouse and also, interestingly, a gallery for exhibitions of local art. These women of easy virtue were favoured by artists and the area housed or was visited by many a talented young man."

I recalled my brief encounter earlier in the evening with the girls in the property across the square but made no mention to Abrinzi of the fact that perhaps the area had not changed much.

He continued, "She was the lover of many

aspiring artists and their masters. In fact, there were rumours that she even bedded Favretto, but that cannot be proven. She spread her, shall we say," he hesitated and licked his thin lips, "'favours' widely, while enjoying the patronage of another of her lovers, a wealthy and ambitious politician. Many years her senior, but rich and besotted, she craved to marry him."

He collected the bottle once again and came across the room to fill my empty glass. Just before he poured the liquid into my glass, he hesitated and said,

"If you want to see her, you can do so at my Gallery. I have a number of very good paintings of her both by Favretto and others."

"Thank you. And what became of her? Did she achieve social acceptance and standing?"

"Initially, yes, but sadly there was scandal and tragedy. She fell in love with a man that the Count could not abide, an artist. It is said that the Count found them together and killed the artist. He was arrested and his estates and fortune were confiscated from both him and his Contessa. She was made impoverished and we do not know what became of her. She was resourceful and determined so I suspect that she survived at a cost to somebody."

My Contessa could not possibly be the

courtesan of whom he spoke. She was flesh and blood, sophistication and charm. I had held her in my arms as we danced last night in the opulent hotel ballroom - the ballroom that I had been unable to locate the following morning. The tale regaled by my host was intolerable and out of kilter with what I had experienced. I was muddled and disorientated, but an intrigue overcame both and I was keen to discover what was reality and what was fiction, what was misdirection and what was illusory. All seem to have become intermingled, indivisible but cogent, rational, and even ethereal.

I decided at that moment of greatest confusion that I must go to this man's gallery; I must see his pictures of the Contessa and confirm in my mind whether she was my Contessa. From my last visit to that dank, foul smelling wharf there had been no evidence of any thriving commercial venture in the derelict buildings that overshadowed the place.

Abrinzi watched me with his beady, black eyes as he continued to alternate his attention between my face and the sketchbook balanced on his knees. He slowly and deliberately turned each page, considering the work before him and then looking back at my face before moving on to the next. It was as if he was trying to fathom out whether the man who had brought this collection of drawings was truly the artist or whether he was a fraud. He had met many highly competent artists but many more expert fraudsters. He clearly could not ascertain into which camp I fell. Feeling slightly uncomfortable under his continued gaze, I enquired if the young artist that he had so admired and who had executed the drawing of Favretto, had a name and whether he had had any success with his art. Abrinzi flipped back the pages until he reached the girl's drawing of Favretto once again.

"Ah, if only we knew. There is no record of his name and so his identity is a mystery. The body of his work appears to have been done around 1870 to 1880. But the trail abruptly ends, and he just seems to have disappeared. Of course, there are conspiracy theories, but none realistically explain his disappearance. Perhaps he just gave up drawing and painting, though personally I find that hard to believe. It is as if he just vanished," he paused again, drank and then continued. "In my opinion, for what that is worth, he was a genius for his penmanship but sadly his work is so very rare. He was one of very few 19th century artists who had mastered such a fine appreciation of detail; the observational qualities are second to none. The penmanship is an art form in its own right. I could study each mark on the paper for hours.... But then I am an obsessive!"

He laughed at his self-deprecation, possibly hoping that I might contradict him to flatter him out of his false modesty.

He waited for my response, which was merely an affirmative nod.

He looked me straight in the eye, his expression serious and professional, delighted to be able to demonstrate his experience and expertise. He took a further draught from his glass,

"Even though his career suddenly came to an end without explanation, the few examples of his work that appear on the market from time to time are greatly admired around the world."

"How do you know, or think you know, that that drawing is his work?" I asked, now quite enthused by his revelations. "Are you basing your judgement purely upon the style? What of the inscription, '*L*'' that appears in the corner of my drawing? Is that on the other examples you have seen? Does that identify the mystery artist?"

Abrinzi closed his eyes and leant his head back against the antimacassar as if to collect his thoughts. After a short while he shakes his head and refocuses on the drawing, holding it softy in his hands.

"Admittedly, I have not had the opportunity to study this piece in detail, but from what I have seen I believe that it is his work."

"Why?"

"Well, there are three reasons in particular. Firstly, the paper, or rather I would prefer to call it the ground. It is not a canvas but is made of shredded material and bonded together with size, which is typical of the few works I have in my gallery and those that I have seen elsewhere. While it is not unusual to find this form of ground in older works, it was rarely used in the late 1800s. Secondly, as I have said, from the detailed nature of the work, the form and application of the marks on the paper, these are all synonymous with his other works. Finally, the 'L' cipher you refer to is indeed seen on all his work, but a competent forger could add this to another work, if the quality could be achieved."

His knowledge and confidence were convincing, and I had to accept his analysis as fact in the absence of any evidence to the contrary.

"May I have another look, please?" I needed to see the picture afresh, with the benefit of Abrinzi's knowledge that he had just imparted to me.

Abrinzi carefully took the plastic envelope from the sketchbook and hands it to me. I looked again at the image and, not just because of what I had learnt that evening, I absorbed the picture with fresh eyes and agreed that I could have mistaken in that the subject was a young Favretto.

But how did Cocola have this work and why had she given it or, more accurately, left it for me to find and then take?

I was feeling the effects of the champagne and put my glass to one side. Abrinzi enthusiastically emptied his glass once again as he continued to travel through the contents of my book.

I wondered how far his examination of my folio had moved beyond the page where Cocola's drawing had been inserted. I considered drawing his attention to the two drawings that I could not recall having completed. While they were to a detail that I was confident that I could have achieved, I still had no recollection of having done the work. This added to my sense of insecurity and so, ultimately, I decided against it as these were on pages bound into the volume and I would not be able to explain their presence. He might think me a forger of the work that he held in such high regard.

Abrinzi suddenly sat up as if rejuvenated,

"Forgive me, I have monopolised you for too long and I must attend to my other guests." He sprang up from his seat and added, "I am so glad that we have had this opportunity to speak. I am serious about exhibiting some of your drawings; I believe that your work on its own also has commercial value. However, this drawing," he points to the plastic envelope, "will have to be verified and I need to know its provenance before I could give you any definitive opinion of value, but it is undoubtedly a very interesting piece. Where did you say you got it?"

Suddenly flustered, I replied without thinking,

"I didn't."

Abrinzi looked at me with renewed suspicion but then quickly moved on,

"Will you come and see me at my gallery, with more of your work? Shall we say tomorrow, around mid-morning, for coffee?"

He held my sketchbook and its additions close to his chest until I extended an open hand for its return. He passed it to me, and then withdrew a large flamboyant silk handkerchief from his pocket and blew his nose with some vigour. After wiping his nose with a flourish, he rose, and I followed suit collecting my cane from where it lay.

It was clear that the interview was over and that he wished me to vacate his study. He gently but firmly ushered me towards the door, which he opened for me. The noise from the adjoining room burst in and surrounded us as we exited, Abrinzi closing the door firmly behind us. He insisted that I helped myself to more drink and enjoyed the evening. Before I could answer he had moved into the melee and immediately engaged another in conversation.

I felt intoxicated and strangely elated. Not purely because of the drink that seemed to have topped up my alcohol level and finally dispelled the remnants of my hangover. Attending this party was to prove a turning point in my life that I had not anticipated. The thought of some of my work being exhibited filled me with excitement, mixed with a degree of anxiety. I was to be judged in public not only on my own work but also, possibly on work for which I had little recall of having undertaken, namely the girl, Cocola, in the canal side restaurant and the old Contessa in her box at La Teatro Fenice. My heart beat a little faster at the possibility of someone accusing me of plagiarism or, worse still, forgery. It was only since being in Venice that I had found the confidence in my work to allow a stranger to flick through the pages of my sketchbook. Little did he know that back in my room were hundreds of other volumes that might provide a living for me in this idyllic city.

However, I had to ground myself by remembering that this had been a conversation at a convivial party with a man who had just met me and who was clearly intoxicated. It was always possible that in the cold light of day he would rescind the expansive offer that he had made at his soirée.

Having been abandoned by my host, I circulated around the room looking for either Cocola or Diablo. I needed to speak with them both to try to find some explanation to the gaps that were appearing, and I felt they held the clues. I found a quiet corner of the room and leant against the wall with my back to the other guests. I opened my folio and referred to the drawing of the old Contessa. The legend remained with the date and time, 11:15pm tonight. I removed Abrinzi's business card from my pocket and compared the two addresses – they were one in the same.

Having attended this party as requested by the absent Cocola, I was steeling myself to move on to the wharf that I so feared. I wanted to make sure that I could locate the premises and not make the same mistake that I had made on the last two occasions when I tried to find Galleria d'Abrinzi. I reassured my disquiet at returning by convincing myself that I had mistaken the true location of the gallery.

I glanced to check the time on my wristwatch and noticed that it was not there. I always wore it but, on this occasion, I must have inadvertently left it in my hotel. I looked around to see if I could ask someone for the time. No one seemed to be wearing a wristwatch but a young man near the door to the stairwell ostentatiously removed a handsome, full hunter, pocket watch from his waistcoat, the heavy gold chain hanging loosely from his other breast pocket. He clicked the cover open and checked the time before snapping it shut with a flourish. I hurried across to him and asked if he could inform me as to the time. He looked me up and down and clearly was not impressed with my unimaginative costume, undoubtedly concluding that I could not afford a timepiece. He informed me somewhat coolly that it was 10:45pm and immediately sought a more interesting and acceptable guest to converse with, rather than this impoverished artist.

I had a mere thirty minutes to get to my 11:15pm engagement and had no difficulty in extricating myself from the gathering to which I seemed to be superfluous. I decided that I had time to walk to the correct Galleria d'Abrinzi, and so collected my still damp cloak and hat, while replacing by sketchbook in the voluminous inner pocket. I slipped on the boots and went to leave the apartment with the party still in full swing and, if anything, getting slightly rowdier as young men and women came and went. As I reached the door, I remembered my cane that I had leant against the pile of wet clothing in the hall. Moving back into the apartment from a brief blast of fresh air, I noticed that the smoke that filled the room had a pleasant herbal aroma that blended deliciously with the champagne, leaving me with a feeling of general wellbeing as I descended the stairs and closed the door to the house to re-entered the dark square.

"I need to get washed and dressed." The old man has finished most of the pastries that the priest had brought and the bottle of Prosecco is empty, but he is still recumbent in his bed. He rubs his veiny hand across the stubble on his chin.

"Can you manage, Giacomo, or would you like some help?" The young Priest stands and then moves to the side of the bed ready to assist.

The old man looks at the priest with one eyebrow cocked as if he is an idiot. The Priest steps back.

"I do not!" he snaps and throws the duvet aside as he starts to get out from the bed. He is wearing a nightshirt that has ridden up and reveals his legs, thin and white. There is loose flesh hanging from his sinewy arms as he takes hold of his stick and stands by the side of the bed. He waits while his legs bear his weight and he is sure of his balance before starting to walk towards the bathroom.

The Priest is alarmed at the physical

deterioration since his last visit. No longer is the old man a robust, fit and healthy nonagenarian.

"Come back this evening." The old man shouts from beyond the door to the bathroom. The door slams shut and his voice more muffled as he calls out,

"I need to finish this thing before I depart."

XXIII
The Galleria d'Abrinzi

It is not until eight in the evening that the young Priest manages to get to see Giacomo. He arrives out of breath, his cassock peppered with drops of water from the rain that falls sporadically outside.

The curtains are open, and the lights of San Marco diffused from across the lagoon. Now and again the French doors flex with a gust of wind and the rain dashes against the panes of glass.

The lamp on the old man's desk is the only light on in the room; it illuminates his face sharply defining every crease and fold of his skin. A heavy, dark shadow looms on the ceiling above his head.

"I thought that you were not coming."

He does not look up from the sketchbook that is in front of him. There is no pencil in his hand and he just sits looking downwards. His face has regained some of its colour and the lamp emphasises the chiaroscuro that was so loved by painters such as Caravaggio, Rembrandt and Da Vinci. The old man sits as a life model awaiting the artist to commit his likeness to canvass. His red smoking jacket, the cravat around his neck, the well pressed shirt and the carefully manicured hands that lay motionless on the desk. His hair has lost its wildness and is well groomed, his beard trimmed, his cheeks smooth and shiny from a fresh shave. When he does look up at the priest, he has a lustre in his eyes that was so missing earlier in the morning. Then they had been watery and had a flatness that made the old man look ancient, almost pathetic.

"I said I would."

"Well, better late than never."

There is a bottle of Amaretto and two brandy glasses on the table by the Chesterfield and the old man nods in their direction.

"Shall we?"

His voice is stronger and more robust, back to his old badgering form, and the Priest is pleased, as he has come to enjoy his encounters with the cantankerous Giacomo Farthing. If the old man was able to do so, he would also admit that he had come to welcome the company of his Priest, even though he was so young and naïve.

The Priest pours two generous measures into the goblets and hands one to the old man before taking his seat.

"Can we continue with your story? You had just left the party in Campo San Silvestro."

"I had a visitation today." The old man cogitates as he gently swills the liquid around his glass. He is avoiding eye contact with the Priest.

"Oh? Who was that?"

"Well, if he has a name, I suppose I would have to say Diablo." The liquid continued to circulate in the glass.

"Ah. I see." The Priest does not expect this and is trying to buy time before responding. It had been a while since the Voice had spoken to the old man and so he should not have been surprised that it would reappear or be heard again. He remembered the advice from his friend in Florence that he should go along with the conversation rather than pose questions or seek to contradict.

"What did he have to say? Did you see him, or did he just speak to you?"

"He just spoke to me, but as you can see, it does have some benefits – these visits, his presence."

The Priest is perturbed by the fact that the old man has returned to a robust state of health that he directly links to the return of the Voice. What unsettles him more is the fact that he cannot find an alternative reason for the change.

"What did he have to say?"

"He wants me to stop talking to you, to completing my confession to you."

"Why?" The Priest sits forward onto the edge

of his seat.

"He says that it breaks the bond that exists between us."

"A bond between you and me?"

"No. The bond between him and me." The old man takes a drink from the glass and then reverts to rotating the goblet to recommence the movement of the Amaretto around its base.

"What bond?"

"Ah, it would be premature if I told you that. I have to decide whether to continue with my confession or to terminate it and continue with my long life."

The apartment has a coldness that the Priest feels but the old man seems impervious to, and without thinking, he fingers the crucifix that hangs from a chain around his neck.

"And have you reached a decision?" He waits for the old man to answer. The mantle clock above the serried ranks of sketchbooks on the shelves ticks away the seconds.

"I have."

The night air was sharp as I left Campo San Silvestro and my breath clouded around my head before it swirled upwards into the sky. The rain had abated but the clouds hung low as they scurried overhead. I gathered my bearings and, having yet again checked the address on Signor Abrinzi's card, set off in the direction of what I still thought was the derelict wharf and gallery. I passed a couple of people who hurried about their purpose, heads down and wrapped in cloaks against the cold, the flood water sloshing up from their boots and dampening hems and breeches. As I continued on my way, a hole appeared in the night sky to reveal a bright white moon. The features of the facades to the buildings became clear and precise in the brief shaft of moonlight, deep shadows were cast which emphasised each intricate architectural detail in a stark black and an eerie bluey white. The paving beneath my feet was even, clean and shone as the water reflected up as if to steer me on my way. I kept to the middle of the streets, the doorways either side appearing menacing and uninviting. Now I found that navigating the narrow passages and walkways; crossing the bridges and traversing small courtyards and squares came naturally. I knew precisely the route I was to take without thinking, almost as if I had walked these streets since childhood.

I checked, fear mixed with excited anticipation held my step, and then I turned the corner into the arched, low ceilinged alley that had led to the wharf. The moonlight beckoned to me at the far end, and the air continued to smell of the damp. Will-o'-the-wisps fleetingly flared in the dark passage and I wrapped the cloak closely around myself to protect me from the invisible imaginings in the enveloping shadows. Stepping swiftly through the foetid water that filled the alley, I emerged onto the wharf side. I had held my breath to avoid having to inhale the putrid gases that inhabited the alley. I exhaled loudly and the walls enveloped the sound, no echo escaped from their hard surfaces.

A thin layer of black limpid water partially obscured a smooth, cobbled surface beneath my feet, the only movement being the splashed ripples that radiated from my boots as I walked. Hanging over the water was a thin mist that veiled the end of the wharf. Along the full length of the façade to the buildings were gaslights, the flames flickering and diffused by the waspish vapour that swirled back and forth. They provided a more welcoming illumination and dispelled some of the depression that had previously hung over the immediate vicinity. Still the temperature remained cooler here and involuntarily I shivered within my cape. Curiosity prevailed over any rekindled fear, even though the knuckles of my right hand were white as

I held a vice-like grip to the head of my stick.

I stood just beyond the exit from the alley, not wishing to venture too close to the invisible edge of the canal.

A transformation had occurred.

There was no scaffolding or hoarding defacing the facade of the buildings. Each was pristine and newly decorated in a variety of soft pastel shades. The water beyond where I imagined the long kerbstones ran was as black as before, but the surface clear of detritus. I wandered slowly down the street marvelling at each building as I passed. The doors had fresh paint; the windows glazed in clear float glass, no boarding and no cracks or shattered panes of glass. Lamps behind some provided a quivering illumination to the scene, a celebration of occupation, resurrection and life.

Halfway along this renaissance, beneath the gold lettered facia that held the legend "Galleria D'Abrinzi", stood my quest. Next to the glazed, modestly bowed window was an intense black painted door with shiny brass fittings. On either side of the door shone two brass carriage lights, glowing onto the lustre of the finished paintwork. A welcoming light that was both warm and inviting flooded out from the half-moon window above the door. The now receding water was barred from entering the building by two stone entrance steps, the edges crisp and newly formed.

Without a second thought, I turned the ornate handle and the wooden door silently yielded, opening on well-greased hinges to reveal a beautiful baroque entrance, lit with highly wrought and ornamented chandeliers fitted with candles too numerous to count, each burning brightly. Rich, elaborate tapestries hung from the walls, a rainbow of threads depicting scenes from nature. Birds of Paradise, stags and hinds, insects and exotic birds of every known and imagined species filled the space. Thick foliage in many hues of green camouflaged these beasts, and in the centre, behind delicate white jasmine flowers hid Adam and Eve. She exuded sensuality and comprehension, while he had yet to succumb to the loss of naïve purity. I softly raised my stick from the stone tiled floor and held it by the shaft, not wishing to generate any unnecessary noise that might disturb the peace within this place.

The door behind me gently swung back into its reveal and the keep clicked shut. A curved, cantilevered stone staircase with wrought iron banisters, and polished brass rail led to the first-floor landing. I climbed the shallow steps, each unworn and newly worked, the nosing fresh and sharp without a chip or scrape to be seen. The only blemish was the trail of wet footprints that betrayed my progress.

A delicate cupola covered the high oval stairwell with crystal clear glazing such that I could see the stars and the soft clouds passing between the heavens and me. The moonlight shone through the imperfections of the ancient float-glass. The diffracted light reflecting onto the curved side walls to the stairwell, throwing intricate silhouettes onto the surface. Everything was perfect without a hint of dereliction; in fact, it was too perfect.

I arrived at the head of the stairs and before me was a pair of tall highly polished, panelled double doors that opened into a large salon. Yet more plaster panels decorated the walls and pictures hung on nearly every vertical surface. More chandeliers were suspended from gilded chains attached to robust hooks within wide, heavily reticulated roses. The bed of the ceiling was a mass of swirling plaster motifs. Wall lamps were symmetrically placed around the room to add a softer, subtler hue. The furniture was decorative but not overly fussy. Each piece was functional, ensuring that the artwork – the focal point of this magnificent room - prevailed. Nothing was out of place and there was no sound from within the building or infiltrating from outside. I appeared to be completely alone and inherently accepted that there was nothing unusual about this state of affairs.

I left my cloak and hat hanging over the back of a low, button-backed Chesterfield sofa. My boots seemed to stop leaving a damp trail on the stairs and so I decided not to take them off. I walked around the room luxuriating in all that I saw before me. This was a salon, designed to exhibit its contents rather than to provide habitation. The plethora of exquisite works of art held me in silent awe as I marvelled at each detailed brushstroke and every mark of penmanship. Each one of the artists who had created these pieces was a master of his calling. There was only the one imposing room on this floor. When I had completed my circumnavigation, and viewed all that it had to offer, I returned to the double doors to climb the staircase to the second level.

This floor was less elaborate and slightly smaller than the one below. At the far end of the room was a door that stood invitingly ajar. The walls displayed yet more wondrous pictures, portraits, finished and unfinished, landscapes, elevations of buildings, street scenes and an interior scene of a salon such as this. Others were local street scenes, of residents and visitors to Venice in bygone days. The market in San Stefano, a canal side restaurant with waiters smirking at the embarrassment of one of the diners, the women were gaudily dressed, the men more sombre but clothed in cloaks and hats such as those I had discarded in the room below. A colossal canvas hung on one side of the salon. It depicted a masked ball, held in a large ballroom with colonnaded sides and windows overlooking a moonlit Grand Canal, the partygoers dancing to an orchestra on a raised dais.

Each picture recounted experiences that were vivid to me. They presented no threat or consternation for me. They belonged here and were a natural extension to my visit. I was to be detained on these walls in perpetuity.

I had reached the far end of the room and pushed the door that was ajar fully open. Before me was a small studio with a number of easels holding incomplete or newly completed works. There was a strong smell of paint and turpentine. It appeared that the artist had only just popped out of the studio, possibly in haste. I felt that I was intruding but the lure of the work displayed was too great and I viewed each one with interest. The genre had moved predominantly to portraiture and life work but had a more personal feel as if I was a voyeur upon a private life, a secret perhaps, that the artist conveyed to canvas in the privacy of this studio. It was comfortably furnished and did not have the feeling of just being a working studio. It was more akin to a study, used for the purposes of painting by a hobby artist. But this was no amateur's work.

Leaning against a side table was a canvas showing a first-floor salon in magnificent detail. As I studied it more closely, I realised that it was exactly like the one I had been standing in some minutes ago, complete to the last detail, including a man leaning forward before a painting to survey the work more closely. Lying, draped across a Chesterfield was his cloak and hat. The man wore knee high boots and held his cane by the shaft behind his back. He seemed to be in raptures over the painting that he was viewing.

I felt an inner calm envelope me.

A tall window that looked out over a narrow canal dominated the end wall. The upper parts and roof of the building opposite was no more than ten feet away, the stucco work crumbling and paint peeling in much the same manner as this building had appeared on my first visit. Beneath the window, a white sheet was draped over some other canvases as if to hide them from prying eyes. I slipped between two easels, each supporting a canvas with the ground completed and initial brush strokes creating the indistinct outline of a face. My breathing had become a little faster as I drew back the cloth that was concealing the three paintings that leant against the wall.

The first was a life study of a young woman, lying naked upon the Chesterfield that currently held my hat and cloak. Her back was to the artist, her long slim legs bent, the mound of her hips raised as she turned towards the observer, a hint of a smile that promised much to the artist who was confining her to his canvas.

The second was a more formal portrait of an attractive, middle aged woman seated, with a stout man standing slightly to her right, one hand proprietarily upon her shoulder. Here the smile was no more, the face stoic and the eyes indifferent or possibly sad and forlorn.

The last canvas was of an elderly woman who had hard, cold eyes and was dressed all in black as if she was about to attend or had attended a funeral.

I knew them all – they were as one.

Cocola, the young woman who I believed had undertaken the drawing of me at the restaurant, the middle aged Contessa Livia from The MonkeyChop Club, her pose was one of entrapment, and finally, the Contessa in old age - elderly and frail, but also with an indomitable, if not triumphant, hauteur.

A life in art, portrayed with such a depth of feeling and love that I stood transfixed for some minutes. I was unsure what story lay behind the pictures, but it seemed to me that I was destined to play a part. Clearly, they were painted as a triptych and must always remain together.

My inspection of the paintings was interrupted by what sounded like muffled voices from the floor above. They rose in volume as if in furious debate. The words were unintelligible, but the anger obvious. I looked around and it was then that I noticed, in one corner of the studio, a narrow arch partly masked by a curtain. Beyond the curtain was a small, unlit lobby with a wooden staircase that rose into the darkness. I hesitated and wondered if I should retrace my steps, gather my hat and cloak and hastily leave the premises. Something suggested otherwise and I stealthily crept across the lobby to the foot of the stairs, the rough timber floorboards creaking under my weight. I paused again and listened, stick held ready, if needed. The lobby and stairs seemed to be enclosed in a cantilevered, timber structure that hung beyond the external walls of the rear of the building. I silently remained motionless at the foot of the stairs. Looking down to concentrate on hearing further sounds of movement above, I realised that I could see between the ancient floorboards to what appeared to be water slapping the solid walls some distance below my feet There was little, if any natural light but a feint glow escaped from somewhere at the top of the staircase.

I tentatively stepped onto the first tread that softly groaned under my weight and I froze. I waited, hardly daring to breath, the arguing voices resumed from above. I still had my cane in my hand, and I used it to redistribute my weight and so avoid point-loading the fragile staircase. I placed my other hand against the wooden enclosure wall for further support.

I advanced to the second step. The timber beneath my hand was roughly hewn, the surface cold and slightly damp. The tread bent imperceptibly to grind against the riser as the timber took the strain. The light above became slightly stronger and as I looked down, I could see more clearly the water of the canal that I now over-sailed. I prayed that this stairway was in regular use and that I had not stumbled upon a redundant or derelict structure, unfit to conveying me to the altercation above.

As I cautiously rose to the mid-point between the two floors, two male voices were now clearly discernible. The enclosing walls and the stair became increasingly dilapidated and the smell of decay in the timber structure more pungent. I had reached a point of no return and reluctantly decided that I had no alternative but to continue upward. The wall to my left was clearly the external wall to the building and the crumbling plaster deposited itself on my jacket, flakes falling through the cracks in the boarding, floating down to the water below.

I had reached a turn in the stairs and the hidden light beyond the corner better illuminated the true decrepitude of the structure that I was irretrievably climbing. With each progressive step the stairs creaked more insistently. Again, I contemplated turning back. The two men's voices rose and became even more strident, one angry, deep and gruff, the other light and defensive.

I was told to push on, to reject any idea of retreat.

Light flooded from around an ill-fitting, ledged and braced door that led from the stairs back into the body of the building. Beyond the door the argument intensified still further.

"Signore, I will not be made a fool of by you or any man."

"That is neither my wish nor intent." Clearly this was a younger man.

"You have the audacity to shame my family name with these disgusting images of my wife, and then plead innocence?" The voice and phraseology is familiar to me.

"It is my profession, I…."

"Profession! Profession!! What in the name of God is professional about that?"

"It is art, to be enjoyed…"

"By God man, my wife is not an object to be 'enjoyed' in a gallery by the masses, leering and drooling. I am cuckolded, Signore, and as such I shall take my revenge."

"No, I beg of you. Please try to understand and appreciate what I am saying."

"Never! Get up and face me like a man!!"

"I will not fight you, sir."

"By God, a coward as well as a philanderer."

There is the sound of a stick hitting flesh and a woman's voice screams,

"Stop, for God's sake stop!"

I know the timbre of the sound, but the blows continue.

I have arrived at the top of the stairs; the small landing slopes alarmingly back from the wall to which it is supposed to be attached. The boards give, chillingly creaking and groaning as I try to decide what is to be done. The younger man's voice starts to gasp for air while the woman screams in a higher pitch the recognition of which jolts me forward and I crash through the door.

Before me is Cocola (or is it a young Contessa)

naked but with her modesty protected by the sheet from the bed upon which she is kneeling. The be-whiskered Conte, strongly built, his face red with rage is standing in dishevelled evening dress, his cloak and hat tossed onto the bare, floorboards, his colossal, powerful hands firmly around the throat of the younger man who is bearded and partially clothed. He is on his knees and stretching his pleading hand out to me for assistance. The tableau is frozen for a couple of seconds, all three looking in my direction - shocked, pleading and defiant.

Standing off to one side is the shadowy figure of Diablo, apparently impotent to stop the events that are unfolding before him. His eyes command me to intervene, to complete the task that he has drawn me into. I take hold of my cane and yell for the Conte to stop.

He looks across at me aghast. This was not meant to happen; this was an unexpected intrusion. The Conte de Wolhertz cannot decide whether to tighten his grip on the young man or defend himself against the interloper. Looking bewildered, he releases his grip and turns to face me. The young artist gasps for air as we stand in silence and mutual indecision. Finally, he charges at me, but I have moved quickly and unsheathed my sword from its stick. The momentum that this beast of a man has created means that it is too late to argue or debate. I step back onto the staircase and then lunge forward a pace, the blade raised, my arm straight and tensed for the inevitable. The point strikes him in the chest, the shaft bends and then straightens as the blade punctures his sternum and enters his heart. He staggers and grasps the blade with his hands. He glances disbelievingly from his victim to me and back again, the look of incomprehension clouding his face, while life ebbs from his eyes as the thick red blood oozes from the wound and slips between his fingers.

I just have time to identify the players to the tableau, to see the Conte drop to his knees, appreciate the Contessa's look of gratitude and the rasping relief on the face of Giacomo Favretto before the decaying floor disintegrates beneath my feet and I am engulfed by the whole staircase enclosure that is collapsing around me. I fall to the landing below, which shudders beneath the combined weight of my body and the rotten shards of timber and plaster that accompanied me on my descent.

There is dust and debris all around me, and my broken body lies shattered on the ground. I try to slowly pick myself up, but I know it is impossible.

There is no pain, just serenity, a peace.

The enclosure supports gives one final tremor of submission and, just as the floor starts to tip me into the canal below, a hand grasps my arm and pulls me free, back into the body of the building.

There is silence in the old man's room, the Priest sits motionless, the old man slumps back into the chair behind his desk, his hands shaking slightly, still encompassing the glass goblet.

"That is my confession."

The old man slowly raises his eyes to look at the Priest, waiting for his reaction.

"Do you want absolution?"

"I think it is too late for that. I have broken the bond."

Epilogue

The Priest went back to the old man's apartment early the next morning, but the bed was stripped, and the room cleared of all his furniture and effects, save for the shelves stacked full of his sketchbooks, all neatly standing so as to fill the available space. He took out the final volume to look at the drawings for one last time. Upon opening the book, he saw nothing but pristine, empty pages. He replaced the volume and took another at random, and then another and each time with the same result.

The Priest arrives flustered at his church and enters the confessional to wait for the first member of his congregation to arrive. The curtain to the next box is pulled back and someone enters and sits down. The Priest offers a brief welcome and blessing. There is silence from beyond the grill.

"What can I do for you, my son? Shall I hear your confession?"

"*No more confessions, Priest. You and I have work to do.*"

The Priest places his hand onto the silver topped hilt of his cane.

The End

Printed in Great Britain
by Amazon